Owen Noone and th

Owen Noone
and the Marauder

Douglas Cowie

CANONGATE
Edinburgh · New York · Melbourne

First published in Great Britain in 2005 by
Canongate Books Ltd, 14 High Street,
Edinburgh EH1 1TE

This edition first published by Canongate in 2006

1

For permissions, see p. 292

British Library Cataloguing-in-Publication Data
A catalogue record for this book is available on
request from the British Library

1 84195 693 7 (10-digit ISBN)
978 1 84195 693 0 (13-digit ISBN)

Typeset in Fournier MT by
Palimpsest Book Production Limited,
Polmont, Stirlingshire
Printed and bound by Clays Ltd, St Ives plc
Book Design by Jim Hutcheson

www.canongate.net

to the memory of
P.Y.T.

Every star that shines
In the back of your mind
Is just waiting for its cover
To be blown.

— Uncle Tupelo, "We've Been Had"

Transcript from WXRT Radio Chicago, January 1, 1999:

We've just received breaking news: guitarist and singer Owen Noone of Owen Noone and the Marauder collapsed while performing tonight in Los Angeles. Nothing about his condition has been made clear to us, and we've received no official comment from anyone connected to Owen or his label. Stay with us — we'll keep you posted with any further developments. Forty minutes of uninterrupted music start right after this commercial break.

PART ONE

PART ONE

Everyone knows the end of the story. This is the beginning.

When I first met Owen Noone it was 1995 and I was a junior at Bradley University in Peoria, Illinois. I was an English major, and believed I was a poet:

> *You've been in my dreams*
> *Three times: once, you*
> *Were lying next to me; in*
> *Another you were standing*
> *In the corner; I don't remember*
> *The third, just that you*
> *Were there. I didn't have*
> *The courage to speak or act,*
> *So I just lay there, breathing,*
> *Watching and waiting.*

This was how most of it went; rhythmless poems about girls to whom I'd never spoken, to whom I'd never speak, but for whom my heart was supposedly aching. Since nobody else understood what a good poet I was I didn't have many friends, and I walked around campus with my fists in my pockets, thinking about the day when I'd be great and all these bastards at Bradley would pretend they knew me when.

I also cursed everyone I knew because they didn't understand music. I worked as a DJ at WCBU, Bradley's radio station, hosting a two-hour indie rock show once a week. They gave me the slot because I wrote a long and pretentious proposal discussing obscure bands, insisting that this music was vital to the community at large and not just to a few obsessed college kids. These bands were far more talented, interesting and, like my poetry, destined for immortality in the ages to come, unlike the lousy jam-bands that the frat boys who scored with the girls I wrote about liked. Everything played on commercial radio – everything – I deplored.

This is how, or rather, why I became friends with Owen Noone, because of a debate about music. It was late January, the beginning of the second semester, and everything in Peoria was dead: the trees, the buildings, the sky; an endless gray mass of cloud pushed across the cornfields and down on the city. The temperature never rose much above zero, and even the factories seemed dead, the cold overpowering their usual stench, which normally served in place of a welcome sign as you crossed the Bob Michel Bridge into the city. Because it was so cold I spent most of my time in my room with the heat turned up as far as it would go. I didn't leave for days, skipping classes and living on ramen noodles and other instant soups.

It was Friday, and one of the student bars was holding an open-mic night. A girl who was one of the subjects of my poems always sang, so I thought I'd go, telling myself I'd work up the nerve to talk to her, although I knew I wouldn't. I put on a thermal undershirt, a long-sleeved flannel shirt, a heavy wool sweater, longjohns under my jeans and two pairs of wool socks, then jammed my feet into my shoes, put on my parka, wrapped a scarf around my neck and face, and finished up with a wool hat, a pair of gloves and mittens. I hated the cold.

By the time I got to the bar my undershirt was soaked with sweat. I opened the door and was blasted as the warm air of the bar collided with the cold outside. I started perspiring even more. The open mic hadn't started, so I peeled off most of my layers, got a beer and sat at an empty table near the back of the bar, watching people arrive with their friends while I drank alone. After half an hour or so somebody got onstage and announced that the singing was about to start. The first performer would be someone called Owen Noone.

Owen took the stage. He didn't have a guitar or notebook; he just stood in front of the microphone empty-handed and said, 'This is a song everybody knows.'

I'd never seen him before, and he didn't seem like a student. He was tall, a little more than six feet, and thin, but well-built, not skinny. He wore faded blue jeans and a white dress shirt, and his sandy hair was long enough to cover his ears. He was good-looking, I thought, the type of guy who could probably pick any girl in the room.

After a pause during which he inhaled deeply, he said 'One-two-three-four,' like he was counting off an imaginary band in his head, and began stamping his foot on the stage and clapping in time. Everybody in the audience started clapping too, even me, but none of us seemed to know why. We were just smiling in anticipation, mild confusion and bemusement, clapping along with this guy we didn't know. Then he started to sing.

His voice was bad. He could barely hold the tune, which was even worse than it might be, because he was right, everybody did know the song. It was Guns N' Roses.

"Sweet Child O' Mine." A few people giggled when he started, but Owen seemed undeterred. He sang slowly, deliberately, and woefully off-key, which was exacerbated by the fact that there was nothing else to cover up his voice. Still, people clapped as he rumbled through the first verse to triumph with the chorus.

'Whoah, oh oh, sweet child o' mine,' he sang, gaining volume and somehow finding a few of the right notes. His voice began to change slightly, transforming into a parody of Axl Rose. He closed his eyes and grabbed the microphone stand, and by the time he hit the second verse he seemed oblivious to everything, the clapping audience, the fact that he was out of tune, even oblivious of himself. His eyes were crushed in his reddening face and his neck convulsed. He looked almost violent, but not threatening. 'C'mon,' he hissed into the microphone between lyrics, 'Sing along with the Roses!'

We did. Or rather, we sang along with Owen Noone and his appalling imitation of a recording we'd all heard a hundred times or more. Now strutting and screaming, he twisted his hips like a hack-Elvis, doubling over so his face was a foot from the ground, pumping his fist in time to a soundtrack that he could hear in its entirety, but of which we were only getting a fraction. The pitch of the bar – the whole bar, from Owen onstage, to the very back where I was no longer sitting but standing, craning my neck to get a better look – was raised to an almost euphoric level. As he screamed out the final sounds – they were no longer notes – drawing out the last word, 'Meye-ee-eye-ee-eye-eye-eye-eye-eyyyyyyyyye-nuh,' everybody rose to their feet and made a fury of sound that eventually drowned out Owen himself, filling the entire building with a cacophony that pushed against the fogged-over windows and into the cold streets outside. Somebody threw a bra at him, but it missed, and he didn't notice.

Then, as easily as he had transformed into a contorted screaming maniac, Owen slid back into the good-looking, unknown guy who'd stepped before the crowd five minutes earlier. He left the stage smiling, oblivious to the people laughing and slapping him on the back.

The next performer was a girl with a guitar who announced that she was going to play Indigo Girls, but no one was paying attention. As she started singing, I heard a hoarse voice addressing me from behind.

'You mind if I sit here?'

I looked up. It was Owen Noone himself, although at the time I had forgotten his name. He held a beer and was soaked with sweat, breathing hard, his hair stringy and damp.

'Go ahead.' I nodded at the empty chair. 'Nice singing, but Guns N' Roses fucking suck.'

He drank half his beer in one gulp and wiped his mouth slowly with his arm, all the while staring straight at me. I stared back as though it were a contest, but with high stakes. I was determined not to lose.

'What would you prefer,' he said flatly.

'Anything.'

'Like the Indigo Girls.' He pointed towards the stage without looking away.

'No.'

'What's your big idea, then?'

I didn't have one, but I didn't want to back down. I breathed deeply to give myself time to think. 'Nirvana.'

'That's original.'

7

I picked something I was sure he'd never heard of. 'Big Black.'

His mouth spread into a wide grin, and he slammed his fist on the table. 'Now you're talking! I'll do something from *Songs about Fucking* next week.'

I was crestfallen. And angry. I'd lost. I kept my eyes trained on him, unable to make the gears in my head lock back together to form some kind of response.

'I'm Owen Noone,' he said, reaching his hand across the table. 'It's nice to meet you.'

I shook his hand and told him my name, and he repeated that it was nice to meet me and offered to buy me a beer. After a few minutes he came back from the bar with a pitcher and set it on the table, the beer sloshing over the sides.

'Are you a student?' he asked.

'Yeah.'

'What do you study?'

'English.'

'Poetry or fiction or both?'

'Both.'

'Which do you prefer?'

'Poetry.'

'Who's your favorite poet?'

'John Berryman.'

'Is he alive or dead?'

'Dead.'

'What should I buy of his?'

'*Dream Songs*.'

'What's your favorite novel?'

'*On the Road*.'

'I've read that. What's your favorite novel that I haven't read?'

'I don't know what you haven't read.'
'A bunch of shit and *On the Road*.'
'*The Sun Also Rises*.'
'Who wrote it?'
'Hemingway.'
'What's your favorite band?'
'Kid Tiger.'
'Have you ever been in love?'
'No.'
'Do you like sports?'
'No.'
'Why not?'
'I have better ways to waste my time.'
'Republican or Democrat?'
'I've never voted.'

Owen's question and answer session lasted the rest of the night. He asked them as fast as I answered, and mostly one question followed the other without any discernible logic, jumping from one subject to another as though they had some connection too obvious to explain. He nodded and listened to each answer and referred back to questions I'd forgotten he'd asked, grinning the whole time. At the end of the night I knew nothing about him except that he might be insane, but he knew everything there was to know about me, including the name of my kindergarten teacher, Mrs. Hamilton.

The performers kept coming and going on the stage but neither of us paid attention. Owen bought two more pitchers in between his questions, and when I looked up the bar was almost empty and the bartender was shouting last call. Owen finished his beer and fired off one last volley.

'Do you ever get the feeling that you're great? That you're going to do something really special with your life? That you'll make a difference?'

'I guess not. Not really. Do you?'

'All the time.'

Owen slapped his palms flat on the table and stood, staring straight into my eyes. He nodded once, picked up his coat and walked away, leaving me alone. After sitting for another minute or two, I stumbled home through the cold, trying to remember if Owen had said what he studied.

I woke up with a hangover, ate a bowl of cereal and drank as much water as my stomach would hold. I had to go to the library to get some books and articles about Robert Lowell for a paper that was due the next week. After bundling up, I stepped out into the cold. It was almost noon, but the campus was empty, everyone avoiding the sun, which, rather than making things warmer, somehow seemed to drag the temperature even lower, reflecting off the thin layer of frost and snow.

I turned down Elmwood – the street had the same name as the hall I lived in, which was more or less a brown brick cube with a few thin trees in front of it, bare and gray against the sunlight. A car passed, swallowed by the steam and exhaust billowing from its tailpipe. I beat my arms against my sides, cursing myself for drinking too much and for waiting until the last possible weekend to start my paper, then turned onto Bradley. By the time I got to the library I was once again overheated from all the layers.

Libraries always look strange, as though at some point in history the architects' guild decided that because they provide such a unique function – storing a collection of knowledge, like a big inert brain – this gave them license to try out every blueprint in their heads, regardless of where the building stood. Cullom Davis Library is proof of this. Surrounded by trees that, in the right season and with a little imagination, make the area around it seem like the countryside, the building itself is a large concrete and glass box. With the trees bare — all except a lone pine, which provided the only variant from shades of white and gray — the library mercilessly reflected the sun off its glass, and I got angry, as though it were all a plan designed against me and my stupid hangover.

The place was empty. It was eerie without even the quiet library sounds of rustling paper, books closing, pens scratching and chairs creaking. I wove through the stacks looking for the call numbers I'd written down.

A book caught my attention. It was shorter than the rest, about half the size, but longer, like a piece of note-book paper. I pulled it out. It was *The Penguin Book of American Folk Songs* by Alan Lomax. The cover had a drawing of a guitar colored like the American flag and with a smiling sunflower in the middle, where the sound hole would be. It made me laugh. The back had red and white stripes and a blurb. I knew who Alan Lomax was, having bought Leadbelly albums after Nirvana played one of his songs on MTV. And I knew some of the songs — "Yankee Doodle," "Old Smokey," "The Midnight Special" — but most of them were completely foreign to me, with great names like "Goober Peas," "Ground-hog" and "I'm a-Ridin' Old Paint." I laughed out loud at this last one, but the sound of my own voice made the library feel even emptier. I tucked the Lomax book under my arm with the others and hurried downstairs to the circulation desk.

*   *   *

There was someone standing on the corner of St. James and Elmwood as I approached. As I got closer I realized it was Owen Noone. He was holding a plastic bag and he didn't seem to be hung over at all.

'Hi!' he yelled as I approached. 'I got those books.'

I was confused. I'd still been thinking about the library. 'What books?'

'You know, John Berryman. Ernest Hemingway. I was looking through those poems. Nuts.' He moved his arms a lot as he talked, even though the bag of books weighed him down. 'Hey, listen, I had an idea this morning. Can you play an instrument?'

I couldn't.

'Neither can I, but I figure we could learn, right? The point is, do you want to start a band? We like the same kind of music and everything, we could get a couple guitars, it'd be a lot better than screaming Guns N' Roses songs at open-mic nights.'

There was no way I could afford to buy a guitar, and I told him so. I was at Bradley on a National Merit scholarship, which was basically the only way I could have paid for college without taking time out to work and save enough money.

Owen paused for the first time and looked down the street. Then he turned and looked me in the eyes. 'I could loan you the money. Pay me back whenever. It doesn't matter. Come on, let's go.'

'Owen, no, I mean, how could you afford it? What do you study, anyway?'

'I'm not a student,' he said. 'I'm a baseball player.'

'A Bradley Brave,' I said.

'No. Peoria Chiefs. Cubs farm team. I'm a professional.

But I live in Peoria year-round, because I've got no reason not to. Come on, let's go buy some guitars.'

I followed him, my bag of books on my back, my paper forgotten. After about a block I asked him what his story was.

'What's my story?'

'Yeah. I must've told you everything about me last night. But all I know about you is that you play baseball.'

Owen shrugged. 'There's not much else to know. I was born in Charlotte, North Carolina. My parents divorced when I was two and I never knew my father. When I was fourteen, my mom got remarried to a tobacco executive. We moved into a big house and when I was sixteen, they moved to the Virgin Islands, leaving me the house and a trust fund. I lived by myself in that big house and continued to play baseball. I was drafted by the Cubs out of high school and played in Michigan for half a summer before being moved to Peoria. I've been here for two years. I know it sounds weird, but it feels pretty normal when it's you. No big deal, really.'

We came to the guitar shop. For a few minutes we stood outside, looking at the instruments hanging in the window: Stratocasters, Telecasters, Jaguars, Les Pauls, plus a bunch of different-colored effects boxes. Inside there were even more. I'd never been inside a guitar shop before, and felt somehow like I was trespassing. In a back corner a guy with long hair, black jeans and a black T-shirt was trying out a guitar, his fingers tapping the strings and then moving on, never lingering for even a second. A blur of notes raced out from a mountain of amplifiers. Guitars hung from every wall – electric and acoustic – and in a back corner, the one opposite from where the guy was playing, were a couple of banjos. We wandered around together, the two of us, looking at the names, shapes and colors of the guitars. Neither of us knew a thing about them.

A middle-sized, balding guy came over to where we were standing and smiled. 'Can I help you, gents?'

'No, just looking,' I said.

'Yeah, can I try that one?' Owen said, pointing at a guitar.

It was a yellow Telecaster with a black pickguard. I knew this guitar. I'd seen lots of pictures of Keith Richards playing one. The salesman took it off its hook and walked with Owen to the corner where the guy with the long hair had just finished his workout. I didn't want to watch Owen try to play it, so I wandered over to look at the banjos.

'How long you been playing?' I heard the salesman ask.

Owen grinned. 'Never played in my life,' Owen said.

The salesman plugged in the guitar and turned on the amp. Owen played a single note. It didn't sound like a real note, though. It sounded wrong, somehow, like it wasn't a guitar note. The salesman smiled again and offered to tune it. After he'd finished, Owen started up again, playing the same single note. Then he got the idea that he could play lots of other so-called notes. The guy who'd been jamming before was at the cash register with another salesman. They looked over, then looked at each other and chuckled. Owen seemed oblivious, stumbling away and smiling. Finally he stopped and said he'd take it, plus the amp. He and the salesman walked over to where I was scrutinizing the banjos.

'You looking to buy a banjo?' the salesman asked.

'No, he's getting a new guitar too,' Owen said, slapping

14

my shoulder, 'Except, unlike me, this guy can actually play.'

I was terrified when I heard him say it. Not embarrassed or worried, but terrified. I was going to have to try to play a guitar in this shop, in front of these guys whose lives were all about guitars. My feet felt like they were stuck to the floor.

'Which one you want to try?'

I looked at the salesman.

'That one,' Owen said, pointing to another Telecaster, black with a yellow pickguard, the opposite colors of the one Owen was getting. 'But we'll just take it. And another amp, too.'

I could imagine the salesman's glee, two suckers walking in and dropping a couple thousand dollars on equipment they couldn't even play. He picked another amplifier off the mountain and walked to the front counter with us. The other salesman was standing by the cash register. He smiled at us.

'Anything else I can do for you, gents?' the salesman who'd helped us asked.

Underneath the glass of the counter were a series of effects pedals. Owen was looking at them and stroking his chin. 'Yes,' he said, 'One of those orange boxes as well.'

'The Fuzz Pedal?' the salesman said. He took a key, unlocked the case and took it out. 'I tell you what. Since you guys are spending so much today, I'll throw this in free. I'll throw in a bunch of cables and some picks, too.'

Owen was ecstatic. 'Great! How much does it all come to?'

The salesman tapped the prices into the cash register.

I felt like I was waiting to hear lottery numbers. 'Two thousand, three hundred and thirteen dollars and seventy-seven cents.'

Owen took out a credit card. 'Do you take Visa?'

We called a taxi and took our new merchandise back to my room in Elmwood Hall. It had clouded over and snow flurries had begun falling and swirling in the wind. There was hardly room to sit once we'd brought in the amps, shoving dirty clothes, books and CD cases aside to make floor space. I had to unplug my computer so we had enough outlets. We were ready, Owen sitting on my desk chair, his guitar running through the effect pedal and into the amp, me on my bed, plugged straight in. Well, we were sort of ready. Neither of us seemed to want to start. We sat facing each other, grinning.

'Do you have any idea what to do?' Owen asked.

Suddenly I remembered the Lomax book. In the back was an appendix that started with "American Folk Guitar Style." There was a drawing of a guy playing guitar, plus a diagram that showed a bunch of different chords, and where you should put your fingers to make them. I set the book, with this page open, on top of my amp. E minor looked like the easiest, so we played that one first. From my guitar it sounded impossibly real and clean, filling the tiny space with music I'd never heard before, recorded or live, as though somebody else had played it.

Owen leaned over to see how it was done, then strummed across the strings. It sounded like multiple grand pianos being dropped off a roof, an assault that felt like the room would explode before it dissolved into a piercing whine of feedback. Owen lunged across and flipped the power switch, ending the torture and supporting himself on the amp to keep from falling.

'I think we should turn it down a little,' he said.

We spent the rest of the afternoon and evening trying to contort our fingers into the right chord combinations. Around nine o'clock we both realized we were hungry, and I realized I had a paper to write. Owen insisted on paying for a pizza, which we devoured when it came.

'Do you mind if I leave this stuff here for now?' Owen asked as he stood by the door, shrugging into his jacket. 'I don't feel like hauling it across town tonight, and besides, I want to do some reading.' He rattled the plastic bag and left, closing the door behind him.

While I worked on my essay I kept looking over at the guitars, one black and yellow, the other yellow and black, leaning upright against the amplifiers. I wondered if we'd ever be any good at playing them. Every once in a while I went over and picked mine up, turned on the amp and plucked a couple of notes, trying to remember a chord or two. Then I'd give up in frustration. But I kept at it, off and on for the rest of the night. I couldn't help going back and picking up the heavy instrument, strapping it over my shoulder, and making sound.

Owen's gear lived in my room into the spring, creating an obstacle course that was hard to negotiate, particularly if I got up in the night. After a while, though, the guitars, the amps and their tangled networks of cables became pieces of furniture, and I didn't give them any thought. Owen came over a couple times a week, working around his baseball schedule, and we rehearsed chords until we had them memorized and could change between them. Then we began working on songs from the Lomax book.

The first one we chose was "Yankee Doodle," because we knew the tune. Neither of us could read music – I'd played trombone for about five weeks in grade school and had a vague recollection of quarter notes and half notes, but that was about it – so we had to rely on the sound of the chords to provide an idea of how the tune went. With "Yankee Doodle" our dependence on this method was limited, and by the middle of April we could more or less play it competently. I strummed and occasionally picked out the arpeggios, and Owen blasted the chords through the fuzz pedal and sang.

'We oughtta play at the open mic next Friday,' Owen said one Sunday.

I looked up. 'No way. Not in front of all those people.'

'Come on, we can play it without trying now. Sort of.'

'No.'

Owen stared me down. 'You won't be embarrassed. We can play it. I've got nowhere to go but up after that performance last January.'

After a little more badgering, I reluctantly agreed. I found it hard to say no. Owen had a confidence about things that I didn't, and he always found a way to persuade me. I spent every free minute going over "Yankee Doodle" that week, even though it was only three basic chords, G, D and C. Owen had the hard part, singing nine verses. By the time Friday night came around, there was no way I could have made a mistake. I was still terrified, though. What if people didn't like it?

Owen didn't concern himself with questions like that. They were irrelevant. As with the first open-mic night, the

18

point wasn't whether or not people liked it, the point was to get on a stage and close your eyes and let go and see what happened.

We were the last name on the list that night, and by the time our turn came, everybody in the bar was glowing with a mix of damp heat and alcohol. I didn't want to be drunk when we performed, and Owen had limited himself to two drinks per evening for the baseball season, but we both raised a toast for courage and slammed down a double Jack Daniel's before we went on.

The master of ceremonies announced us as 'Owen Noone and –' Here he looked to the side of the stage where we were standing. Owen tried to mouth my name, but the guy couldn't understand, so he said, 'Owen Noone and friend.'

People remembered Owen from January and cheered and whistled, some of them yelling about Guns N' Roses. I shuffled after. We plugged our guitars directly into the PA system, Owen running his through the orange fuzz pedal, and stood facing the crowd. My entire body was shaking, and I felt sure I would collapse; I didn't think I'd be able to hold the guitar, much less make the chords. I looked at Owen, who looked back at me, then leaned into the microphone. 'We're Owen Noone and the Marauders,' he said, then looked over at me again. 'Marauder. This is a song that you all know, so please sing along on the chorus.' He took a deep breath, counted one-two-three-four, and we began.

People giggled, and nobody sang along on the first trip through. Without Owen's pedal on everything sounded clean and strange to me. I kept my eyes on my guitar, as though I could will my hands to do the right things if I held them within view. Then, when we got to the second chorus, Owen stepped on the pedal and a blast of noise and energy pulsed through the bar. I froze and looked up sharply, stunned by the outburst of noise. Owen had his eyes closed and was singing in a sing-songy way like it was a lullaby or nursery rhyme, but off-key. Still, nobody was joining in. I looked back down and kept playing, and when we got to the next verse, Owen stepped on the pedal again. Then we returned to clean chords until the third chorus, when he stepped on it a third time. This time the bar joined in, a choir of voices rumbling to the stage and supporting Owen's. The whole thing was discordant, but people were clapping, knocking time on the table with their glasses and bottles, Owen's voice rising and becoming a hoarse yell. Then the calm of the verse. The pattern continued through the rest of the song, becoming more and more boisterous as it went along, and I even forgot that I was playing and strummed along automatically, watching Owen, watching the crowd watching Owen, pumping along to the rhythm of our guitars, his voice, the audience's clapping and bottle thumping. On the last chorus, which we went through twice without even thinking, I sang, my voice disappearing off the stage and into the audience without a microphone. I didn't care. I was happy.

Two weeks later Owen knocked on my door. I was reading *Measure for Measure*, and every thought I had, and everything I said seemed to be in iambic pentameter.

'Good morrow, sir,' I said after opening the door.

'Huh?'

I held up the book, a big mustard-colored *Complete Shakespeare*. 'Never mind. Too much of this, methinks.'

Owen scratched his head. 'Listen, I've got bad news.

I've come to pick up my guitar and stuff. I've been promoted to Triple A.'

'But that's good,' I said.

'Yeah, good for baseball, bad for the band.'

'What band? It's just the two of us, anyway. I mean, it's been a lot of fun, but I'd say you've got more important things going.' I felt like I was trying to convince myself as much as I was him. That night playing "Yankee Doodle" had been one of the best moments of the past few years. I'd felt confident, and when we'd finished, people had told us how much fun it was, and I'd felt like I was something more than this shy kid who walked around with his hands in his pockets, looking at the pavement. All of this was because of Owen. He'd bought the guitars, he'd insisted we play, he'd brought me a fraction of an inch out of the shell I'd created. And now he was going. 'Where is Triple A, anyway?'

'Iowa.'

'Iowa's not so far. Where in Iowa?'

His eyebrows crumpled down and he turned his head slightly sideways. 'I have no idea.' We both laughed. I helped him gather together his guitar, amp, pedal and the various cables. 'I tell you what,' he said, standing just outside my door, his things clasped to his side with his arms. 'You graduate in another year and a half, right? If I haven't made it into the majors by then, I'll be back, and we'll hit the road and make this band thing work.'

'Yeah,' I said, chuckling through my nose, 'right.'

Owen smiled, set down the amp, gave a mock salute, picked up the amp again, and walked down the corridor, disappearing around the corner on his way to the stairs. I closed the door and returned to the Duke and Isabella.

*   *   *

21

I spent the rest of my college career as I'd spent most of it already, writing bad poetry, doing my radio show, reading and writing papers. And playing guitar. I managed to steal the Lomax book from the library by turning it back in, then going back a while later, peeling the "Due for Return" slip off another book and fixing it into the Lomax, then playing innocent and showing that it wasn't due for another two weeks when the security alarm caught me. I learned all the chords listed in the back – there weren't all that many, anyway – and practiced the different styles. I also learned to read the music by beginning with songs that I knew the tune to, more or less, and working it out. By the time graduation day rolled around, I knew a couple dozen songs, although not all from memory. I'd also managed to get a job at Caterpillar in Peoria, writing and editing their internal newsletter and press releases.

The graduation ceremony was long, hot and boring. It was almost 90 degrees that day and sitting in the sun wearing a robe over a suit – my mother had insisted I wear a suit – made it almost unbearable. The commencement address was given by some state senator who told us that the world we were about to enter was ours to fashion to our greatest ideals and that we had more opportunity than any generation before us. We would all be going off to different futures, some of us into business, some of us to further education, some of us, like him, into public service, but we'd all, each in our own way, be contributing to the singular future of America and, indeed, the world. 'The world is yours,' he concluded; I remember this exactly. 'Don't let anyone stand in the way of your vision of it, your dreams.' And vote Republican! I hoped he'd add, but he didn't. After the speech, we spent hours listening to people's names and achievements as they walked across the stage. At the end, hats were thrown.

After taking me to a deli for a supper of subs and french fries, my parents left. They had 200 miles to drive because Dad had to be at work early the next morning. It was out of the question to take a day or two off in the run-up to the summer shut down, even if it was your only kid's graduation. After supper they dropped me off at Elmwood Hall – I had two days before I had to leave and move my stuff to my new apartment. My dad shook my hand and said he was proud. I was the first one in the family to finish college. My mom cried and gave me a hug. I stood on the sidewalk, watching their car as it rolled away towards Main Street and I-74, which would take them home. Staring down the street until they disappeared, I suddenly felt empty and alone. I hadn't known very many people at Bradley, but the few people I did know were all leaving for different places, cities like Chicago, St. Louis, Indianapolis, some of them even as far as New York or San Francisco. I was staying in Peoria, a place I'd hardly left in four years and only a few hours' drive from where I'd lived my entire life. Of course, it was by choice that I was staying, but something made me skeptical, or scared, about venturing wider into states, regions, cities to which I'd never been, places that were names and postcard pictures, places that were television news footage. No, I preferred to stay in Peoria, work at Caterpillar, a respectable job with a respectable company, and save some money. I could always go to those places later, when I had experience, money and something about myself to sell.

'I hoped I'd find you here.' I recognized the voice and turned. It was Owen Noone, unchanged from the few months I'd known him a year and a half before, except he was tanned and wearing sunglasses. I couldn't think of anything to say, but then I remembered what he'd said before he'd left. He grinned, and took off his sunglasses. 'Have you been practicing?'

'Yeah,' I said. Owen was taller than me, and it made me feel younger than him, standing there answering his questions.

'All right,' he said. 'Where are we off to then: east, west, north, south?'

'Owen.' I was speaking slowly. 'What are you – I can't –'

'I told you I'd come back if I didn't make it, and I haven't. Baseball's getting boring, anyway. Catching a ball, hitting a home run, stealing a base. People cheer. I've been playing lousy too, and I think they were about to send me back here, so I just saved them the effort and expense.' He pushed his hand through his hair and I could see small dark patches in the armpits of his gray T-shirt. 'So, which way are we headed?'

I phoned my parents the next morning from Iowa City. It seemed like a good place to go – college town, decent sized, we could probably find cheap rent and gigs easily enough. And it wasn't Peoria. Eventually, we'd head west, either to California or Portland or Seattle, but not until we'd memorized a complete set of songs. That was the plan.

My parents weren't impressed. 'Oh, son,' my father kept saying over and over, 'Oh, son,' making it sound like I'd just been sent to prison, 'Oh, son.' My mother didn't speak at all, but I could hear her sobbing on the other line. 'Go back to your job, son,' my father said after he'd composed himself. 'You've done so well. Don't blow it. You don't get a lot of opportunities like that. Go back to Peoria, to your job.'

I was on a payphone and didn't have any more coins, so it cut me off, those last words hanging over me in the small glass cube. I looked through the glass at Owen, who was standing on the sidewalk in front of the diner where we'd just eaten breakfast. He was looking at the pavement and trying to kick something loose from the crack between the slabs. I began to forget my father's voice as I stared at the bottom of the phone booth, where the glass stopped a foot short of the ground. I took a deep breath and replaced the receiver before rejoining Owen, who was still kicking at a penny that was lodged in the crack, kept partly in place by a flattened piece of chewing gum.

*   *   *

We moved into a house on Gilbert Street, not far from either the campus or the downtown area. The landlady was in her seventies and had long, wispy gray hair. She insisted we call her Miss Kitty and, for the entire time we lived there, never wore anything except long-sleeved floral cotton dresses. The house was a three-story wooden square with a steep black-shingled roof. It looked like it hadn't been repainted since the turn of the century, huge patches of bare board showing through where the green paint had flaked away. Once-white shutters were grimy and gray. Owen and I were given adjacent rooms on the top floor, surprisingly large, each with a single bed and mattress and a bare light bulb hanging from the middle of the ceiling. The floorboards were so worn that only the very edges, near the walls, had any varnish. Owen and I were the only two residents on the top floor, and we had a bathroom just for the two of us. 'The hot water ain't so good, 'specially not up here,' Miss Kitty said as she shuffled ahead of us, opening doors and pointing to every light switch and electrical outlet. 'But my boys all seem to make do.'

'My boys' is what Miss Kitty called the other men who lived in her house – six in all, including us. The others were all older and seemed to live in varying degrees of destitution. Al was a pink-faced fifty-year-old feed salesman who traveled all over Iowa, Minnesota and Illinois during the week and only appeared on weekends, when he spent two days parked in front of the television watching baseball with Miss Kitty. Brett was a thin guy of about thirty with brown hair and a pencil mustache. He managed one of the Iowa City McDonald's. Carl, forty and recently released from prison, never left his room except when he had to go see his probation officer. We didn't know what he'd been in prison for, or how long he'd been there, and didn't want to ask any more than he seemed to want to volunteer the information. Dennis, the fourth of our house-mates, was Miss Kitty's nephew. He didn't seem to have a job although he left the house every morning at eight, shouting, 'Bye, Aunt Kitty,' and returned every night at seven, dark stains spreading out across his blue shirt from his armpits, shouting, 'Phew, what a day,' and sweeping his black hair over his bald spot. Nobody seemed to know where he went, least of all Miss Kitty, who spent most of her time telling him it was high time to get a job like a man. Brett said he came into McDonald's once in a while, never at meal times, but always in the middle of the after-noon, and always ordering three cheeseburgers and paying with a twenty dollar bill. I thought he probably made his money betting on horses or dogs, or maybe selling drugs, but Owen didn't think he was smart enough for that.

By offering to paint the entire outside of the house, Owen convinced Miss Kitty to let us stay rent-free for the first two months. For the rest of May we got up at six, spending the first few days scraping off the old paint, then taking the next two weeks to splatter three coats of pea-green Glidden onto the boards, which soaked it up almost as fast as we could put it on. After a day of painting we were too tired to move, much less pick up our guitars and practice. I started to feel as though I'd made a terrible deci-sion, that like my father had said, I'd blown it. Here I was in Iowa City, the middle of nowhere, painting a house that was falling apart, the guitar that I was supposedly playing in a band leaning in a corner unused since we'd arrived. In a moment of supreme stupidity I'd followed Owen Noone a hundred miles, giving up a decent, albeit boring job, for what? It occurred to me that I didn't even really know Owen all that well, and I started to dislike him simply for that. I started to wonder if anything he'd told me was actually true, or if, like the rest of Miss Kitty's boys, he was just another deadbeat, and if I, following his every move, was even worse, a deadbeat's fool.

As the sun burned my neck and arms, and as the constant climbing up and down on the ladder began to make my back hurt more and more, I would silently curse myself for being stupid, and even more, curse Owen Noone for dragging me into his idiotic plan. Every night, though, sitting in one of our rooms, drinking beers that Owen had run down to the store to buy, we'd flip through the book of folk songs, laughing at some of them, tearing pieces of paper to mark ones we liked, half listening to the baseball broadcasts that came from the AM stations in Chicago, and I'd forget about my daytime cursing, feeling somehow like I was living a different life, in a different time, sitting on a bare wood floor listening to the radio and drinking cold beer with my friend. Neither of us really knew what we were doing, but when we finally finished on the first of June – our handiwork wouldn't have passed muster by most standards – Miss Kitty was so pleased she gave us the third month free as well.

Finally, on the second of June we started playing our guitars again. We'd planned to get up early, go to the same diner where we'd eaten our first morning in Iowa City, then go back home and play all day. Miss Kitty agreed to let us clear a space in the basement where we could practice. It was the only place in the house that didn't allow every sound to escape through cracks in the walls and thin floorboards. The basement was big and cluttered with a jungle of broken appliances, unused garden tools and boxes that were covered in thick layers of black dust that we didn't want to touch more than we had to. Fifteen minutes' work with a hammer and some nails fixed a couple of broken chairs and we were ready to get down to what we'd come to do. Owen had plugged a power strip into an extension cord that weaved between a pile of boxes and around an old refrigerator to the wall socket. Into the power strip we plugged our amps. Like our bedrooms, the basement was lit by a single bare light bulb that wasn't bright enough to spread much further than a few feet. It was hard to read the chords in the book without leaning over and squinting, so we propped it on another broken chair.

Owen switched on the amps and we heard a loud pop. The light went out. Across the room a small flame licked up the wall from the end of the extension cord, or the socket, or both. We rushed over, banging into boxes as we tried to avoid them in the dark, and Owen tore the cord from the wall, then stamped on it to make sure the flame was out. He laughed. 'We didn't even start yet. It's not fair.'

An hour later, after a trip to the hardware store to buy an extension cord and a new fuse – Owen insisted we buy a half dozen, to avoid future trips – and after reassuring Miss Kitty that there was nothing to worry about, we got back to it, starting with the only song we both knew: "Yankee Doodle."

It felt like that night in Peoria, when I'd stood on a stage for the first time in my life, watching Owen as I strummed chords on the guitar he'd bought me a couple months before. In that moment I felt like I knew what I was doing, that I knew where I was going and who I was.

That feeling would continue for as long as I knew Owen, self-confidence, maybe, and with nothing more than a nod, and sometimes just by sensing it, we would slow down, speed up, change volume or style, mid-song, without missing a beat. The basement was dark and dirty, but I hardly noticed, the space consuming me with the sound of my — our — music.

We added songs to our repertoire all summer, practicing from nine to five every weekday like it was a regular job, except for two weeks in July, when, on a recommendation from Miss Kitty, the next door neighbor hired us to paint his house. By the beginning of August, besides "Yankee Doodle," we knew "Old Smokey," "The Wild Mizzourye," "The Erie Canal," "Ground-Hog," "East Virginia," "Worried Man," "The Old Gray Goose," "Blue-Tail Fly," "Green Corn," "Godamighty Drag," "John Henry," "My Government Claim" and "Careless Love," thirteen new songs, plus "Yankee Doodle," which made fourteen. A lot of these songs shared the same few chords, which made them easier to learn, and Owen didn't seem to have much problem memorizing the words. Most of them followed our successful "Yankee Doodle" pattern: soft, clean verses followed by loud, Owen-distorted me-clean choruses, although some, like "Green Corn" and "My Government Claim," we just played loud, and some didn't have choruses, so we just monkeyed around, trying different patterns until we found one we liked. We did "Old Smokey" very softly, with me picking out arpeggios against Owen's lightly strummed chords.

One morning in mid-August Owen was waiting in the living room when I came down to eat breakfast.

'Come on, we've got to get going.'

I rubbed my eyes, trying to wake up. 'Go where?'

'Bars.'

'Owen, Jesus, it's –' I looked at my wrist, but I wasn't wearing a watch – 'early. I'm not going out drinking.'

'No, we've got to go around and try and get some gigs. It'll be the school year soon. We've got to do this before all the students come back.'

Of course, none of the bars were open that early, but Owen didn't let it stop him. We went into coffee places, stopped at record stores and just wandered around looking for places to go back to later. When the bars began to open mid-afternoon, we went back to places to try and get hired. The first bar we went to was called Fuzzy's, a big, dark place with a long bar, tables in the front half and a two-foot-high stage in the back. Owen, as usual, did all of the talking.

'We're Owen Noone and the Marauder,' he said, and pointed at me. 'He's the Marauder.' I sheepishly half-smiled.

'What kind of music do you play?' The owner was around thirty, blond and about the same height as Owen. He wore a blue dress shirt and jeans and despite his easy demeanor, I was petrified.

'I guess you'd call it, I don't know, alternative-folk-rock-pseudo-punk. I think that covers it, don't you?' He looked at me.

'Yeah,' I croaked.

'We have a good following in Peoria,' Owen added.

'Do you have a demo?'

I panicked. Owen didn't. 'Yeah, sure. Not with us, though. We can bring it around tomorrow.'

I tried to kick Owen, but my legs wouldn't work. I alternated my gaze between the two of them.

31

The bar owner smiled. 'Okay. Bring it by tomorrow, I'll have a listen, and decide. Thanks, Owen.' He looked at me. 'Thanks, Marauder.'

'See you tomorrow, Fuzzy.' I couldn't believe Owen said it, but the guy laughed, so he must not have minded.

Outside, Owen turned to me. 'We need to buy some sort of recording device right away.'

'Yeah.' I felt sick. Putting songs onto tape was somehow a bigger, worse step than playing in front of people. In a bar people were drinking, not paying a lot of attention if they didn't want to, and any little mistake went by, if not unnoticed, at least quickly forgotten. On tape everything was preserved. It could be scrutinized over and over.

We went to a music shop and Owen bought a four-track. These expenses never bothered him. Between his baseball salary and his trust fund he was used to having enough money for things. Of course, he didn't have his baseball income anymore, but I suspected that he'd saved a lot of money over the few years of his career, enough not to have to worry about it for quite a long time. And the trust fund money came every month; it was, I inferred, more than a livable wage. He always paid for things, equipment, meals, beer, and I felt somehow like his child, or like he was my legal guardian, but he was never patronizing. I was constantly thanking him for paying, but he'd just wave me off, sincerely, without putting himself above me. For Owen, it was just a matter of course.

In Miss Kitty's basement we looked over our list of songs, trying to decide which ones to put on the demo. "Yankee Doodle" was essential, belonging as it did to the genesis of playing and our friendship. The three others we chose were "East Virginia," "Ground-Hog" and "Erie

Canal," all of which sounded the most like real rock songs. For the first time it crossed my mind that what we were playing was in fact not rock 'n' roll at all, but folk music, played in a rock style.

Recording them was easy enough. We just draped microphones we'd bought along with extra cables over our amps and plugged them into the four-track, then had Owen sing into another mic. We didn't have a stand or anything for it, so we looped it over a water pipe that ran across the ceiling, letting it dangle at mouth level so he could play and sing at the same time.

The next afternoon we took the tape into Fuzzy's. Fuzzy greeted us as Owen and Marauder and told us his name was Mike. Fuzzy was the guy from whom he'd bought the bar. He put the tape into a deck, and after a second of hissing, the chirpy chords of "Yankee Doodle" started up, followed by Owen's voice. Mike's face crumpled into a grimace of confusion, then opened into a grin.

'Is this — "Yankee Doodle?"'

'Just keep listening,' Owen said.

Our recorded music filled the empty room, but still sounded spare and hollow. At the far end of the bar a girl was putting away clean glasses. She stopped and listened, a quizzical look on her face, as though she was trying to decide whether it was a joke and whether she should laugh. Then we hit the second chorus, when Owen stepped on the fuzz pedal and the volume doubled. I imagined the needles on the receiver jumping into the red. Behind the fuzz of Owen's guitar I could still hear my own playing. Everything sounded amazingly good, I thought. "Erie Canal" was the next song, an all-out rumble of noise, more in the punk vein in which Owen had advertised us and less recognizable as a folk song. Mike drummed lightly, keeping time on the shiny wood of the bar. By the time the tape ended with the ridiculous, off-kilter shouting and stamping of "Ground-Hog," in which you could hear my background shouts and Owen keeping time with his foot on the floor, Mike had a huge grin, and the girl had come over to see who we were.

'I like it, boys,' he said, 'But I have no idea how it'll go over with the college crowd.' I felt myself sink inwardly.

'We had a good following in Peoria,' Owen reminded him, even though it wasn't technically true.

'Yeah, well, anyway, what I'll do is hire you for one gig, and then we'll see how it goes. If it works out, we can make a deal for a longer-term thing. Sound good?'

It sounded great to me. Owen scratched his head, though, and I thought maybe he was going to push for more than one guaranteed gig. 'You won't be disappointed,' he said. 'Sounds good.' We spent a few more minutes working out the details, and when we walked out of Fuzzy's we had a deal for the first weekend of the semester with a two dollar per person cover charge, of which we'd get half. Owen was very businesslike when working out the details, sounding as though he negotiated these things all the time. We stepped back into the sunshine of the hot afternoon and walked down the street.

'Can you believe it?' Owen shouted suddenly, after we'd crossed onto the next block. 'This is great! We'll pack the place.'

I was excited too, but I didn't share his optimism. 'How? We don't know anybody here. There's no reason for anyone to come.'

'We'll advertise. Put up posters everywhere, hand out

flyers. Make it sound good. Plus, it's the first weekend of the semester. There'll be loads of people anyway.'

'What if they don't like it?'

Owen stopped walking and turned to me. 'They've liked it so far.'

'Who? A bunch of drunks in Peoria, and that was only one silly song, and a bar owner.'

'Plus a pretty girl behind the bar.'

'Still, it's not exactly a strong survey.'

'Don't worry so much. Besides, we don't have time to worry. We've got two weeks to learn more songs. Fourteen isn't going to last very long.'

We doubled our repertoire in two weeks, practicing a few of the songs we knew to start out with, then spending most of the day working on new ones, flipping through the Lomax book to find anything we could learn quickly. The new songs lent more variety, more balance and a few more chords to our set, and the two of us were concentrating so hard during our rehearsals, and working so well together, that we memorized them without too much trouble. We spent the last few days before the gig working out the order and playing the whole set through to figure out if we had enough to spread over three hours. We also made posters and flyers, sticking them onto any empty space and handing flyers to anybody who'd take them.

OWEN NOONE
AND THE MARAUDER

FUZZY'S
Friday August 29

10PM

PSEUDOPUNKFOLK

Plus:

"YANKEE DOODLE"

✕

(FAMOUS IN PEORIA)
(SOON TO BE IN IOWA CITY)

People would take the flyers automatically, then, after walking on a few paces, turn and look at us, trying to decide, I guess, what the hell it meant and whether we were Owen Noone and the Marauder. I didn't look much like a marauder, but I suppose Owen did.

The twenty-ninth of August came. We decided not to practice that morning, so we didn't ruin whatever freshness we might have for the gig. It was the first morning in almost three months that our day didn't begin under the bare light-bulb in Miss Kitty's basement. We spent most of the day in Owen's room finalizing our set list and getting nervous.

'What do you think we should wear?' Owen asked.

I hadn't thought about it. 'This, I guess.' I was wearing jeans and a short-sleeved blue and gray plaid shirt. Owen had on khaki shorts and a white T-shirt.

'It's not much of a rockstar outfit.'

'We're not much of rockstars.'

'Yet. Good point though.' He picked up the paper on which we'd written the set list. 'But don't you think we should dress the part?'

'What's the part look like? I mean, pseudopunkfolk doesn't even mean anything. I don't know what the dress code would be. Overalls with leather jacket and a fedora? Besides, I don't feel like putting on some ridiculous costume, and I don't have much else besides things like this anyway.'

Owen grunted. 'I guess. It just seems like a shame not to wear something special, since we're getting paid and all.'

We got to Fuzzy's at six in order to set up and do a soundcheck. We didn't really have any idea what to do, so we hung microphones in front of our amps like we had when we'd recorded the demo tape, and strummed a little while Owen sang. I stood in front to see if it sounded all right, which it seemed to, very loud and big with everything coming through the bar's PA system. By seven we were finished, and had three hours to sit and wait and drink beer and try not to get drunk. We more or less succeeded, and when we got onstage at ten we had enough alcohol in our systems to be relaxed but still coherent. Until we actually looked out at the crowd, that is.

Or until I did. We stepped up onto the low stage and turned on our amps, strumming a couple of chords by way of checking the sound and turned to face the audience. The tables towards the front of the building were all taken and the area directly in front of the stage was densely packed. It was dark enough that I couldn't make out the faces of the people further back, but the first few rows were clear. I didn't know anybody, but I was petrified, looking out at what was around a hundred people jammed into the bar on their first Friday night back at school, or their first Friday night out, period. I went over to Owen and tapped his arm.

'I'm fucking nervous,' I whispered, away from the microphone.

'What for?' he said, stepping back and leaning towards me. 'We don't know these people. Besides, we're good. If they don't like it, fuck 'em.' Then he stepped back to the microphone. 'Hi, everybody. I'm Owen Noone.' He pointed at me. 'This is the Marauder. We've never played in front of this many people, and he's a bit nervous, so be nice.' I could feel my face turning red as he said it. 'This song is called "John Henry."'

'Jaaaaaaaaaaaawwwwwwwn,' Owen started, drawing it out as I formed a C-chord on my guitar, and on the quick syllables of "Henry," I played furiously, banging out the C while Owen sang, 'Was a little baby boy, / You could hold him in the palm of your hand.' I hunched over my guitar, alternately watching my left hand, which was forming the chords, and my right, which was a blur as it slid across the strings, my arm pumping urgently to make the chords push down through the cable and out of the amp.

On the first refrain Owen belted out, 'Gonna be a steel-drivin' man, Lawd, Lawd,' and stepped on the pedal, the wall of sound crashing into me so I no longer had any idea of my surroundings. I was just hammering my three chords, C-F7-G7 and back to C, sweat rolling down my face and arms. Only when we got to the end of the thirteenth and final verse, with Owen proclaiming that John Henry was 'nothin' but a Lou'siana man, / Leader of a steel-drivin' gang, Lawd, Lawd,' and with people howling and clapping and whistling, did I remember anyone was there. I smiled, remembering my nerves. As they crept back down my arms and legs, I took a deep breath and let them go.

Owen said thank you and we launched into "Careless Love," Owen's voice doing a parody of a crooner against the slower, melancholic blues chords. I played without thinking for the rest of the night, listening to our sound and singing along under my breath, lost in the fun. We finished with "Yankee Doodle," and everybody sang along to the parts they knew. When we finished, some of them shouted for one more.

'We don't know any more,' Owen said, and unplugged his guitar. The cable made a sharp cracking sound through the amp as it hit the floor and lay near Owen's effect pedal making a buzzing whine. He switched off the amp and the whine disappeared, leaving only silence on the stage and the background sounds of people talking and finishing their drinks.

When I was twelve years old, I used to daydream about being in a rock band, like Mötley Crüe or Poison. My friend Ben would play drums, his older brother Jeff and I would play guitar, and I'd sing. I'd lip-synch to tapes or the radio with an imaginary guitar in my hands, imaginary long hair flailing around, imaginary crowd pumping their fists and holding up lighters, every eye on me. Without the costumes and makeup, that childhood dream came true on August 29, 1996, in a bar in Iowa City.

After that first gig, Mike hired us to play at Fuzzy's once a month for the rest of the semester. We also played a few other places around Iowa City and a couple of fraternity parties, although those weren't successful because people wanted to dance, and the music Owen and I played was inherently undanceable. We were starting to make a decent amount of money, around three hundred bucks per show, but less than that at Fuzzy's where we always got a hundred plus half the cover charge and usually pulled in around 150 people. Fuzzy's was guaranteed income, though, and since that was the first place we'd played, we didn't mind getting a little less. We liked it there. It felt like home. I tried to pay Owen back for the guitar, but he refused. 'Wait until we've actually made something,' he'd say. Holding a hundred and fifty dollars cash in my hand was something, I thought, keeping my mouth shut.

When spring came, the cold, dry winter gave way to rain, mud and an altogether worse kind of cold, a coldness that, because it was warmer and wetter, seemed to hang in the air and seep through the skin. We were well known and had a gig every weekend. We were also getting bored.

'I think we should move on,' Owen said one afternoon while we were practicing, learning "Come All You Virginia Girls," which we thought would be funny to sing as 'Come All You Iowa Girls.'

'What do you want to play?'

'No, I mean move on, get out of town, go somewhere else where there's more people, more places to play, more money.'

'Okay.' I didn't know. I liked being in Iowa City. It wasn't too big, we were making enough money. It was comfortable, if kind of dull. I thought of places like New York and Los Angeles, far away places to which I'd never been, or Chicago, where I'd been once, and was every bit as big and intimidating in my mind. Iowa City, a little more than a hundred miles from Peoria and three hundred or so from where I'd been born and grew up, felt like far enough away from the center to me. But I didn't tell Owen. 'East or west?'

'Not west. I don't want to go through Des Moines.'

I couldn't think of anything offensive about Des Moines until I remembered that Owen had quit baseball there. 'There's other ways west.'

'I thought we could go East, though, to Charlotte. We can live for free there, in my house.' Owen had been renting out his house ever since he left, but it had been empty since the New Year. I was amazed at his business sense. He always seemed to know what he was doing when it came to these kinds of matters, things about which I knew nothing, never having been taught them, never having had the need to learn.

Returning to North Carolina, I thought, would be the last thing Owen would want to do, but Charlotte didn't seem big or frightening, so I decided to go along with it. Besides, a free place to live, a new home already taken care of, made it less foreign. On March 30 we played one last gig at Fuzzy's, and on April 6, we set sail.

Excerpt from University of North Carolina-Charlotte *University Times*, Tuesday, May 6, 1997:

... Owen Noone and the Marauder, as they were listed on the posters, proved the only original, if entirely befuddling act of the evening. Consisting of only two guitarists, they played a dozen or so songs, alternating between jerky, jangly strumming and something approximating grunge, throwing in a sweet love song towards the end for good measure. The lyrics, sung out of key by Noone, were anachronistic, conjuring up images of Erie Canal shipmen and jilted backwoods lovers before they led the crowd in a protracted sing-along of "Yankee Doodle." Half the crowd had left by the time this moment came, but for those who stayed it was worth the puzzle of figuring out what these guys were doing singing "Yankee Doodle" accompanied by a distorted guitar, an out-of-tune bandleader and a real live Marauder ...

Looking at it now, this was the most important, most defining moment of my life. More important than when I'd given up the job in Peoria, more important than what college I picked. Leaving Iowa City, going to another part of the country, I was pushing into something unknown, going out far enough that there was no option of returning. Despite what our graduation speech said, the truth is that the world wasn't really mine. I had no idea what it was. It belonged to other people who did know, and facing this, a world full of so many things and expectations, things I didn't understand, didn't care about or that just seemed wrong, there were three things, as I saw it, that I could do: get a job and join it, sit in a big empty room and avoid it, or play in a rock band. Owen Noone and I played in a rock band. Whether or not this was any different from the first and second options, I don't know.

On April 6 we moved out of Miss Kitty's, packing our clothes and guitars and equipment into Owen's white Ford Bronco before giving her a check for the April rent, which she tried to refuse, but Owen insisted. 'Bless you, boys,' she said, giving us each a hug. 'If you come back to Iowa City, you've always got a home with me. Miss Kitty will look after you.'

It was ten o'clock in the morning. We had a lousy map that only showed federal highways and interstates. Our plan that first day was to drive as far as Champaign and depending on what it looked like, try and get a gig, then move on. We drove down I-74, going back the same way we'd come, out of the Iowa River valley and back across the border marked by the Mississippi River and a sign that said, THE PEOPLE OF ILLINOIS WELCOME YOU TO THE LAND OF LINCOLN. Following the white dashes as they led us from one river valley to another, the Illinois, suddenly we were racing past Peoria, and the land flattened out and there was nothing except bare, muddy cornfields and a horizon line. I folded the map and tossed it onto the back seat.

Champaign was a city that didn't seem to have any reason to exist. No river, no industry. Just a collection of buildings, a university and a railroad junction in the Illinois farmland.

We checked into a room at the Holiday Inn and drove around town looking for bars that might listen to our tape. The first one we saw was called Scruffy's, a name containing echoes of Fuzzy's, which seemed like a good omen. It was a small, one-room bar with a pool table in the center and pinball machine against the back wall. Two middle-aged men were setting up the balls on the pool table but otherwise the place was empty. Owen and I walked over to the bartender.

'You ever have live music in here?' Owen asked after ordering two beers.

'Every Friday and Saturday night,' he replied, then put the glasses in front of us and took Owen's money.

'We've got a band you might like to hire.'

'Yeah? What do you play?'

'We're a rock band.'

The bartender alternated his gaze between the two of

us and I tried not to look away. 'Just the two of you, or what?'

'Yeah, it's just us two. We're from Iowa City, where we've been pretty successful.' Owen sounded like a circus promoter looking for a place to pitch his tent.

'You got a tape?'

Owen handed a copy of our demo across the bar then took a sip of beer. My glass was already half empty. The bartender put the tape into a deck and pressed play. 'Is this – "Yankee Doodle?"'

'Yep. One of our most popular songs back in Iowa. Peoria, too.'

The bartender looked skeptical. When the first song finished and "Erie Canal" came on his expression altered from skepticism to distaste, like he'd eaten a crate of lemons. To his credit he heard out the tape, then pressed the eject button and handed the cassette back to Owen.

'Look, boys.' He scratched his head and the right corner of his mouth turned upwards into a pose of mild discomfort. 'I don't think my clientele are going to have much truck with listening to a couple of Iowa boys playing "Yankee Doodle" and singing about Erie Canals and ground-hogs. I mean, it just doesn't make a lot of sense.' He tapped the cassette, which Owen had put on the bar. 'Good luck, though, boys. You're all right. Just not for here.'

One of the pool players cursed, and I looked over at the table. There were three stripes, one solid, no eight ball. The other grinned and put more quarters in the slot as his friend shook his head and chalked his cue. Owen and I finished our beers quickly and left, Owen taking the tape and shoving it in his jacket pocket. It felt like it should be raining, but it wasn't. The sky was bright with only a few curls of thin cloud slowly shifting shape as they rode east on the wind. I wrapped my arms around my ribs and shivered. We tried another bar, but they weren't interested in having live music. A few others said they might be interested, but were booked for the next couple months. After five attempts I felt like going back to the hotel. The town was a dump, and I just wanted to sleep and leave as soon as possible. We weren't wanted. Owen insisted we try two more places, which we did, without success, so we stopped for pizza on our way back to the hotel and spent the rest of the night watching the opening game of the baseball season, the Cubs losing to the Braves three to nothing.

We left early the next morning, our goal to get as far as possible, hopefully to Nashville, which was around 400 miles. By eight o'clock we were back on I-74, passing through a farm town called Danville and crossing the border into Indiana, which had a sign that welcomed us to THE CROSSROADS OF AMERICA. These signs were starting to feel like the only thing that differentiated one state from the next, the terrain hardly altering. Just mile after mile of muddy farmland, always the green tractor rumbling along, furrowing the ground to make it ready for planting. In another season it would be different, yet somehow just as uniform, fields of tall corn giving way to low-lying soy, the occasional cow pasture or pen of hogs, always a barn that needed painting, with an ancient oak or two in front of the house but never more than that. In a couple of hours we were circling Indianapolis, its glass office buildings rising from the flat land and reflecting the sunlight.

This, our second day driving, seemed much more full

of purpose. The first day, we just drove, hoping to end up somewhere, anywhere. Now we had to get somewhere specific – Nashville, a place, a destination, a star in the middle of a green area on our map. I drove after lunch, the first time I'd driven a car since Christmas of my final year of college, the last time I'd been home.

'How do you think they choose the colors?' Owen said as I merged back onto the interstate. I had no idea what he meant. 'For the map. How do they decide that Iowa should be pink, Illinois orange, Indiana yellow, Kentucky pink again, and Tennessee green? Why do we drive across two pinks before we get to our first green?'

'What if we'd gone north or south or west? Then it might have worked out better.'

'A little better, but still not perfect. But why those colors? Only one primary color.'

'It's easier on the eyes,' I said with the authority of someone who'd been reading the map for a day and a half.

'I think you're right.'

He folded the map and threw it on the dash as though, with that question out of the way, we didn't need it anymore. I was concentrating on the road, passing and being passed by semis that dwarfed the few cars. After an hour and a half we were climbing another bridge over another river into another state, only this time it wasn't just the Bluegrass State we were welcomed to, but also the City of Louisville, home of the Slugger, the Derby, the University of. Just after the bridge we passed Churchill Downs, and Owen said he wished it were the right time of year to go to the horse races.

We sped through Louisville, heading southwards through Kentucky. After another hour we'd gotten to

Mammoth Cave and were ready for a break, so I left the interstate and looked for a place to stop. Every shop we passed advertised cigarettes, groceries and cave souvenirs. We came to a low, rectangular diner with a large white sign that said RANDALL'S in green letters. Several tables with vinyl-upholstered chairs lined one side of the dining area, and a sandwich counter ran along the other. We sat at the counter and ordered french fries and Cokes. A couple of families sat in the booths and a truck driver sat next to us, eating a chicken-fried steak and fries. The tall, bald, muscular man with a mustache who had taken our order came back and put our drinks in front of us. When he brought the rest, Owen asked him if he was Randall.

'I am,' he said, running his thumb and finger along his facial hair.

'I'm Owen Noone. I noticed you've got an electrical outlet outside. You mind if my partner and I plug our guitars in and play a few songs for people as they come and go?'

Randall squinted his right eye and stroked his mustache again. 'What kind of music you boys play?'

I looked at Owen. 'Folk songs,' he said, 'Whole variety of folk songs.'

Randall stopped stroking his mustache and gave a half-smile. 'I don't see why not. If I don't like it, though, I'll send you on your way.'

'Understood.'

We ate our fries and took the glasses of Coke outside to the truck, where we unloaded our guitars, amps and the power strip. The orange fuzz pedal was in the bottom of a milk crate, covered by coils of cables and extension chords, the microphones and four-track. 'I think I'd better leave that thing in the truck,' Owen said.

We set up near the door and left a guitar case open in front of us. I prepared to start "Yankee Doodle," forming my fingers into a G-chord. Then I thought better of it. 'Owen,' I said, 'We can't play "Yankee Doodle," can we?'

'Why not?'

'Aren't we in the South?'

He looked at me and shrugged. 'I guess, sort of. North of the Mason-Dixon, though, aren't we?'

'We don't want to piss anyone off.'

'Yeah, I don't know if I'd play it down in Carolina. We should learn "Dixie."'

'But right now. Let's skip it. Just to be safe.' I was starting to get anxious just thinking about it, let alone playing. I'd never been this far south and realized that I didn't really have any idea what it was like. I'd always assumed for one reason or another that it was a different place, the South. A different country, almost. "Yankee Doodle" wasn't something I wanted to test out.

We started with "The Big Rock Candy Mountains" instead, which we'd always played without any distortion. It was warm that day. After we finished playing that first song I took off my jacket and played in a T-shirt, feeling the sun on my skin and playing guitar and smiling to the people who stopped for a minute or two on their way in or out of Randall's to listen to a few choruses of "Blue-Tail Fly" or "The Midnight Special" before heading in for their meal or back onto the highway. Most people put some change in the case, a few dropping dollar bills. I always smiled and nodded a Thank You when they did. We played "Come All You Virginia Girls" as "Kentucky Girls" and a couple of teenagers giggled when they heard it. We played for about an hour and a half, until the late afternoon. Some passing cars honked their horns. Occasionally one stopped and the driver, or sometimes a family, would get out and listen for a while, then continue on after dropping some change in our case and buying some fries or Cokes. There were still a hundred miles to drive to Nashville, and we didn't want to get there too late at night, so we finished with "Old Smokey" and started packing up our gear.

Randall came out smiling. 'Boys, that was real nice. We could all hear it in the restaurant there and really enjoyed it. You just passing through?'

'Yep,' Owen said, 'Just passing through. On our way to North Carolina.'

'Well, good luck to you. Thanks for the entertainment.' Randall shook hands with both of us and gave Owen ten bucks. We packed our things into the truck and got back on the interstate and headed towards Nashville.

'I was thinking,' Owen said, changing lanes to pass a slow moving truck. I'd been leaning against the window, feeling a light, empty happiness from our afternoon. Playing outside Randall's was like being transported in a time machine to a place that seemed to belong more to the fifties than to the end of the century, and we were something like the town barbershop quartet, or a traveling Dixie band, fitting into Mayberry, in some weird way.

'I was thinking,' Owen repeated, and I turned my head to look at him. 'We could do that anywhere. Play just normal like that, without the distortion. That way, we can bill ourselves as fits the situation. Punk rock type stuff for those places, folk act in the sticks.' He grinned. 'All things to all people.' I laughed and agreed and looked back out the window at the patches of wildflowers that sped past our truck.

Crossing into Tennessee was like crossing into Indiana. No river, no bridge, just a series of signs welcoming us to the Volunteer State, stating the speed limits and announcing the welcome center one mile ahead. Nashville lay another forty-something miles further along.

'Mason-Dixon,' Owen said.

I didn't understand right away.

'We're south of the line now, the real South. The place you're scared of.'

'I didn't say I was scared.'

'You looked pretty worried, whispering in my ear outside that diner in Kentucky.'

I felt my jaw growing tense, and my right hand gripped the armrest. 'I just didn't know, is all. I didn't want to — offend anyone. There's a difference.'

'Sure.' Owen had one hand on the steering wheel, the other resting upright against the window. He glanced over at me. 'Jesus, you're really pissed about it, aren't you.'

'No,' I lied.

'Look, I didn't mean anything. I just meant we're actually there now. I wasn't suggesting anything, that you were really scared. I was just having you on. Sorry I pissed you off.'

I mumbled something unintelligible and stared at the back of the car in front of us. Neither of us said anything until we got to Nashville and even then, it was only perfunctory. We found a motel and went to sleep.

The next morning I awoke before Owen and felt bad. I took a shower and thought about whether I was actually angry about it, and why. Maybe I was scared, crossing into so much territory I didn't know anything about towards a destination that I'd only heard about from

Owen. He'd touched a nerve when he'd said that, and it made me feel alone, even with my friend a few feet away, because he seemed to know more than I did. He seemed in control, and I was floating along with him, behind him, racing to catch up, and always moving further away from something, even as I caught up with Owen Noone.

I opened the bathroom door, letting the steam escape. Owen was already up and dressed. I stammered something about being sorry, but he told me to forget it, it didn't matter. 'Besides, I've got an idea.' I picked up my toothbrush and waited for him to explain. 'We're in Nashville, right? Home of country music. We ought to be able to use this folk-act thing to our advantage here.'

'Yeah,' I said, squeezing a glob of toothpaste onto the brush, 'But they're not the same thing, are they? Country and folk, I mean.'

'There must be room for all shades of country, folk, whatever, in Nashville. We should stay a couple days, go around to some places, recording places, labels, bars. See what we can drum up.'

After I brushed my teeth we went out, got breakfast and looked up some record labels in the phone book. Owen was sure we'd be on to something by lunchtime, but it didn't turn out that way. Nobody had any time for us. Mr. So-and-So was always in a meeting, could we leave a number, sorry, folk acts aren't our thing, this is Nashville, we do country and country only. One recording studio boss must have seen shades of Elvis in Owen and imagined himself as Colonel Tom Parker, because he actually let us play for him. We did half of "My Government Claim," until he cut us off and told us we were talentless crap and he was looking for a good country act to promote. One guy told us we'd be okay if we changed our look, and suggested a shop where we could 'outfit ourselves in some nice duds'. We went by, just to see. The window display had mannequins with tall cowboy hats, jackets of various colors and fabrics, but all with fringes down the arms and pants that had patterns stitched into them. It would've been funny if it weren't the end of the day, if we hadn't been kicked out of every place we'd tried, if it hadn't seemed like an insult to get clothes that would make us look like the Village People's cabana boys.

Getting into Nashville had seemed like a good idea, an easy way into the recording business. We'd heard enough country music to know they weren't discerning. But you can't just walk in and take it over like it's a bar in Peoria. Even Owen's usually unstoppable optimism couldn't keep up.

We got up early the next morning in order to be in Charlotte by the end of the day. Owen was gloomy. We were on the road by seven o'clock, going East on I-40, the low-hanging sun staring me down as I drove. I didn't have sunglasses and had to squint hard to keep my eyes from aching with the light.

I put in a tape of a radio show I'd done a couple years before and listened to songs I'd forgotten about completely but that were among my favorites at the time. Bands about whom I was telling everyone who'd listen, and now made me smile to hear and remember. Owen fell asleep, his head tilting to the right and supported by the shoulder harness of the seatbelt. It was the first time since we'd started across the country four days ago, other than before Nashville, that Owen wasn't talking or singing over the music, and it seemed strange to be driving with my friend silent and sleeping in the seat next to me.

Three and a half hours later we were almost out of Tennessee and into the Great Smoky Mountains, the interstate climbing and winding. It was raining. I drove with the headlights on and the windshield wipers furiously pumping back and forth. As we wound over the mountains, the road bending and weaving before ducking into tunnels that cut right through the rock, I would occasionally glance over the guard rail into the valleys, which, with the weather, were too deep to see entirely, the fog settling in and making the treetops look like they were floating on a murky sea. But they were far enough down that I could imagine the steep descent to the very bottom. I'd never been this high before, with an abyss like that looming below, and after a while I had to stop sneaking looks. I found myself gripping the steering wheel more tightly, my teeth set hard against each other. I wished Owen would wake up so I could tell him I was too tired to drive any further, or at least so I could have someone to talk to. All I could think of was the valleys, the rain and the insufficiency of the guard rail.

We cleared the mountains, descending into Asheville and then back up, but not as high as before. Finally we left the Great Smoky Mountains for good, the land more or less flattening out. It was early afternoon, my arms ached and I was hungry. In a town called Hickory I stopped for gas and woke Owen. I couldn't remember crossing into North Carolina, but it must have been somewhere in the mountains when I was busy staring at the road in front of me. After refueling, we went to a Subway and sat there for nearly an hour eating and taking advantage of the free drink refills. Owen drove the rest of the way.

It was sunny again now, and soon we were turning into the driveway of Owen's house. It was the biggest house I'd ever been in. The first level had a large entryway and the floor was shiny and wooden. From the high ceiling hung a chandelier. There were also two big, carpeted living rooms, a smaller dining room and a kitchen, both with pine floors. Sliding doors opened out from the kitchen to a patio and the backyard, at the back of which ran a creek. A wide staircase curved up to the second floor, where there were four bedrooms and two bathrooms, and the basement had a couple couches and a pool table. My jaw must have been dragging across the floor because Owen chuckled and said, 'Yeah, well, it's not all it's cracked up to be.'

We set up the basement as our practice room by moving the couches around to define a border between the playing space and the rest. We recorded two new demos, one that was just a better replica of the first, the other emphasizing the folk style we'd played at Randall's in Kentucky. That way we didn't have to rely on one tape when it didn't fit the situation. We spent a month and a half rehearsing all of our twenty-five songs and scouting out the best places to play. Owen said that now we were in a bigger city and should try to approach the whole thing more professionally.

In May, pretending to be students, we managed to get a gig at an end-of-year party at the University of North Carolina-Charlotte. Slotted after a jangly acoustic/electric light-rock band and another group that did classic rock covers and turned every instrumental break into a self-flagellating guitar solo followed by keyboard solo followed by drum solo followed by another guitar solo, we were very much out of place.

The event was staged on a practice field next to the baseball diamond, a huge grassy area with Toby Creek – the same creek that bordered Owen's backyard – running along the edge. There were a couple of carnival rides plus other distractions – people in outfits that made them into sumo wrestlers, a bouncy castle – but there were hundreds of students watching the gig, probably because the other bands were their friends, fraternity brothers or classmates. The master of ceremonies was some guy from the student government, and he introduced us as 'Owen Noone and the Marauders,' then looked a bit puzzled when only two of us came out. There was some polite applause from the crowd and we started straight into "Worried Man," playing the whole song through the distortion pedal. This uncomplicated, evenly paced song seemed to hook the crowd in, and they cheered and whistled and clapped. It was hard to see their faces because of the lights of the stage, but I could see shapes, bodies moving around.

'Thank you,' Owen said into the microphone. 'I'm Owen Noone, and this is the Marauder. We're the Rucksack Thracians.'

My head snapped around and I stared at him in confusion. He hadn't mentioned the name before. I didn't have much time to think about it, though, because we launched right into "East Virginia."

Since I couldn't see the crowd, there wasn't any point in being nervous. I watched my hands moving across the strings, forming the chords, and I watched Owen, who

57

closed his eyes whenever he sang, but glanced my way during instrumental parts, needlessly making sure we were still together. Needlessly, because we were always right together, or rather never exactly together, because without a drumbeat it was difficult to keep a steady beat onstage, but always close enough, which made our songs jerky, like we hadn't quite rehearsed enough, like anyone could play them. Of course, anyone could play them – they'd all come out of a book. But that, I think, was the charm, the idea that if these two guys could play these songs and be entertaining, so could anyone else.

The tempo and volume changes of "East Virginia" didn't translate well into this environment – a big stage, a big field, a big crowd – and the applause and cheering sounded more polite when we finished. The next song was the rambunctious "Erie Canal," though, and people started to clap along, which made us play more urgently, more forcefully. But next was "Ground-Hog" and again, changes in pace and distortion had the audience wondering what to do with themselves. The whole hour-long gig continued this way, by turns engaging and alienating, and the reactions grew quieter as it went on and people began to leave. We finished with "Yankee Doodle," Owen announcing that the Marauder was in no way condoning the Yankee lifestyle by playing this song and therefore should not be lynched. His voice when he spoke to the audience between songs regained some of the Southern drawl that had faded during his time away from Charlotte, and it seemed to go over well, a few people in the front laughing and scattered voices floating towards the stage on the chorus. After the final chord, I managed to improvise the melody to "Dixie," ending the song and provoking a huge roar from the collection of people who'd stayed to the end. Owen looked over at me and smiled and laughed.

We unplugged our guitars and amps and took it all backstage. The classic rockers had left, but the jangly acoustic light-rock band was still there drinking beer. They gave us sympathetic smiles as though we were young up-and-comers and they a seasoned group of veterans. 'Nice going, guys,' their singer said. 'It was, uh –' he took a long drink from his beer. 'It was interesting.' He and the others broke out laughing.

I started to open my mouth but Owen stepped in and grabbed the guy's T-shirt by the neck. 'As opposed to your brainless, meathead shit-rock, which is why you'll never be more than a frat-party clown.'

I wasn't quite sure he made sense, but the way he spoke, even-toned, almost under his breath and very deliberate while staring straight into the guy's eyes from about six inches away, made it seem like sense.

'Remember that when you see us on the cover of *Rolling Stone*.' One of the guys in the band tittered. Owen shot him a look. 'I'll let you clean my toilet when I've taken over the world.'

He let go of the guy's T-shirt and walked away. I picked up my gear and followed, ignoring whatever they shouted after us. Owen had scared me. I was as mad as he was, but these guys didn't really matter. It wasn't worth it. We packed our stuff into the Bronco and Owen drove home, cursing and changing the radio station every ten seconds. I didn't say anything.

At home we drank beer and played pool in the base-ment. Owen beat me, but I played well enough to make it close once in a while.

'What the hell is Rucksack Thracians, anyway?' I asked him after he'd won his fourth game in a row.

He shrugged. 'I don't know. Thracians, it's got something to with mythology, I think, and Rucksack, well, it just gives it a kind of rambler quality. It just popped into my head. It doesn't really make any sense, does it?' He laughed. 'I don't think I'll use it again.'

We got a few gigs around Charlotte and made some money. Most of the places were bars like Fuzzy's where the clientele were students who liked our music. We sent our demo tape to a few small record labels but didn't really expect to hear anything. Answering an ad in the newspaper, we sent the folk version of the demo to a place in Asheville that was hosting a music festival. The tape featured "Old Smokey," "Wild Mizzourye," "The Big Rock Candy Mountains," "Blue-Tail Fly" and "I Love My Love." To our surprise, we got a phone call from the organizer telling us we'd be put up in a hotel and paid an additional two hundred bucks if we came. Towards the end of July, we drove to Asheville to take part in the Great Smoky Mountains Music and Art Festival.

Asheville was tacky. Whatever it may have been at one time, it was now wholly devoted to tourism, selling T-shirts, jewelry and leather products to the tourists who passed through. The lines of shops with their covered wooden walkways were reminiscent of a Wild West outpost, except instead of serving any municipal function they all sold the same things at the same prices with little discernible variation. As part of the festival, some places had special displays of paintings and crafts – hand-woven baskets, quilts, carpentry projects such as small tables or chairs – by local artists and in a few designated areas, the actual artisans were at work, talking to passersby as they painted or chiseled or sewed.

The music part of the festival turned out to be a loosely organized event. It was spread over two days and each act – we never figured out how many there were, especially because some seemed to consist of the same lineups, anyway, but with different names and playing different styles – played one daytime slot, and an evening slot on the other day. Owen and I played during the first day and served as a warm-up act for the festival's main attraction, a group of local bluegrass legends, on the second evening. The daytime slot was the most fun, playing in the street as people roamed around, a musical version of what the artists were doing. We had a bucket for change and the occasional dollar or five dollar bill. For three hours we played songs using the outlets in one of the shops as a power source. Occasionally a group of twenty or so people would be gathered watching and listening, but for the most part people just drifted past, and we provided background music, a soundtrack for the art-making, the craft-buying and the T-shirt selling. The money in the bucket was split among all the performers at the end of the weekend. It earned Owen and me an extra fifty dollars each.

We slept late the second day and spent the afternoon wandering around. Our gig was scheduled for seven o'clock. We had to show up at six to set up and talk to the organizer, a guy named Bill Freem. Bill was a sixty-year-old carpenter and fiddle player and had a bushy black beard, but no moustache. He covered his bald head with a blue corduroy cap that looked like something a ship's captain would wear, except faded and worn, and the bill floppy with age. He wore blue jeans and a checked shirt that held in his sagging gut. Before we played he gave us the check for two hundred dollars and thanked us for coming. 'It's nice to see younger folk, and city folk like yourselves taking part in something like this, taking an interest in the folk music. I have to admit, I was a bit wary of this electric guitar thing, but I like it. It works, a little something new mixed into the old formulas.'

For the nighttime gigs there was a stage and about a hundred folding chairs all of which were occupied, with people standing behind and to the sides as well. Bill introduced us, saying we dropped the average age by about thirty years and increased the power output by several hundred watts. We played a more or less sedate set, the songs on the demo tape plus "I'm a-Ridin' Old Paint," "Hush Little Baby," and a couple more up-tempo songs, "The Midnight Special" and "Green Corn." The audience sang along with every song, something Owen and I had never heard before nor expected. When we played "Yankee Doodle" to the bar crowds the singing pushed us on and was a drunken, stumbling, hollering affair. The singing here was more of a chorus, people singing because they knew the songs in many different versions, because they liked these songs, and it felt as though we weren't so much performing or entertaining, but rather, providing an opportunity, a space, an accompaniment to the entertainment that they created themselves. When we finished, with "I Love My Love," people clapped and whistled enthusiastically. Bill came back onstage, smiling and clapping, and shook our hands. We quickly unplugged our gear to make way for the bluegrass group, a collection of older men playing banjo, double bass, guitar, a small drum kit and fiddle. It was a humid night, and Owen and I swatted mosquitoes as we watched from backstage, listening to the music and the occasional rumble of distant thunder.

'Holy shit.' Owen's voice woke me up. He'd been awake for an hour or so, watching the television news quietly. I rolled over and saw him sitting on the edge of his bed, staring at the television, his mouth hanging open. 'Hurricane Danny,' he said. I wasn't quite awake yet and didn't understand. 'Hurricane Danny hit Carolina last night. Hard. There's flooding everywhere, even as far inland as Charlotte. Guess whose house they just showed flooded almost to the second floor.'

Hurricane Danny had been a tropical storm when we left for Asheville. I looked at the television, just in time to see Owen's house – our home – peeking out of the water, the first story half-submerged. Toby Creek had turned into something of a lake. They showed other houses, trucks submerged almost to the roofs, people rowing dinghies through the streets.

'I guess we should get home,' Owen said.

It seemed like the thing to do. We each had a turn in the shower, packed up our stuff, checked out and drove for home, silently wondering what we'd find.

By the time we got to Charlotte the water had receded somewhat. We waded through two feet of brown water to the front stoop, which was just above the water level, and stood for a minute, both of us afraid to open the door. I imagined a cartoon-like scene, water cascading out the open door, fish flopping in the torrent. I held my breath as Owen put the key in the lock and turned it. The result was anticlimactic. There was no standing water in the house. There was, however, a layer of dirt and pebbles covering the entire floor. The carpets were soaked, dirty water squelched up as we walked across each room. The water marks on the furniture weren't very high, so we figured the first floor hadn't been as flooded as it looked on television. A swampy odor, the smell of muck and rotting plants, filled the house. We went through to the kitchen and looked out at the backyard, which was a lake as far as we could see, the creek indistinguishable from anything else.

Suddenly I thought of the basement. I practically ran to the door, as though if I could get there fast enough it wouldn't be too bad. Owen followed. I sucked in a breath and opened it. He reached for the light switch then thought better of it. Water came halfway up the stairway.

Owen stared down into the flood like he was trying to read a secret message in it. 'Was there anything important down there?'

Other than the pool table, the sofas, the refrigerator? 'Recording equipment.' I could virtually feel the color drain from my face. 'Recording equipment.'

We remained at the top of the stairs, both of us now staring into the darkness and the water. 'I took the microphones with us,' Owen said quietly, thinking aloud more than talking to me. 'They're in the truck. So's my pedal. And the master tape.'

'But the four-track.'

'I know.'

'The songbook.'

'I know.'

We stared into the water for a while, then I went and got a flashlight and shined it into the space below us. A cream-colored circle spread across the brownish water where I pointed it.

'The songbook.'

'I know.'

'No – I see it.' It was floating just beyond the stairwell. The smiling flower face on the cover had caught my attention as I swept the flashlight back and forth.

'We've got to get it.'

Owen took the flashlight and kept it focused on the book while I went down the stairs. The book was out of reach. I held the railing and reached out as far as I could, but it was still a couple feet beyond my grasp. Owen ran upstairs and came back with a baseball bat. Holding it by the fat end, I once again held the railing and stretched out across the dirty floodwater towards the songbook. At first I just tapped it, and I thought it was going to sink, but it didn't, and I hooked the far edge with the handle of the bat and pulled it close enough so I could grab it. The pages were waterlogged and dirty and a layer of grime coated the cover, but after it dried it would be okay. We'd still have songs to play.

We went to the dry upstairs and sat in Owen's room, me on the floor, Owen on his bed, neither of us saying a thing and just staring at the walls. It was obvious the house was going to need a lot of work, a lot of money, a lot of time. It was insured, but ours wasn't the only house that had been flooded, and we obviously couldn't live there without electricity, with a basement full of water and who knows what diseases waiting for us in the grime that covered the first floor. We sat like that for at least an hour before Owen broke the silence.

'Let's go.'

I'd been tracing a circle in the carpet with my finger, absorbed in this idiot's task, and didn't hear what he said the first time. But then his voice broke my spell.

'Let's get out of here,' he said. 'Out of Charlotte. I hate it anyway. The day my mom and stepdad left, I hugged my mom and shook his hand and watched their limo back down the driveway. Then I just sat down on the front steps for the rest of the day, wishing I felt happy or free. But I didn't, and that's how I feel now. We're doing nothing here, conning our way into college gigs, going to folk festivals, boring ourselves to death in this shithole. I don't know why we came here anyway, it was a bad idea, I should've never come back to Charlotte.'

I looked at him. He was talking not to me, but to the space between us, his eyes not focusing on anything but invisible particles of air. His face seemed to squeeze entirely towards the center as he pushed his eyelids together as tightly as he could before opening them and relaxing all his muscles. He looked at me. 'Tomorrow we go to New York.'

I was never any good at arguing with Owen. He had made a decision for both of us, and there was nothing to do but go along with it. New York. New York equaled Big in my mind. Not just a big place, but Big itself, a proper noun accompanied by Dangerous and Unknown. A place that existed in movies and on television, but not a place where anyone normal lived. Neither of us had ever been there, we didn't know anybody there. We would, for the first time, be in a big city without a place to stay, and we wouldn't be able to just walk into bars and tell them we were popular in Iowa or Peoria or Charlotte without getting laughed out of town. In New York we would find out if we really were any good, or if I'd have to go slinking back to my parents, the prodigal son who would not be welcomed, but would be allowed to stay until I found a lousy job, worse than the one I'd never been to in Peoria. Sitting on the carpet two floors above a flooded basement in North Carolina, I knew that I'd be traveling hundreds of miles again, not sure whether I was pursuing something or being chased myself, but knowing that I'd find out in New York.

It was dark when Owen shook me awake the next morning with the flashlight in my eyes, saying, 'Come on, wake up, come on,' over and over. When I finally opened my eyes, he turned off the flashlight and I tried to look around the room, but without lights, without streetlights shining through the window – the whole neighborhood was without power – I couldn't really get my bearings. The room was just an empty blackness and flashing spots as my pupils tried to shake away the effect of the flash-light.

'Pack up your stuff. I want to get out of here.'

In half an hour we were back on the road again, our first long journey in almost four months, not east this time, but north. The change in direction seemed important to me that morning as I looked at the map, trying to estimate how many miles we'd have to drive to get to New York City, where we'd have to change roads. I temporarily forgot my fear as we raced out of Charlotte, out of the flood-water towards dry land. Another new beginning.

'Where do you want to get to today?'

'New York.'

'All the way?'

'Yes.'

'Owen, it's like seven hundred something miles.'

'We can do it.'

'Fourteen hours, at least.'

'We can do it.'

'You're the boss.' I folded the map and flung it on the dashboard and let the headlights of the oncoming cars and trucks lull me into sleep.

When I awoke it was early afternoon and the sun was baking the side of my face through the window. Owen had his arm drooping over the side of the truck. We weren't on the interstate but driving down the main strip of a small town, marked by fast-food joints, grocery stores and gas stations. I rubbed my eyes and mouth and sat up straight in my seat.

'Where are we?' I asked, rolling down my window.

'Good afternoon,' Owen said. 'Welcome to Martinsburg, West Virginia, home of your lunch.'

'West Virginia?' I reached forward and grabbed the map, trying to unfold it quickly and smoothly. An impossible combination. 'What the hell are we doing in West Virginia?'

'The road goes through it.'

'Yeah, but that doesn't make sense. What road? Where –' I managed to get the map open and look. To my surprise I-81 went through the very eastern end of West Virginia. I refolded the map and put it back on the dash.

'Everything kosher, smart guy?' Owen grinned like he always did when I panicked over nothing. 'How about McDonald's?' He swung the car into the McDonald's parking lot and parked.

We hadn't eaten breakfast and now it was one o'clock in the afternoon. We both ordered Big Mac meals plus apple pies, which we scarfed down in about ten minutes. The fried, greasy food sat in my stomach like a rock and made it ache.

'Listen, I don't think we can make it to New York today,' Owen said as we stepped back into the hot afternoon. 'Have a look at the map and figure out a place –'

'My pig!' somebody yelled.

Owen stopped talking and we exchanged confused looks.

'My pig!' we heard again. From behind the McDonald's appeared a pig, racing flat out across the parking lot towards us, grunting and squealing and trailing a rope behind it, ears pinned back from the force of the wind. Just behind it ran a middle-aged, silver haired man wearing faded blue jeans and a white T-shirt, his belly bouncing with every step as he bellowed, 'My pig!'

Owen swung over the rail that separated the sidewalk from the parking lot, staring at the pig as it sprinted up. When they were almost even he dove, his shoulder driving into the side of it, knocking it over and causing more squeals and furious grunting as it rolled and he pinned it. The whole maneuver looked like some absurd football play.

'Oh, thank you, son, thank you.' The middle-aged guy trotted over and grabbed the rope, which, it turned out, was a leash. 'I don't know what I would've done if old Frances here had darted into that road. She's like one of the family.'

Owen stood and wiped his jeans. His elbow was scraped and bleeding. The pig – Frances – tugged hard at the leash, which was wrapped several times around the guy's hand, and squealed. She didn't seem to be hurt at all. Owen looked at his arm, at the pig, at me, at the guy, and smiled. 'I do it all the time.'

The guy laughed. 'You're a good man, good man. Here –' He reached into his pocket and took out his wallet – 'Let me give you something for your trouble.' He held a twenty dollar bill towards Owen.

'No,' Owen said, waving his hands in front of his chest, 'No. That was just a reaction. If I'd been thinking, I sure as hell wouldn't have done it. I don't want any money.' He looked at his elbow again and flicked some gravel from the wound. 'We've got to get going. On our way to New York.' He unlocked the door and I jumped in and we drove away, leaving the guy and Frances, squealing and pulling on her leash, behind in the parking lot.

'Owen,' I said five minutes later, scrutinizing the map as we merged back onto I-81, 'We can make it to New York today, easy. It's only a few hundred miles.

'Yeah,' he said, 'But we'll get there at night, and we don't know where we're going or anything. It'd be better if we stayed close by, so we could get there in the morning and have time. Maybe even reserve a place ahead.'

We decided on Philadelphia, a big city and easy enough to find a cheap room, and got there in the early evening, checked in, ate dinner, bought a New York City map and reserved three nights in a hotel. The next morning we were on I-95, driving through the rain towards our final destination.

New York City had more cars in one place than I'd ever seen. By the time we got to where we were staying we'd spent at least two hours in the city sitting in traffic, listening to car horns and engines. It was like being inside a living cliché – yellow taxis, frustrated motorists, everyone going nowhere.

Our hotel was actually a couple of rooms – we each

71

had one to ourselves, mine with a bathroom – above a small restaurant on East Houston Street, a big, busy road dominated by Korean restaurants and groceries. But all the streets were busy regardless of how big they were or whether they were one- or two-way, and every corner seemed to open into a different ethnic area defined either by restaurants or apartment buildings. Cross the street and turn right, everyone was Puerto Rican. Not too many blocks away, the neighborhood was Indian and a row of Chinese stores lay not too far beyond. The biggest city in America, I kept thinking, and here we are: what are we going to do?

What we did was go to a nearby bar and get very drunk. Owen said we were celebrating, and I asked him what there was to celebrate, exactly.

'Being in New York.'

'That's it?' I'd had four beers and was feeling sour. Being in New York seemed lousy, seemed lost, seemed meaningless, especially with nothing to do, nowhere to play, and no easy way of talking ourselves into a gig.

'And being out of Charlotte.'

'We're always getting out of somewhere, though. We never stay anywhere.'

'We stayed in Iowa City for a long time.'

'Not even a whole year.'

'But close.'

'And we were in Charlotte for all of a few months.'

'But Charlotte was dead, and our house was –'

'So what? The house would have been fixed up after a while. It's insured.'

'Yeah, but –'

'But what, Owen? But you didn't want to stay, you wanted to move on.'

'So did you.'

'Did I say that?'

'No.'

'Did you ask?'

Owen looked into his beer. 'No.'

'So what the fuck are we doing here?' My fists were clenched and I was staring at Owen, who was still divining the messages in his beer. He didn't answer right away but when he did, he looked up at me, speaking quietly and slowly.

'We'll stay here, I promise. And we'll get some gigs soon. We'll be making real money, we'll be a real band, no more of the bullshit we've been doing. We'll start tomorrow.'

'We'll fucking see.' I regretted it as soon as I said it. Owen was being genuine and I wrote him off. He looked back down into his beer, and when we'd both finished, neither of us having said another word, we stood and left.

I awoke sometime in the afternoon and lay in my bed for another hour, not wanting to move. My skull felt like it was wrapped too tightly around my brain, and my eyes ached. Eventually I got up and drank a glass of water while sitting in a chair by the window and staring at the street below. After an hour or so, Owen flung open the door and marched into the room carrying a small plastic bag.

'Great news,' he shouted or seemed to shout. 'We've got a gig.' He came over to the window. 'And I met a girl.'

I turned and looked up at him. It was obvious he had a story to tell and, hangover or no, I was going to hear it.

Owen woke up early, slightly hung over and unable to sleep anymore, so he decided to go for a walk to clear his head and to get some breakfast. It was already hot even though it was only nine o'clock, and humid, which made it hard to breathe. The only sound was that of the cars — engines, squeaking brakes, horns — as they traveled down Houston Street. He turned down Avenue B and went into a convenience store and bought a bottle of water, then continued up the street until he came to a park — Tompkins Square. The sidewalks and the park were crowded but nobody seemed to mind. Lots of people had dogs. After walking around the park he crossed over to Avenue A where he found a bagel shop and stopped to eat.

He felt better after he ate and continued his walk, trying to get the lay of the land and see what kind of shops and restaurants there were. It seemed like every corner had either a convenience store or a bar or both, and there were tons of record stores too — good ones. On St. Marks he went to a guitar shop and looked at a couple of four-tracks and bought some strings. They had business cards that listed how much Elvis would weigh on every planet, and he took one of those, too.

Eventually his route took him down Bowery, and he suddenly realized he was at Bowery and Bleecker, walking past CBGB's. He stopped and stared. He knew the club wasn't very good anymore, not like it was in the seventies, but still, when you've never been to New York before, and when you know the history — it was something like going to Graceland, or the Parthenon or the Coliseum. Or more like going to the bar where Jefferson wrote the Declaration of Independence, or Yankee Stadium or Wrigley Field, a historical place where things had happened and your heroes had made themselves heroic. Whatever the analogy was, Owen stood across the street, looking at the place, the sign, imagining what it must be like inside. Country Blue Grass Blues. He crossed the street.

They weren't open, but he tried the door anyway. It was unlocked, so he went in. It was dark; only a few lights were on. A couple of guys were pushing equipment around and another guy was sweeping the floor. He came over to Owen.

'We're not open.'

'I know,' Owen said, 'But I want to talk to the manager.'

He stopped sweeping and leaned on the broom. 'You looking for a job or what?'

'Yeah, sort of.'

'Shit, you're not in a band, are you?'

'Yeah.'

'Shit, kid, if I had a dime for every guy with a band –'

'Yeah, look, I'm sure a bunch of shitty bands are always coming in here, but I'm not that. Let me talk to him.'

'Yeah, right. I know the schtick. Screw off.'

Owen took twenty bucks out of his pocket and pushed it against the guy's chest. 'I want to see the manager.'

The guy's eyebrows went up and he took the bill. 'You're serious, huh? I'll bet you this twenty bucks you're wasting your time and money, kid.'

Owen smiled. 'I'll let you keep the twenty you're holding and when I walk out of here with a gig, I'll give you another twenty.'

The guy laughed and called over his shoulder to the other guys, who were lifting a case onto the stage. 'Wait 'til you hear this story, fellas.' He turned and looked at Owen. 'All right. But I'm not holding my breath.' He put down the broom and led Owen through a door and up a stairway, then knocked on another door. They heard a voice and the guy opened the door. 'Somebody here to see you,' he said.

'What's he want?'

'I don't know. Says you're expecting him.'

'I don't remember – well, send him in.'

The guy looked at Owen and said, 'I wash my hands of it now, kid. Good luck.'

Owen walked into the small office, which was basically just a desk and a safe and a sofa. The manager was forty-odd, mostly bald but with a monkish half ring of black hair, and wore a blue dress shirt and black jeans. He stood and shook Owen's hand. 'What do you want, Mr. –'

'Noone. Owen Noone.'

'Right. Do we have an appointment?'

'No, that was a lie, but I had to tell him something, and I wanted to see you so I could tell you that one of the best decisions you could make would be to hire my band, Owen Noone and the Marauder, to play a couple of gigs in your club.'

The guy sat down. 'Right. Kid, do you know how many shitty bands like yours come here wanting to –'

'Not like mine. We're not shitty. We're not the same. We're different.'

'Just like everyone else.'

'No. Owen Noone and the Marauder are something new, and we've got a good following in –'

'Hold on a second.' The guy opened a drawer and started rummaging through its contents. He pulled out a cassette. 'Did you say Owen Noone and the Marauder?'

Owen nodded. 'Yeah.'

The guy held up the cassette and smiled. 'I have your tape.'

Owen, probably for the first time in his life, couldn't speak. He stared at the demo tape. He repeated one word: 'Tape?'

'Yeah. You sent it to Pulley Records, right? A friend of mine there liked it and loaned it to me the other day, to see what I thought. I guess he tried calling you, but the phones and everything are knocked out in North Carolina. Have a seat.'

Owen fell into the sofa. His whole body felt slack, almost paralyzed. He hadn't really expected to get very far, and he didn't know what to do at this point. The guy pulled a large book from another drawer and scanned a page with his hand. 'You based in the City now?' he asked, turning the page, his eyes and finger still scanning.

'What city?'

The manager looked up. 'New York City.'

'Oh,' Owen said, grinning in embarrassment. 'Yeah, yeah, we are.'

'Great.' He looked back down at the book, turned back a page and stopped, holding on a spot with his finger. 'One week from Friday.' He looked up. 'Kid Tiger are playing. You know them?'

Owen nodded. 'They're the Marauder's favorite band.'

'Well, you're the warm-up act.'

They spent a few minutes working out the details and when they were finished, Owen shook his hand. 'Can I ask a favor?'

'Sure, what?'

'Can I borrow twenty bucks? I owe that guy downstairs.'

He laughed. 'Yeah, sure.'

Owen went downstairs and felt like he was floating as he strode across the floor to the guy, who was still sweeping.

He walked up behind him and tapped his shoulder. 'Your twenty bucks,' he said. 'See you at the show.'

Outside the hot, humid air, which earlier had seemed to press in on him, now felt like it was wrapping itself around him. He whooped and a woman walking by turned sharply to look at him, then hurried on. He wasn't exactly sure how to get back home to tell me the news. The only thing he could think to do was retrace his steps until he got to a street he recognized. He ended up walking back to St. Marks and crossing over to where it ended at Avenue A and Tompkins Square. A girl with a black labrador stood next to him on the corner as he waited to cross. She had brown hair and was wearing sunglasses, a gray T-shirt, soccer shorts and sandals and had a small knapsack on her back. Owen smiled at her, and she smiled back. Then her dog lifted its leg and pissed on him.

'George!' she shrieked at the dog, then turned her attention to Owen. 'Oh shit, I'm really sorry.' She took off her sunglasses. 'Really sorry.'

She had green eyes. 'Um,' Owen said, lost for words for the second time in less than an hour.

'I'll give you money to get them cleaned,' she said, pointing at his wet blue jeans. George's tail swished against her bare leg.

'No, that's okay. It'll – I'll live. It's fine.' He looked at his leg, then at her. 'Do you want to go for a coffee?'

She smirked. 'It's a bit warm for a coffee, isn't it? And I've got George here. He's not my dog, he's my neighbor's. I walk him during the day for a little extra money.' She pulled on the leash. 'Do you want to go to the dog run?'

In the dog run she let George off his leash, and he raced across the area to where a group of dogs were smelling each other's behinds. Owen and Anna had introduced themselves and Anna kept an eye on George, who would race back to them every once in a while before tearing back across to another group of dogs. She told Owen she worked in a Manhattan restaurant. He asked her what kind of music she liked.

'Oh, I don't know. I don't really listen to that much music. I guess whatever's on the radio. There's this station, WFMU. It's pretty weird. I listen to that sometimes.'

'I'm going to this concert a week from Friday. A couple of really good bands. Do you want to go?'

'Who are they?'

'Who?'

'The bands.'

'There's two. Kid Tiger?' He looked at her to see if she'd heard of them, but more to try and think of something to say for the second band, realizing that he'd look like a jerk if he told her his own name. She made a confused face, and he said, 'Well, they're good. A friend of mine's favorite band.'

'What's the other one?'

'Oh, the other one. I haven't really heard them.' He remembered a name he could use. 'Rucksack Thracians, I think they're called.'

Anna shrugged. 'Haven't heard of them, either.' She looked across the dog run to where George was squatting. 'Shit,' she muttered, pulling a wad of newspaper from the knapsack. She looked at Owen. 'Yeah, sure, I'll go.'

'Great! I have a friend who works there, so I'll get your name on the guest list, and we can just meet inside there, okay? It's at CBGB's. Do you know where that is?'

She smiled. 'Yeah.' George finished his business. 'I've got to go clean up after him.'

'I need to get going, anyway. See you a week from Friday.'

They both stood, and Owen started to reach his hand out to touch her arm, but then he let it drop. She smiled and said goodbye, and he walked to the gate, where he stopped and turned just as she was scooping up George's poop with the newspaper.

'You didn't get her number or anything?' I asked.

'No. I guess I should've.'

'I'll say. Hope she turns up.'

'Yeah. Hey! What about that? Great gig, huh?'

It hit me. In just over a week we would be playing at CBGB's, opening for my favorite rock band. I began to shake and feel queasy. I stood and sprinted to the bathroom and flung open the toilet but only coughed a couple of times, flushed, washed my face, and walked back into the room, feeling a little stupid. Owen laughed.

We spent the whole weekend and next week practicing. We couldn't play very loudly, so we just strummed our guitars without plugging them in, and Owen sang quietly. Being the warm-up band, we only had forty minutes, so we picked ten songs to play: "John Henry," "East Virginia," "Erie Canal," "Jesse James," "The Big Rock Candy Mountains," "Careless Love," "The Midnight Special," "Worried Man," "Wild Mizzourye" and of course, "Yankee Doodle." A lot of our practice time was spent bickering over what the best order was – only agreeing that "Yankee Doodle", as always, should be last. Owen maintained that we should open with "Worried Man," for the sake of irony, because we sure as hell would be shitting ourselves. I, on the other hand, wanted to start with "John Henry," remembering that first gig at Fuzzy's and how when Owen had bawled out the first words, I'd completely lost myself in banging the chords. I knew playing in New York City, opening for my favorite band in front of more people than ever, or at least more important people, more discerning people, people who knew and liked good music, I knew I'd be terrified.

By the time Friday came we'd rehearsed the songs so many times I was seeing my fingers forming the chords as I lay in bed at night, trying to fall asleep. I awoke early on Friday like a little kid on Christmas morning, unable to lie still once I realized what day it was, and got up and slipped out to take a long walk and get some breakfast. It was raining a heavy mist that seemed less to be coming down than it was just hanging in the air, making it feel like I was walking through television interference. After ten days in New York I still hadn't seen much of anything – the Statue of Liberty, Yankee Stadium, the Empire State Building – but I had a fairly good idea of the layout of our little corner of the Lower East Side. I went to a restaurant on the corner of 7th and A and ate a huge breakfast of eggs, bacon, sausage, potatoes, corned-beef hash, coffee and orange juice. I sat facing a window and watched people hurry by in the rain, some with umbrellas, others holding newspapers over their heads or just hunched over, eyes to the pavement as they rushed by. Afterwards I wandered around the area for a little while, passing by record stores to see if they had posters in their windows or flyers inside. I'd been wanting to do this all week but had kept myself from it. Now I had to see, I had to indulge. I wanted to see my name – well, not my name, but some part of me, our name, Owen Noone and the Marauder, displayed in public, on paper, something permanent, something that we hadn't made ourselves.

All the shops had flyers and a couple had posters in their windows, but none of them mentioned us. There was one with a sort of stick-figure cat and in large letters across the top it said: KID TIGER. Beneath that, much smaller, was written: PLUS SPECIAL GUESTS. Then all of the what-when-where information. In one shop I picked up a flyer and asked the clerk as casually as possible, 'Do you know who the guest band is?'

'No,' he said. 'Nobody important.'

I tried to smile and said thanks, and walked back out into the rain, all the way down to Washington Square, then up to Union Square where I stopped for a few minutes in a bookstore. I picked up a *Village Voice* to look at the listings in the hope that they, at least, would have our name. No luck. Only Kid Tiger was mentioned, and not even Plus Special Guests. I walked home. Owen was awake and gone, so I took a shower to wash away the rain and sat in my chair by the window, absently strumming a few chords on my unplugged guitar, waiting for him to return.

'Do you know our name isn't on one goddamned flyer or poster in this whole city?' he announced, banging the door shut behind him, water dripping from his matted brown hair.

I stopped playing. 'Yeah. I guess we shouldn't have expected much else.'

Owen was in the bathroom now. 'Soon enough,' he called as he turned on the shower, letting it run for a while so it could get warm. 'Soon enough our name will be on those things.'

It was almost noon by the time Owen had showered and dressed. We spent a couple of hours running through our set twice, once unplugged and then again with our amps on, playing the familiar songs, which we could do without even thinking about it, just an automatic movement of fingers, Owen tapping his pedal every so often, our minds struggling to stay focused. It would be different onstage, which was why we needed to practice; the ability to play on autopilot would become a necessity when the nerves kicked in. Plus onstage was always fun, partly because we weren't worrying about this change or that, or whether we were keeping in time together. We just sat back and listened to ourselves, and enjoyed it almost as if we were the audience, disassociated from the parts of us that were actually making the sound.

At three o'clock we walked down to a deli and had sandwiches, then came back and packed our gear into the truck. At four-thirty we were unloading it at CBGB's.

'It'll be cool for you to meet Kid Tiger,' Owen said.

'Yeah.' I was trying to be nonchalant about it but inwardly it was all I was thinking about.

After unloading our gear we set up and did a sound check. We'd never done a proper sound check with an engineer before. Basically we just played "Worried Man," which had lots of dynamics changes, over and over until the engineer had the levels marked. Since we didn't have drums or anything it was much simpler, he said. Then we moved our amps and guitars off to the side so when Kid Tiger came they could set up and do their sound-check. We had a few hours to kill, so we got a couple beers and wandered around the club, Owen imagining aloud what it must have been like in the seventies, with the Ramones, Television, New York Dolls and bands like that playing all the time. To us it was like stepping onto the field to play at Yankee Stadium. I wondered if Owen saw it that way, if one dream was replacing another, and

I tried to imagine how he felt about it but didn't want to ask him.

'Do you think Anna will show?' I asked, finishing my bottle of beer.

'I hope so. I put her name on the list.' Owen looked up at the ceiling, then back at me. 'Do you think she'll be impressed?'

I shrugged. 'Either that, I suppose, or she'll think you're an arrogant prick.'

'Am I?'

'No. She'll probably dig it.'

Kid Tiger showed up late and there wasn't any time to talk before we had to set up our stuff and get ready to play. I was disappointed, but they didn't really seem that interesting in person anyway. Just four regular guys in vaguely bad moods. Seeing them and with our time to play getting closer, I started to get nervous. This was a real gig, not some bar or college campus or folk festival, and the more times this thought looped around my head, the more worked up I got. I drank a beer as fast as I could. Owen did the same. His face was pale, and he stared at the floor. I imagine I looked the same.

'It'll be fine,' I said to myself as much as to Owen, 'Once we get out there and start. 'Steel-drivin' man, Lawd, Lawd,' I added.

The guy who was in charge of coordinating everything came over. 'You guys ready?' It wasn't so much a question as a signal to get out there and start the show.

Owen took a deep breath. 'Here we go.'

We picked up our guitars and walked onto the stage. The lights made it hard to see, but I could tell the place wasn't full yet. A smattering of applause and an aimless cheer or two greeted us. Nobody knew who we were. We plugged in our guitars and both strummed a couple chords to reassure ourselves, to confirm that yes, these things worked and yes, we could play them. We looked at each other and tried to smile.

'Hi, I'm Owen Noone and this is the Marauder. This song is called "John Henry." Owen tapped his foot a few times and began. I shut my eyes and pretended we were in Fuzzy's. 'Jaaaaaaaaawwwwwwwwnnnnn Henry was a little baby boy –'

I slammed my hand across the strings, my C-chord ringing through the amp, through the monitors and into the audience, not thinking, my eyes shut, curled over my guitar, playing the chords and listening to Owen singing and playing, our guitars marking out a choppy beat against his scrapey voice until the refrain, when, stepping on the pedal, the sound and energy pushed up a level and I opened my eyes and looked out to the front of the audience, where people tapped and nodded along to our music. We blazed through that song faster than we ever had, picking up speed because of our nervous energy, so that at the finish my arm was just a blur trying to keep up with Owen's, and as I let the last chord ring out, I dropped my right arm to my side and shook it a little, trying to loosen it up. People applauded and Owen said thank you and I stepped towards him.

'Let's slow it down, huh? We'll be finished in three minutes at this rate.'

'Yeah. Set the pace.'

I began strumming the opening G-chord of "The Midnight Special," deliberately playing slower than I thought we usually did, assuming that I was probably playing faster than I thought. Owen began singing this song without playing, only adding his distorted guitar chords to the choruses, and I sank back into autopilot, looking out over the first couple rows of the audience, where the unfamiliar faces all blended into each other. In Iowa City the same people would show up at our gigs, and I could look out and recognize faces and feel comfortable. In Charlotte I'd never really cared. Here, they all looked like the same face, New Yorker, and because we weren't the main attraction, the expression was indifferent.

We played on. As the set progressed and more people showed up, the audience response grew bigger, more enthusiastic, so that by the time we finished the stomping "Worried Man" the faces were no longer blank but smiling, cheering and whistling. The next song was "The Wild Mizzourye." I strummed the first couple of beats, but Owen cut me off.

'Hold on a second,' he said. 'I met a girl the other day called Anna. This song is for her.'

He nodded, and I started playing again. We'd changed the way we did it. I played the whole song, Owen adding his guitar only on the 'Away, You Rolling River' and 'Across the Wild Mizzourye' refrains, creating the intermittent short blasts of noise that, by the next year, ended up becoming familiar to a few hundred thousand people. It was the first time we played it that way, and when we reached the end, the final E-chord blasting from both of our guitars, the audience was ecstatic, cheering wildly and clapping. Owen and I grinned like idiots at each other. The next song was the tamer, undistorted "Big Rock Candy Mountains," followed by "Careless Love," which ended with Owen howling, his voice cracking as it strained to be heard over the chord, lamenting, 'See what careless love will do,' which we blended straight into the assault of "Erie Canal," playing them almost as a medley and creating a wave of energy to carry us into "Yankee Doodle."

We always saved "Yankee Doodle" for last. Part of the reason was apprehension. We were never sure how it was going to go over. Another was that there was nothing to follow it up; the gimmicky sing-along nature of it left a good impression and feeling on which to depart, leaving everybody happy. The audience response was always the same, and CBGB's was no different: Owen invited people to join along, but without telling the name of the song. We'd both start playing, and there would be puzzled looks followed by general bemusement when Owen started singing until eventually, one by one, voices would rise out of the crowd and filter to the stage, singing with every trip through the chorus, rising in volume and energy until that final line, when everybody, even myself, would be shouting along with Owen, the last words erupting from 'with the girls be handy' into a roar of approval through which Owen would say, 'Thank you, that's all,' and we'd unplug our guitars, switch off our amps, and walk off the stage.

We collapsed into a couple of chairs, exhausted both physically and emotionally. We'd played for forty-five minutes, the whole thing a blur of impressions and emotions. Kid Tiger had two roadies who pulled our amps and cables off stage before beginning to set up the other equipment. The bassist and lead guitarist in the band came over to us and told us we were great.

'Really liked it, dude,' said the shaven-headed, skinny bassist.

'Fuckin' great,' said the guitarist. He was tall and peered over his sunglasses as he talked.

It felt like Christmas and my first kiss put together. I

stammered a thank you and tried to think of something interesting to say, but couldn't.

'I'm going to try to find Anna.' Owen got up and went through a door and into the audience.

Kid Tiger took the stage, and I sat alone drinking a bottle of water and watching my favorite band at work, lost in a pleasant void. But before the end of the second song, my reverie was broken.

'Nice show, man.'

The voice jolted me to attention, and I turned from the stage to see its owner, a guy about thirty and my height, dressed in a short-sleeved plaid shirt and jeans.

'Thanks,' I said, wondering who he was.

'I'm Dave Ferris.' He stuck out his hand, and I stood and shook it. 'I run Pulley Records. You guys sent us a demo? I'm interested. Very interested. Is Owen around?'

I was exhausted, and my brain wasn't quite keeping up with his talking. 'Owen? He's – no. I think – I don't know where he is.'

'Well, never mind that. I don't really need both of you for this. What I'd like to do is get you guys in the studio to rerecord this demo, put it out as an EP, see how it does and then get to work on an album. Now we're not a big label, as you probably know, but we're doing well, getting a lot of bands good airtime on college radio and some promotional touring. I think you guys would fit in well with us. What do you think?'

I scratched my head aimlessly. 'Yeah. I mean, I guess. I should probably talk to Owen and see –'

'Yeah, yeah, of course. We'll talk it over with Owen before we work out the contract proper. What I'd like to do this evening is write out an agreement between us to say we've got a deal, and then we'll have a meeting next week and work out a contract. How's that sound?' His hands moved a lot as he spoke, and I followed their movements more than I paid attention to what he was saying, watching them inscribe spirals and arcs in the space between us.

I gazed out at the stage where Kid Tiger was finishing another song, then looked back at Dave Ferris. 'Yeah, sure,' I said, wondering what Owen was doing.

Owen told me later. After our set was over he went to find Anna. He stood at the edge of the audience, which, as people went to the bar or the restroom, was breaking up into smaller, looser clusters. After scanning the faces but not finding hers, he wandered towards the bar, ordered a beer and paid for it, forgetting that he could have had it free. He leaned one arm against the edge of the bar and noticed that a few people were looking at him and talking. While he was enjoying being recognized, he saw her.

She was standing alone near the back wall staring down the neck of a beer bottle. Owen bought another beer and walked over. She didn't notice him until he spoke.

'Anna. Thanks for coming. Did you like it?'

Her head snapped up. 'Huh? Oh – Owen. Hi.' She smiled and looked at the two beers he was holding.

'Is one of those for me?'

He looked at his hands and then at her. 'Yeah.' He held the fresh one towards her and took her empty bottle. 'Did you like it?'

She took a sip of beer and swallowed. 'Um – well, I guess not, really, I mean, it's not really my type of thing.' Owen felt crushed. 'It was fun, though,' she added,

'Thanks for inviting me. Everybody else seemed to like it. The guy next to me kept at his friend about how great you were. Anyway, I only came to hang out with you, not to hear some silly bands. Not, uh, that you're silly.' She smiled.

Owen's chest pumped back up and he could breathe again. It occurred to him that he should be dejected – she hadn't liked it – but he was too caught up in her smile to care.

Dave Ferris wrote something on a piece of paper and then copied it onto another. I can't remember what it said. Something about Owen Noone and the Marauder, as represented by me, agreed to a contract with Pulley, blah blah blah, details to be discussed. I couldn't really focus on it. I signed the bottom of both papers and so did Dave Ferris, and he gave me one and pocketed the other. Then we shook hands. He gave me a business card and told me to give him a call on Monday to set up a time for both Owen and me to come in and 'do up a contract'.

Suddenly there was a loud, dead thunking sound – it sounded something like "kerunnkk" – followed by another similar but smaller sound and then the angry, piercing buzz of high-treble feedback. I looked out at the stage where Kid Tiger had stopped playing. The singer-rhythm guitarist was stalking off towards me, holding the neck of his broken guitar in his left hand and scowling. The rest of the band was still onstage watching him leave, their faces pale, the remains of his guitar dead on the ground in front of his microphone stand. Somebody – probably the sound engineer – ended the feedback. The guitarist slapped the broken neck against my chest and into my hands as he passed.

Onstage, the bass player walked over to the microphone and kicked the rest of the guitar to the side. The audience watched, silent. 'I think Rob's no longer in the band,' he said. 'We'll keep playing without him.' The drummer counted off and they started a song, the bassist doing his best to sing but messing up a lot, and the whole thing sounding hollow without a full rhythm section. They finished, announced that this next song would be their last, and played another empty version of one of my favorites. As soon as they finished I started moving our gear to Owen's truck to avoid having to see them or hear what they said. I packed everything in, locked it, and went back inside to find Owen, but he wasn't there. I waited around for a while talking to no one, thinking about what I'd just done, what I'd just seen, and wondering where Owen had gone. Finally I left, knowing he was off with Anna somewhere.

It seemed like it was impossible for me to sleep late in New York without the aid of alcohol. I was wide awake at eight o'clock and restlessly moving around my room, rearranging the way the guitars leaned against the amps, which stood against the wall where I'd put them the night before. Picking up Owen's guitar, I suddenly remembered with full clarity the events of the gig as though they were a single picture: playing, Owen skipping out to find Anna, Kid Tiger breaking apart, signing the memo. Signing the memo. I dug into my pockets and pulled it out. One piece of eight and a half by eleven plain white paper, with a bunch of words that effectively said we were a Pulley Records band as represented by the two signatures at the bottom. I wondered if it was actually legally binding or what. It wasn't clear to me which way would be better in our favor. Having a record out seemed like a good thing, and I knew Pulley Records was decent from my radio work at Bradley, so it must be good. But I didn't really know anything about the legal stuff, I mean, we could get ripped off – it all depended on how honest Dave Ferris was. He seemed like a good guy and he certainly didn't come across like some creep of a businessman, but then, you never know. It'd have to wait until we had a meeting with him.

'What are you looking at?' Owen had come in without me realizing it. He was wrapped in a towel, standing by the bathroom door.

'It's – well, I kind of signed us up for a record deal last night.'

'You what?' Owen shouted, holding the towel at his waist as he bounded towards me. I couldn't tell if he was happy or pissed off.

'With Pulley Records,' I said. 'Dave Ferris.' I realized I wasn't making any sense. 'They want to put out a record.' Owen picked up the memo and started to read it. 'This isn't a contract,' I continued. 'It's just – just a statement, a prelude, I guess, to a deal. We have to set up a meeting next week. I've got his number.'

Owen stopped reading and looked straight into my eyes with an intensity that I couldn't figure out. 'What time is it?' he said.

'Nine o'clock.'

'Okay. I've got to shower. We're meeting Anna in an hour for breakfast.' He started for the bathroom door, and when he got there he turned. 'This is great news,' he said and shut the door.

When he got out I showered, and when I finished he

was sitting on the bed reading the memo. 'This is great,' he said over and over, and then, folding it and leaving it on the bed, he stood. 'Come on, already, we've got to meet Anna.'

'I thought you'd brought her home,' I said as we walked down the stairs and stepped out into the street, into the humid, bright morning.

'No way.' Owen peered at me through his sunglasses. 'Wouldn't be right. Not on the first date.'

'Okay,' I said, and that was the end of it.

Anna wasn't at the café yet, so we picked a table near the front by a window and ordered coffee, but nothing to eat. Yesterday's *USA Today* sat on the table, and we each picked up a section and leafed through it without really paying attention. After a couple minutes the door opened, and we looked up, and I knew it was Anna. She wore khaki shorts and a blue tank-top that betrayed faint tan lines on her shoulders. She smiled and came over to our table, and she and Owen kissed shyly, almost embarrassedly, and she shook my hand when Owen introduced us. The waiter came over and poured more coffee and took our orders. Owen excused himself to go to the restroom, and Anna and I were left alone sitting across from each other, without anything to say. We sat smiling at each other apologetically, trying to fill the silence.

'Is this today's paper?' she said, picking up the front section.

'No, yesterday's,' I said.

She started leafing through it aimlessly, not really reading. Then she stopped and peered closer at it, her expression changing from one of detachment to close scrutiny, frowning slightly as she leaned in. 'That's funny,' she said.

'What's funny?' Owen eased back into his seat across from me, next to Anna.

'This guy running for the Senate in California has the same last name as you.'

USA Today, Friday, August 8, 1997:

CALIFORNIA: Jack Noone, Republican Congressman for the 9th District, has announced his candidacy for the Senate seat being vacated by the retiring Democrat Alf Reiniger.

It was just a sentence. One of the inside pages had a one or two sentence news item for every single state, and that was California's. Somehow it had caught Anna's eye. We passed it around several times, none of us really believing it was there at first. Owen, of course, must have thought about his father sometimes, but he never mentioned him aloud after that first time he told me the whole story. I just kept looking around the table, first at Anna, who was looking at Owen, and then at Owen, whose mouth hung open, his eyes blank. He was still wearing that expression when our food came, and we had to fold up the paper.

'That –' Owen slid his knife and fork from the napkin that encircled them. 'That –' He sighed and sunk back into his chair. 'That son of a bitch.'

Neither Anna nor I knew what to say. We began eating our eggs and toast, and the scraping of knives and forks against the plates seemed like fingernails on a chalkboard. The waiter came and refilled our coffees and asked if everything was okay. I mumbled something vaguely affirming and tried to smile reassuringly.

'Owen, don't worry about it. It doesn't really change anything, does it? I mean, he's been in Congress all this time anyway,' I said.

Owen leaned forward and glared. 'It changes everything. He's in the goddamn national paper. He'll be on TV. Spouting some self-aggrandizing crap. Forcing his way into my life. And I don't want him. I won't let him.' He dropped his fork onto the plate. 'We're going to California.'

'Whoa,' I said. 'We just got here. We're setting up this deal. We're not going anywhere. Besides, what's chasing him all the way to California going to do?'

Owen was squeezing his napkin in his fist and his knuckles were turning white from the effort. 'Make him remember me. Let him know what it's like. Make sure he doesn't get elected.'

'Owen –' Anna reached over and touched his arm.

'He doesn't deserve it.' Owen looked at Anna, then at me, then back at Anna. 'Do you want to go to California?'

Monday morning we were driving again, and I was in the back seat. Owen drove, while Anna sat next to him. We were driving west on Interstate 80, planning to be in California by the end of the week. I'd phoned Dave Ferris to tell him we were going to be gone for a while, but that we were definitely interested and would be back, soon. I did my best to reassure him, even though I knew that we might never be back, or at least not for a long time. He said he was disappointed, but we should do what we needed to do, and he'd hang on to the memo we'd signed. If we were going through Chicago, he said, he could pull some strings and get us a gig there on short notice, so I said we were, we'd be there on Tuesday, and he told me the name and address of the place.

So we were driving again, this time heading west, chasing some vague ideas in Owen's head. Owen and Anna chatted in the front seat. I didn't like the fact that she was there, in my seat. She was an interloper. I couldn't figure out why she'd come, anyway. She didn't even know him.

Or she hardly knew him. And now she'd just quit her life to follow him across the country? But I'd done the same thing. Owen Noone pulled people with him, made people want to follow him. Maybe I was just jealous. I could hear their voices but not the actual words, and I watched the blur of landscape out the window until it made my eyes heavy and I fell asleep.

We made it to Cleveland that day and got a hotel. Before Owen and I had always shared a double room, but now Owen and Anna took a room, and I had one to myself. We had to get up early the next morning to be in Chicago in time for our gig at eight, so at ten o'clock I was lying in bed, watching a baseball game on television and feeling lonely. For a year I'd spent every single day with Owen playing music, driving, arguing, horsing around and now, suddenly, there was a divide. I felt diminished, as though overnight, because of things outside my control – outside his control too – we were chasing down a dream again, but the dream wasn't Owen Noone and the Marauder, it was Owen Noone with the Marauder and Anna as an after-thought, or maybe I was the afterthought, or we both were, but anyway, the dream we were chasing wasn't anything positive. At that moment it seemed destined to end up a nightmare.

The telephone rang with my wakeup call. I was still dressed and the television was on, showing some kind of breakfast news show. I could taste sleep in my mouth. A couple minutes later, there was a banging on my door. I opened it and Owen and Anna were standing there arm in arm, showered and smiling.

'You look like you slept in your clothes.'

'Shut up, Owen.' I scowled. I wasn't really awake yet,

and some foggy remnants of dislike for Owen were still floating in my head.

'You did sleep in your clothes, didn't you?'

'Shut up, Owen.'

'Can you be ready to go in ten? We're starving.'

Fifteen minutes later we were eating breakfast in a McDonald's and ten minutes after that we were leaving Cleveland, heading for Chicago and our second big-city gig. Anna sat in the back seat, leaning forward to talk and listen to us talk. Owen and I were arguing as usual about the order of songs and how we were going to play them. We'd phoned ahead to make sure we were really playing. We were, with a couple of local bands at a place called the Metro. Ohio unfolded in front of us and then disappeared as we crossed into Indiana. It wasn't even noon.

I got a shiver when we crossed the border and saw the sign CROSSROADS OF AMERICA.

Anna must have noticed. 'Are you all right?'

I turned in my seat. 'Yeah. I just realized we're in Indiana.'

'So?' Owen said.

'My home. My parents.'

'When was the last time you saw them?' Anna asked.

I slouched down. 'I don't know. A year and a half or something. When I graduated. And then the next day — when I called them from Iowa City —' I didn't know what I wanted to say.

'Are we near?' Owen asked. 'Do you want to go see them? We can stop.'

'No,' I said. 'No. No. I can't. They'd — I don't think I should.'

I don't want to would've been closer to the truth. I

100

was afraid to show up at my parents' house and try to justify my life. To look them in the eye and tell them I was playing guitar, living off someone else's money and heading to California for someone else's reasons with a girl we'd picked up along the way. How were they supposed to react to that? I loved my parents, and I didn't want them to be disappointed, so I wasn't going to say anything to them until I could prove – to them and to myself – that I'd made the right decision.

We crossed over a toll bridge and down into the city of Chicago, welcomed by Richard M. Daley, Mayor, or at least by a sign with his name on it. Driving along the highway, running parallel to an elevated train track and surrounded by tall buildings, it felt like we were driving through a very narrow and steep valley. Then we exited the freeway onto Lake Shore Drive and the skyline of Chicago presented itself as a wall on our left, with Lake Michigan spreading out from our right, all the way to the horizon, so it looked like a great calm ocean. We navigated our way to the Metro, which was within view of Wrigley Field.

'I went there once,' Owen said, standing on the sidewalk and looking down the street at the baseball stadium, its red sign proclaiming it HOME OF THE CHICAGO CUBS. 'When I was with Iowa. Just to visit. I walked around the field, spent some time in the locker room. That was the only time I was actually in a major league stadium, except as a spectator. That's the closest I got.' He was staring down the road and seemed to be talking to himself rather than to Anna and me. 'I miss it sometimes, you know? Do you – is there anything like that, that you miss?' he asked, turning to us.

'Cowshit,' Anna said, a grin spreading on her face. 'I miss cowshit. The smell. Every spring and every fall when we'd hose out the barns, this massive cleaning before and after winter, and it would send all those little particles in the air. All the farmers did it around the same time, so for a whole week the air would smell like cowshit. I left for college in New York City, and then after I just stayed, because there were more jobs I guess. I've been working as a waitress for three years and only go back to the farm for Christmas. It sounds stupid, but the thing I really miss is that smell.'

'It's not stupid,' Owen said. They both looked at me. 'What about you?'

'No,' I said, even though it was a lie. 'Not really. I can't think of anything.'

On my twelfth birthday my father came home from work in the evening towing a heap of rusted, broken automobile that had once been a '74 Chevelle SS. By the time you're sixteen, he told me, we'll have this thing beautiful and running and you can take your driver's test in it. For the next four years we spent summer evenings and weekends out in the garage, lying on our backs underneath the car or bending over the engine, my father pointing out the different parts and showing me what tools to use. Sometimes we went to junkyards to get parts, spending hours sorting through the leftovers of other broken cars to find what we needed. On my sixteenth birthday I passed my driving test in a perfectly running, shiny royal blue Chevelle SS. After my seventeenth birthday I sold it and bought a Ford Escort, telling my father I didn't care about cars, and I was sick of wasting Saturday afternoons fixing this or that. There were better ways of spending my time.

It began a marked descent in our relationship, a descent whose most recent valley was a phone call from Iowa City that ended when I ran out of quarters.

We unloaded our gear into the Metro and spent an hour walking around the neighborhood before heading back to do our soundcheck. Anna insisted on helping carry things and plugging in the amps and guitar cables.

'Good of me to hire a roadie, eh?' Owen joked, and she hurled a coil of cables at him, striking him in the chest.

We played for a little over an hour between two local bands. They had a decent following, and the place was packed. It was the best crowd we'd played to yet. A DJ from one of the Chicago stations was introducing the bands, and after we'd set up, he walked up to the microphone and said: 'We don't know anything about this next act except that they're on their way through town and they're the talk of New York. We've been promised something special. So please welcome Owen Noone and the Marauder.' As we walked out to energetic applause he passed by us and said, 'Good luck, guys. I hear you're good.'

We were good. As was slowly becoming habit, we started with "John Henry," not pausing at the end but going straight into "The Midnight Special." Owen's voice was coarser than usual, which made it sound better, and every time he stepped on his pedal, I stopped strumming and picked out arpeggios, giving a slight imbalance to the sound that somehow lent more energy to it. We played "Erie Canal" third. 'This next song,' Owen said before we started, 'is about a part of the country where, according to my girlfriend, the cowshit smells divine.' He looked over to where Anna was standing at the edge of the stage and winked. We roared through our set, adding a couple

103

songs we hadn't planned on and when we got to the end, and started playing "Yankee Doodle," the voices of the audience drowned out Owen's. Finishing with three rounds of the chorus, I plucked out the "Dixie" melody – we still hadn't learned the song yet – and pulled the cable out of my guitar. But Owen was still standing at the mic, his guitar buzzing with low-level feedback. He started singing, unaccompanied and out of tune. "Ding-dong, the witch is dead," he sang, out of tune. "Ding-dong, the witch is dead, "Ding-dong, the witch is dead."

I plugged my guitar back in and shouted, 'Which old witch?' at the top of my lungs.

Owen giggled. 'The wicked witch.'

He said it, he didn't sing it. I guessed which chord to play and strummed as we both sang, Owen into the microphone, me into the air, "Ding-dong, the wicked witch is deaaaaaaaaad."

The audience cheered and we started from the beginning, Owen's guitar still buzzing, with just me playing and the audience yelling out, 'Which old witch?' on cue, everybody laughing, clapping, playing, singing. I have no idea how Owen knew all the words.

'Fucking great!' Owen yelled when we got off stage, wrapping me in a sweaty hug. 'You. Only you could've done it. It was great. The way you came in right on the right chord at the right time, just spontaneous like that. Great, great, great!' He squeezed me again and grinned at Anna. 'Sorry, darling, I think I love him more.'

'I guess I'll just go do my roadie shit, then,' she said, smiling, and walked past us two hugging, grinning fools to drag off the amps.

I realized then that whatever doubts I'd had about

Owen and me were stupid. We were a band. We were friends. Anna and Jack Noone – they didn't change that. We had our music.

We stood at the back of the audience listening to the final band, a four-piece punk outfit. I was aware as we stood there that people were watching us. They'd glance and stare as they walked past or simply turn where they were and nudge their friends, trying subtly to point. Owen was staring at the stage listening to the music with his arm around Anna, but I could hardly pay attention. A kid who looked a few years younger than Owen and me came over.

'Hi,' he said. 'Nice show.'

'Thanks.' I turned my eyes back to the stage.

'So – you guys are from New York?' He smiled nervously. His head was down, but his eyes looked up at me.

'No – yeah. New York.' I had to shout to be heard over the music.

'You got an album out?'

'No – well, not yet. We've got a deal.'

'Cool. What label?'

'Pulley. We haven't worked it all out yet, though.'

'Cool.'

He seemed to be out of things to say, which was fine with me. With this kid treating me like some kind of rockstar I'd found myself telling lies – well, not lies, but half-truths. I didn't like it.

'Cool,' he said again and then added, 'Well, thanks, dude. Nice talking to you,' and pushed his way back into the crowd.

'What did that kid want?' Owen asked, leaning towards my ear.

'I don't know. Just to talk to a rock band, I guess.'

'Cool.'

'That's what he said.'

'Hey, where the hell are we going to stay tonight?'

It hadn't occurred to me. We didn't have anywhere to stay. We hadn't thought to find a hotel. 'I guess we can sleep in the truck or something.'

'That sucks. If anybody else wants to talk to a rock band, ask them if they want to put one up for the night, too.'

We ended up staying with a friend of one of the other bands. They had an extra room with a double bed in their house. When we got there I wondered if we wouldn't have been better off sleeping in the truck. The house was nice from the outside, even though the lawn was more of a jungle, plastic bags and paper food wrappers clinging to the overgrown clumps of grass. It was a small, brown brick, two-story house that looked like it had been built in the fifties. Inside was a mess. The living room, immediately inside the front door, was strewn with dirty dishes and more fast-food wrappings: pizza boxes, McDonald's containers, paper cups. There were two sofas riddled with cigarette burns, and on the coffee table between them lay a few syringes, spoons, lighters and what I assumed was a bag of heroin.

'Uh, I guess I'll show you guys your room,' said one of our three hosts, tugging his thin brown hair. 'Unless you want to –' he swept his arm towards the table.

'No,' Owen said. 'Thanks. We've got to get moving early tomorrow.'

'Yeah, sure, okay,' the guy said and led us to our room.

The room was empty except for the bed. Other than the layer of dust on the wood floor, it was clean. Our host showed us where the bathroom was and said he'd be downstairs if we changed our minds or needed anything.

'Do you think our gear is safe?' I asked Owen after the footsteps got to the bottom of the stairs.

'Yeah. We locked the truck, right?'

'But still. I don't know. I think I'll sleep in the truck. Just to be sure.'

'Come on, don't worry about it.'

'I will, though. I won't sleep. I think I'd better.'

Owen shrugged. 'Okay. More room for us, I guess. Three in the bed would have been a bit cozy, anyway.'

I said goodnight and went downstairs, making my way across the living room to the front door and nodded at the three people sitting on the sofas, two of them slouched into the cushions, cigarettes dangling between their fingers, the third – the one who'd shown us to our room – cooking a dose of heroin in a spoon. 'You change your mind?' he asked as I walked past, but I just said nothing and walked out the front door into the humid night air. It was still too hot to be comfortable. I stood on the front stoop for a minute, slapping at the mosquitoes that landed on my arms and neck, then opened the truck and climbed into the back seat. I rolled down the window halfway, locked myself in and tried to sleep. Despite being tired, I must have lain there for a couple hours listening to the night air and staring into the streetlight that blinked on and off every few minutes before I finally fell asleep.

I was startled awake by Owen banging on the side of the truck. 'Come on, wake up, sleepy boy,' he shouted. 'Time to get a move on. We's gots to gets to Californee by sundown.'

'Owen,' I said, rubbing the crud from my eyes and trying to orient myself. 'California is days away.'

'I know. It was just a figure of speech.'

We drove back through Chicago to I-55 and headed south towards St. Louis, where we would pick up I-70 West and cut across Missouri, Kansas, Colorado, Utah and Nevada before hitting California to find Jack Noone and whatever else. We'd gotten four hundred bucks for the Chicago gig and felt good about it. By midday we were passing through St. Louis, and by evening we were checking into a motel along the highway near Kansas City.

We left at five the next morning, hoping to get all the way to Denver by the end of the day, a trip, as we figured it, of around 700 miles or roughly eleven hours. Kansas was flat, long and uninteresting, a stretch of prairie for as far as we could see. It felt like we weren't really going anywhere but just marking time, the same farmhouse flying by every so often, the sun creating shimmering pools of water on the road ahead that always dried up before we got to them. I thought that Colorado, once we got there, would be an exciting change, the snow-covered granite of the Rockies climbing into the air, a natural version of the peaks of the Chicago skyscrapers. But when we crossed the border in the early afternoon, other than the welcoming sign and the new color on the roadmap, there was nothing to distinguish it from Kansas. Just miles more of flat farmland.

Then outside of Limon, something happened. There was a grinding noise from the engine. 'What the hell?' Owen pulled onto the shoulder and slowed to a stop. We'd been listening to music and he turned it off. The engine scraped and ground.

'Try turning it off and restarting it,' Anna said.

Owen did, with no effect.

'I'll check the oil.' I got out and Owen released the

hood. We didn't have a rag or paper or anything, so I took off my T-shirt and wiped the dipstick on it, then checked the level. Nothing. 'Owen, when did we last change the oil?'

'New York.' He was right; we'd had it changed only last week as a diversion from rehearsing for the gig.

'It doesn't make sense,' I said. 'Start it up again while the hood's open, so I can hear it.' He turned the key and I could hear the oil-less pistons grinding in the engine. 'It's fucked.' I slammed the hood shut. 'We need a new engine.' I leaned my elbows on the hood and propped up my chin. 'Or a new truck.'

We all stood on the shoulder leaning against the truck and stared out across the wheat field, afraid to articulate what we knew was true: we were stuck. I squinted against the light and started to wonder, again, what I was doing broken down in Colorado when I could be anywhere else. Especially now when we could be in New York, all of us, Owen and I recording an album, making real money, playing real gigs. No more of this shoestring crap, stumbling with luck into gigs while racing across the country to yell at a father we didn't know for doing something that didn't concern us. Maybe that was unfair. Maybe it did concern us, or at least Owen, but he never talked about his father and I always just assumed he didn't care, until we'd opened that newspaper.

'What are you going to do when we get to California, Owen?' Apparently Anna was thinking about it, too.

There was a long silence, and I listened to the semis on the highway behind us. The truck rattled with their passing, and I stared across the land.

'I don't know. I don't know what he'll be like – well, I don't think it matters what he's like. I just know that I have to go, have to talk to him, have to make him know that he can't just – ignore me. Pretend he's something he's not. He's gotten away with it too long. I think I've got this – we've got this tool, you know? People like us and our music. We have to somehow use it as a way to make them pay attention, make him pay attention. I guess that's what I'm going to – what we're going to do.'

Anna turned to me. 'Is that what you want to do?'

'Right now, I just want to fix this damn truck and get moving,' I said. I didn't know what I wanted to do in California.

A tow truck pulled up on the shoulder in front of us and backed up to where we were. A shaggy-haired, thin man got out and walked towards us. 'You folks need a tow?' His blue shirt had a patch above the pocket that said "Barry" in script.

'Yeah,' Owen said. 'But –'

'Trucker radioed me. Said he saw a broken down outfit. Here I am.' He hooked the Bronco to his truck and we all piled onto the bench of the tow truck. 'Where you folks headed?'

'California,' I said.

Barry whistled. 'Long way to go then. Any ideas about your outfit, there?'

'Threw a rod,' I muttered, embarrassed that I knew.

'Bitched it, then.'

'I guess.' I took the initiative. 'You know somewhere we can buy a new one? Get a decent trade-in?'

Barry grinned, exposing the gaps where most of his teeth should have been. 'You've stumbled into the right man, folks. My old man and me, we fix up wrecks. I got some decent ones – no shit, I'm not hustlin' here. I got

110

some real heaps, too, but I ain't gonna press 'em on you.'
He didn't seem capable of not talking. 'See you've got a
lot of equipment back there. What is it you folks do?'

'We're a rock band,' Owen said.

Barry whistled again. 'That so? What kind of music
do you play?'

'Rock.'

A mile turned over on the odometer before Barry
spoke again. We passed a group of white crosses clustered
next to a fencepost. Barry pointed. 'That there's the worst
wreck I ever pulled out. Bunch a kids hit by a drunk driver
weekend before high school graduation. Awful. The whole
outfit flattened out, all those kids killed. Drunk died in the
hospital. Fixed 'em up though. Took some time, but I got
a decent price for 'em in the end.'

Twenty miles and several stories down the highway,
Barry exited and drove a mile or two down a small local
road before turning off in front of a barn. There stood
about a dozen different cars and trucks and above the
door was a sign: NORTON & NORTON TOW SERVICE. Behind
the barn about a hundred yards stood three trailers. 'Here
we are, folks. I think I got just what you need. Come have
a look at these outfits.' Barry jumped out of the truck
and we piled out the other side and followed him over to
what looked like the newest vehicles in his fleet. One was
a navy blue Ford F-150, the other a red Jeep Cherokee.
Barry rattled on about the wrecks these two particular
"outfits" had been in, but his wreck stories all sounded
the same. I tuned him out until I got the chance to ask,
'How much?'

'Well, I've been asking two grand for both of 'em. Two
grand each. I mean, not for the both together, but I figure

that Bronco you got's worth seven hundred, so you take your pick and we'll get you into it for thirteen hundred.'

'Great,' Owen said, stepping towards the pickup.

'Hold on.' I put my hand on his chest and looked at Barry. 'You know for a fact, busted engine or not, this thing's worth more than seven hundred. You can have it for twelve, and we'll give you eight hundred for whichever of these we decide on.'

Barry squinted at me and stroked the bristles on his chin. 'You know your outfits, eh? I'll up it to eight-fifty, how's that?'

'A thousand. It's worth more than that, and you know it. You're getting a perfectly good Bronco there aside from the engine, which is easily fixed in time, plus another grand from us. Take it or leave it.'

Barry grinned and stuck out his hand. 'Deal.' We shook hands.

An hour later we were heading back towards the interstate in the F-150, Owen driving, Anna next to him and me facing sideways in the flip-down seat behind Anna's, my legs stretched across the cab. The bed of the pickup had a cover over it so our gear was safe from the elements. Before we left Anna got out her camera and took a picture of the white Bronco, our former outfit, as Barry called it. Now our priority was to get to Denver as soon as possible.

'Do you want to get married?' Owen said. We were sitting on one of the double beds in our hotel room looking at the map, trying to figure out how far we could get the next day.

'I guess eventually,' I said, not looking up from the red and black lines. 'Not for a while, though.'

Owen swatted the back of my head. 'Not you. Anna. Do you want to get married? In Vegas, I mean. We could get there by tomorrow night.'

I looked up from the map. Owen was staring at Anna, a wide smile on his face. She stared back, but her expression was more complicated. Then it broke into a smile, and she threw her arms around his neck and kissed him.

I drove all the way from Denver to Las Vegas, through the mountains and down across the desert, something like seven hundred miles in one day, twelve hours in all, Owen sleeping in the back seat most of the time, Anna next to me, talking about the landscape, what she'd done in New York, the farm where she'd grown up.

'Do you think I'm stupid to marry Owen?' she asked while we stood leaning against the truck at a rest stop, waiting for him to come out of the restroom.

'No. I've been practically married to him for two years now.'

'After such a short time, though.'

I looked across the parking lot towards the interstate. 'What made you come with us?'

'It seems weird, doesn't it? But – I just couldn't think of any reason not to. My life wasn't mine in New York, and I guess I always thought that when I was twenty-six I'd be doing more than waiting tables. And Owen – it sounds stupid, but I think I really love him. I knew it almost right away. After your concert he and I went out and had a couple drinks, and I just knew it. Guys come and go but with Owen it's a whole different thing. I can't really express it. I mean, it was kind of a spur of the moment decision coming with you guys, but it just seemed right and now this seems right, and I don't think my gut reactions are usually wrong.'

'We've been living on gut reactions for two years,' I said, 'and even though it scares the shit out of me half the time, I can't think of anything that I regret.'

I watched a semi back out of its parking spot, then turned to Anna. 'Maybe that's the point.'

Owen jogged out of the building towards us, and the conversation stopped. 'What're you two talking about?' He smiled and kissed Anna on the mouth, me on the cheek. 'Don't want you to feel left out.'

Las Vegas. It glowed from a distance like a spaceship in the desert and when we got closer what we saw was overwhelming. Neon signs with lights racing around their edges, casinos everywhere, from the classy, famous ones to the seedy ones. Women in cocktail dresses, men in suits and tuxedos walking the sidewalks and turning to go through the elaborate entrances of massive hotels. We found a place to stay somewhat away from the main strip and pulled out the Yellow Pages to find a wedding chapel that was nearby. It was ten o'clock and we figured if we could find a place soon, we'd still have plenty of time to go out celebrating and then get up in the afternoon and continue to California.

We found one within walking distance and reserved a time, even though the guy on the phone said it wasn't necessary. At ten-forty we were at the Fortune's Love Matrimony Chapel signing the guest book and paying the Reverend Jimmy Swale a hundred dollars cash before the ceremony could begin. The chapel, such as it was, was entirely white on the outside with various shades of white and pink on the inside. The altar was white and had a white cross, and there were two rows of three white folding chairs on the pink carpet. The walls were white and trimmed with pink.

Owen and Anna stood in front of the Reverend Jimmy Swale and I stood behind them, next to the Reverend's wife who was the second witness. There were two sticks of awful smelling incense burning on the altar and thin wisps of dark smoke rose into the air and wafted towards us, the breeze of the air conditioning spreading the cheap odor through the room. The Reverend Jimmy Swale made a few token remarks about the holiness of marriage and the importance of honesty, then cut to the ceremony, asking if you – and here Owen had to fill in his own name – took this woman – and Anna had to say her name – to be your lawfully wedded wife. The Reverend Jimmy Swale grinned in a way that made it look like his mouth had been surgically molded into that position. The incense got worse, drifting into our eyes and making them tear, even the Reverend's. Owen and Anna were both wearing blue jeans and T-shirts, Anna's gray, Owen's orange and emblazoned with an advertisement for Fuzzy's. Finally the Reverend Jimmy Swale pronounced them husband and wife under the laws of the state of Nevada and the Lord our God and told them to kiss and we raced out of the chapel, our tears becoming tears of laughter as soon as we got out the door.

'It's done!' Owen said, wrapping his arm around Anna's shoulders. 'We've done it.'

I had the certificate and I held it up in the air as if to prove that Owen was telling the truth.

'Keep that somewhere safe,' Owen said, and I folded

it twice and put it in my pocket. Then we went across the street to a casino where they provided us with free cocktails for the rest of the night as long as we pretended to be gambling.

At four o'clock the next afternoon, after a long sleep and a long brunch, we crossed into California and were greeted by a sign that welcomed us to THE GOLDEN STATE. We didn't feel like going very far, so we spent the night in Barstow, a town that, like Champaign, Illinois, seemed only to exist as a junction of railroad lines and interstates. Owen made a couple phone calls and tracked down the newly set-up campaign headquarters of Jack Noone.

'Congressman Noone is back in Washington now, sir,' the woman who answered the phone told Owen in a businesslike tone. 'May I be of assistance?'

'When will he be back in California?'

'Not until December, sir.'

'Do you have a contact number in Washington?'

'Sir, I'm not authorized to give such numbers out. May I ask who you are and what business you have?'

'What's your position?'

'Sir, I'm Congressman Noone's campaign spokeswoman.'

'Oh, good. See, I'm his son. Could you tell him I phoned to say hello and that he might want to contact me?'

'Sir, what son? Congressman Noone doesn't have a son.'

'That's what he'd like to pretend. Just give him a message please. Tell him Owen said good luck, and he might grow to regret ever having given me that guitar.'

Owen dropped the phone into its cradle and turned to Anna and me. 'We've got until December to get ready.' Ready for what, he didn't say.

PART TWO

Somewhere, somehow, we forgot what we were doing. I think it started the morning we heard it on the radio and after that it just crept up little by little until we had no idea what was going on. We'd found a house to rent in L.A. and had been living there for about two weeks doing almost nothing, just sleeping late and sitting around all day, playing guitar when we felt like it and going to a local bar every once in a while. Then one morning shouting from downstairs woke me up. I thought Anna and Owen were arguing and tried to cover my ears by pulling the pillow over my head, but it didn't work and I could hear footsteps pounding up the stairs. Owen exploded into the room shouting at me too loudly and quickly to be understood. I rolled over and tried to focus. He paced around my room saying, 'Turn it on, turn it on, where is it, turn it on,' over and over. I thought maybe he was drunk, but then he switched on my radio and I heard the stutter of different frequencies as he moved the dial to the station he wanted. 'Listen!' he demanded with a huge smile, pointing at the radio, his other hand on his hip. I sat up and as I realized what I was hearing, I felt like I'd been given a shot of pain killer; my whole body tingled and felt alien, detached from the rest of me.

'Is this – "Yankee Doodle?"'

'Yes!' Owen yelled. 'It's us. Us! On the radio – the fucking radio!'

Anna had come upstairs by this time and the three of

us listened, Anna leaning against the doorjamb, Owen next to the radio, still pointing at it, me sitting in bed with my knees drawn up to my chest, my chin resting on them. There was no doubt that it was us – the jangly guitars, Owen's off-key voice, the assault of noise on the chorus. It was us.

We listened, none of us saying anything more until the song was over. I'm not sure what we expected – balloons falling from the ceiling, a special announcement, apocalypse – but when the last chord finished another song came on, and somehow it felt anticlimactic, somehow unfair and disrespectful. Give us the praise we deserve, don't just put on somebody else's song. But that's what happened, because that's what radio stations do. Somebody else was playing it, putting it in a queue with other songs by other people. It felt like both an injection and a deflation at the same time. Owen ran downstairs to call the radio station.

'What was that, that last one?' he asked after getting through to the DJ.

'I don't know,' the guy said. 'Something new we got in this morning. Let me find it. Hold on.' Owen could hear the clatter of CD cases being pushed around. 'Here it is. Owen Noone and the Marauder. It's just a four-song EP. Pulley Records. What'd you think?'

'Excellent. Fucking excellent. It's fucking great.'

'All right then. What's your name?'

'Owen Noone.'

The DJ laughed. 'Yeah, right,' he said, and Owen hung up.

We spent a few minutes standing around the telephone absorbing it all. Then Owen pointed at me. 'Phone Dave Ferris. Find out what's going on.'

I got hold of Dave Ferris and as soon as he heard my voice he said he'd been waiting for us to call.

'Yeah,' I said. 'I heard something interesting on the radio this morning.'

'Where are you?'

'L.A.'

'Great. We only officially released it yesterday. We would've had a party or something if you guys were around. Glad it's on the radio so fast, though.'

'Yeah.' I couldn't think of anything else to say. All of a sudden I wasn't sure why I'd called. I already knew that our demo had been released; I'd heard it on the radio. I didn't need Dave Ferris to tell me. I felt stupid listening to the silence on the phone line.

'Are we getting paid for this?' Owen said, then repeated himself, 'Are we getting paid? Ask him if we're getting paid.'

'Dave,' I said, 'Are we getting paid? I mean, what are we getting paid. There wasn't a contract really ever, was there?'

'No. I mean, yeah, you're getting paid. No there wasn't a contract. We've got one all drawn up though, and we can send it out to you. Once you get it read it over and give me a call. We'll discuss anything. Don't worry, I'm not out to screw you guys over.'

Dave Ferris was right. He wasn't out to screw us over. The contract came in a couple of days and we looked at it, trying to understand some of the language. We figured out that we would get fifteen percent of the sales, which seemed good enough. We didn't get an advance or anything, but I guess we didn't really need one since there wasn't anything else to do, and the EP was already out being played and, we hoped, bought. The contract also bound us to record two more albums with Pulley, which also seemed good. We were a professional band now. We signed it and sent it back.

"Yankee Doodle" started getting more and more airplay, mostly on college radio and small stations. A few of Pulley's bands were touring, so when they came to Southern California we'd open for them, and from that we started getting well known in both Los Angeles and San Diego, selling a bunch of CDs at the gigs and, after a couple of months, hearing our songs – not just "Yankee Doodle," but the others – "Erie Canal," "East Virginia" and "Ground-Hog" – played on smaller radio stations in the area. Anna always came with us and helped to drag our equipment around, watching every gig from backstage. Then one night she sang.

We were opening for a band called Neptune at a gig in Los Angeles. We'd come to the next to last song, "Careless Love," and just as I started the first chord Owen told me to stop. 'Ladies and gents,' he said, 'Please welcome to the stage, Anna.' People started cheering and clapping, and I looked to the shadows beyond the stage where Anna was pointing at herself and shaking her head, mouthing, 'No,' while Owen nodded and waved his right arm in a beckoning gesture. Finally, coerced by the growing cheers, Anna walked onstage. She was shaking as she passed me and, remembering those first gigs at Fuzzy's, I said, 'Just close your eyes. It'll be all right.' Owen nodded to me and I started playing again. We hadn't rehearsed, and I'd never heard Anna sing. He sang the first line, 'It's on this railroad bank I stand,' but Anna stood mute and I wondered if she'd start. Of course she knew the words – they were simple, repeated a lot, and she'd heard us play the song a thousand times. Then, after the first chorus, she began.

It started as a straight duet with both of them singing in unison. The thing was, Owen couldn't sing – his voice was always out of tune with our guitars – but Anna, as it turned out, could. She floated above the scratchy, almost tuneless voice of Owen with smooth, connected, beautiful notes. The song started quiet and got more and more raucous as it developed, and Anna went right along, abandoning the unison and echoing parts of the phrases until the last chorus, which turned into almost relentless noise, Owen banging as much feedback out of his guitar as he could and screaming the words into unintelligibility, when she grabbed the microphone stand and started wailing herself, her voice turning gravelly like a genuine blues singer, or a damned soul in hell. The audience responded with shouting, clapping, whistling, stamping and more shouting. Without stopping we rolled right into "Yankee Doodle," the audience singing on the first verse and choruses, Anna staying in front of the microphone and almost outsinging Owen, a feat I'd thought impossible.

Backstage, Owen wrapped his left arm around Anna and they kissed. His guitar clunked against the floor and scraped along it as they staggered back a couple of steps under each other's weight. The Neptune roadies cleared our gear off the stage and began to set up for the rest of the show. I stood nearby, watching Owen and Anna, watching the roadies, my guitar still strapped over my shoulder as though I were about to play. The PA system was pumping out some kind of techno music and the throbbing bass line and drums felt like they were beating into the back of my head. I put my guitar away and wandered around to the back of the audience where I could watch the band and feel anonymous without feeling alone. Neptune was a punk band that played a succession of two- or three-minute, two- or three-chord songs. The crowd was jumping, pushing and shouting along with the singer, and I stood at the back drinking a bottle of water, watching and listening.

'Good band, huh?' I turned to see a guy standing next to me, grinning like an idiot and waiting for a response.

I shrugged. 'They're okay.'

'Not as good as you guys, though.'

'That's not what I meant. Just that they're okay.' We were both shouting over the churning guitars and drums and leaning towards each other to be heard.

'No, but you guys are better. I mean it.'

'Whatever. Thanks.' I turned back to face the band but felt his hand tapping my shoulder. 'What?' I said, turning back to face him, irritated.

He stuck out his hand but I didn't reach to shake it, so he let it drop to his side. 'Stuart Means,' he said. 'I do A&R for Pacific Records. We're always looking for up-and-comers like you guys, and I think you'd fit us great.'

'We're already signed,' I said.

'Yeah, yeah, to Pulley. I've heard the EP. That's why I'm here. It doesn't matter. How much you making with them? Next to nothing, I bet. A few grand. A major label like Pacific, we can do a lot for you guys.' He put his hand on my shoulder and made a gesture to follow, which, inex-plicably, I did. We walked through a door into the foyer where it was quieter, and we – or, rather, Stuart Means – didn't have to shout to be heard. 'We've got a lot more resources than them,' he continued. 'A bigger team. We can pay you more, invest in you more, get you a bigger name producer who knows what he's doing. We've got connections at MTV, we can make a flashy video, get it airtime – in short, we can offer you everything that'll make you guys big.'

'Yeah, well, Pulley's been good to us so far. I don't think we're unhappy with where we're going. But thanks anyway.' I started back towards the door.

'Hold on a second, man.' He put his hand on my shoulder again, and I stopped. 'How far do you really think you're gonna get with them? I'm sure we can offer them enough that there won't be any hard feelings. Why settle for being a warm-up act when, with the right help, you can be playing places a hell of a lot bigger than this, and headlining?'

'Look, I'm going to go back inside now. Anyway, I don't make any decisions without consulting Owen first.'

He waved his hands in front of his chest defensively, palms out. 'Okay, yeah, great, I understand. Here,' he produced a business card. 'Take this, talk it over with Owen, give me a call. If you're worried about anything, just ask me, all right? I understand, man. I used to play in a couple bands myself, I know you want to be in control of things and everything and believe me, I want you to be. That's my job, that's why I'm here – to help you be exactly what you want to be, and make a decent living at it, too. Give me a call after you've thought about it. You won't be sorry.' He tried to shake hands again, so I made my hand unavailable by putting the business card into my pocket and watched as he raised his hand to his head, scratched, and walked back inside, a blast of Neptune escaping from the door as it opened and closed behind him.

When I came downstairs the next morning Owen was sitting at the kitchen table, drinking a cup of coffee and turning Stuart Means's business card over and over between his fingers.

'What's this all about?'

I took a cup from the sink, rinsed it, and filled it with coffee. 'Some guy from Pacific gave it to me last night.'

'I can see that. You didn't sign any contract or anything again, did you?'

'No. I told him we were with Pulley. I told him I wouldn't do anything without you there.'

He set his cup on the table. 'You did before. With Pulley. In New York.'

'That was different, though.' As soon as I said it, I tried to think of how, if at all, it was different.

'How?'

I stood leaning against the counter sipping my coffee and holding it in my mouth for several seconds before swallowing and letting the liquid heat rush down my chest. 'It just was.'

'No, it wasn't.'

'Owen, why are we arguing about this? I told the guy to fuck off, more or less. He kept hounding me and gave me his fucking card. I didn't agree to anything, I barely even said anything. He just rattled on about how much money they'd give us and what fancy videos they'd make for us and all that shit.' I took another sip of coffee in order to shut myself up.

'Okay, I'm sorry. I just – wanted to make sure that I had a say in things. It's not your band, it's not my band, it's our band, right? I'm glad about that thing with Pulley, anyway. But I thought maybe you'd been conned into something or whatever when I saw his card sitting here. That's all. Sorry. I got carried away.'

'Yeah, well, so did I.' I rubbed a spot on the cream-colored linoleum with my big toe. 'It's no big deal. Hey – where's Anna?'

Owen started laughing. 'She went to the store to get something for her throat. She could barely even talk this morning. I guess she shot her vocal chords last night.'

We heard the door open and close and Anna came in carrying a grocery bag and a newspaper tucked under her arm. Both Owen and I were staring at her and grinning. 'What?' she whispered, and we both started laughing. 'Fuck you both,' she whispered again, slamming the bag and newspaper on the counter, which made us laugh harder.

'Nice singing last night,' I said.

Anna's grimace broke into a smile, and then she started laughing. She picked up the newspaper and swatted my arm with it. She was still laughing a little as she unfolded it, but suddenly her smile dropped and her eyebrows crunched down, her eyes getting big. She threw the newspaper onto the table in front of Owen, almost knocking over his coffee.

Los Angeles Times, Friday, October 24, 1997:

Noone Declares War of Words over Morals

WASHINGTON, D.C. – Congressman Jack Noone, the Republican candidate to replace the retiring Democrat Alf Reiniger in the Senate next year, has started the war of words early, denouncing the California Democrats as 'a party of loose morals'.

The comment came as part of a speech to donors at a fundraising dinner in Washington last night. Noone, Congressman for the 9th District, is running unopposed in the primary and is seen as having a good chance of winning back the seat for the Republicans.

In what began as an anodyne review of his past accomplishments and goals for the remainder of his term, Noone shifted towards the end of his speech to a broad and heavy-handed attack on his potential opponents. 'Let there be no mistake,' he said, 'that the coffers of the Democrats are filled by the dirty money of Hollywood, of the music and television industries. They are directly indebted to and controlled by the same interests which corrupt our children with offensive, smutty, violent trash that they would have you believe is art and free speech. Not this man.'

Although the comments come more than a year before the election, they are seen as setting the tone for what is expected to be a tough and bitter battle.

Noone, who has served in Congress since 1980, is known for his conservative views on Hollywood and the entertainment industry, as well as other key Republican issues, such as abortion and tax cuts. Reached for comment, his spokesperson stated, 'Congressman Noone expects to campaign and win on the issues he has always supported and defended. That he has begun to reassert his position so early reflects his deeply-held commitment to the American way of life and to American families as a whole.'

Owen read the article aloud while I rocked back and forth, shifting my weight from my toes to my heels and cradling my coffee cup. I expected him to slam his fists on the table and break something, or at least to yell and curse, but he didn't. When he finished reading he folded the paper at its crease, then folded it in half lengthwise, carefully pinching a second crease along the fold. The hum of the refrigerator was the only sound as Anna and I stood still, watching Owen. The words of the article – the words of Owen's father – turned over in our heads. 'Corrupt our children' was the phrase that I kept hearing Owen reading, and Owen hearing not his own voice but his father's, the man who was too busy to see him on his sixteenth birthday.

Owen creased and recreased the edge of the paper, then looked up at both Anna and me.

'We're going to write a letter,' he said.

'What do you mean, "we,"' I said. 'To whom?'

Owen smiled and spoke softly. 'To Congressman Jack Noone, plus assorted others, like the *Los Angeles Times*, the television news, whoever. By "we" I mean you and I – you're the English major.' He slid his chair back and stood, picking up the paper and empty coffee cup. 'Let's get started.'

'Now?' Anna and I said in unison.

'Yes, now.'

The telephone rang but nobody moved to answer it. After three rings, Owen went into the next room and picked it up. The conversation lasted about five minutes and although only Owen's half was audible, I could tell he was being asked a string of questions because there were long pauses after which he made short responses: 'Yes, about two years. No, too many to mention. I hope so. I don't know. Professional baseball player, yes. Change the world, yes.' Then he called into the kitchen, 'Does the Marauder want to answer a few questions for *College Music Journal*?'

'He does not,' I called back.

'He does not,' Owen repeated into the telephone. 'No, thank you.' He set the phone back down and came back into the kitchen, grinning his smart-alecky happy grin. 'We're going to be in a magazine.'

'I gathered that. What for?'

'I didn't ask. The lady just said, "We want to do a short feature. Do you mind answering some questions?" and I answered them." The telephone rang again. 'Your turn,' Owen said.

It was Dave Ferris. 'Hey, listen,' he said. 'Somebody

from *CMJ* wanted to do an interview with you guys, so I gave her your number. I hope you don't mind.'

'Too late, Dave,' I said.

'They phoned already? Jesus. Anyway, I also wanted to talk to you guys about getting into the studio. Now that this thing is going well, we ought to get working. I don't want to pressure you guys or anything, but have you thought about it? Do you have more songs?'

'Yeah, sure.' I was itching to do something more than sit around the house in Los Angeles, and of course we had songs – a whole book of songs. 'I'll talk to Owen about it and we'll get back to you next week, Dave.'

Owen wasn't as enthusiastic. 'But we've got to write this letter.'

'It won't take months to write a letter, Owen.'

'I guess not. But what if other things happen?'

'Like what?'

'Like – other things. I don't know. Things.'

'Owen, I think we can handle the other "things" as they come. The point is, this is what we're here to do, isn't it? Be a band, make an album? It's not like there won't be time for other stuff. It'll be good to be doing something, anyway, instead of sitting around all day. It'll be more like when we were in Iowa City when we got up every morning and made music.'

'Yeah,' Owen said, sitting down at the table and picking up the paper. 'You're right.' He waved the paper. 'Let's write the letter now.'

Owen Noone
352 King Street
Los Angeles, CA 90010

Congressman Jack Noone
9th District, California
Rayburn HOB
Washington, D.C. 20515

October 25, 1997

Dear Congressman Noone:

Remember me? I used to be your son. On my sixteenth birthday
eight years ago I drove from North Carolina to Washington
to see you. Your lackey brought me a guitar, which I turned
into firewood on the steps of the Capitol.

Well, I've got a new guitar now and I make money playing
what you recently called the 'interests which corrupt our children'. Nice try, Congressman. It seems to me that other interests were corrupting your children long before rock 'n' roll and
movies got to them.

No doubt you'd prefer it if I were still wallowing away in
obscurity somewhere pumping gas and scraping to get by, too
busy to pay attention to who's running for the Senate in
California. Too bad for you. You don't deserve to get elected,
sir. There are already too many hypocrites in politics.

You can safely assume that this letter is a formal announcement of an independent public campaign against your election.

Sincerely, your son,
Owen Noone

Cc: Los Angeles Times
San Francisco Examiner

Owen wrote most of the letter. I just made the grammar nice. The last line especially was his. I tried to dissuade him, but he insisted. When we'd finished we showed it to Anna. She tried to convince him to take out the last line, too, but he wasn't changing his mind. She and I both asked him what the guitar-smashing was all about, but he just waved a hand and said it was nothing, not a big deal, and something about the way he said it made it clear that we shouldn't ask any further. We typed and printed four copies at a printing store and mailed them to Jack Noone and the newspapers that afternoon, keeping a copy for ourselves. Owen seemed happier after that, less agitated than he'd been after Dave Ferris had phoned. We spent the weekend looking through the book to decide what songs to record and if there were any new ones we wanted to add. On Monday I phoned Dave Ferris and on Thursday we went to a place in Los Angeles called Mindful Studios to start recording our first album.

This was a process neither of us knew anything about and it was unlike anything I'd expected. When we'd made our demos, we just plugged in our guitars and microphones, tuned our guitars more or less and pressed record. This was far different. The producer was a tall, skinny guy named Steve Wood, and he seemed to know just about everything about how to record an album. Owen and I expected to be able to get the whole thing banged out in a couple days, but by the end of Thursday we'd only done two songs. First, Steve had us play through the song to hear what it sounded like. Then he'd run around the studio positioning microphones, adjusting the amps, taking our guitars and retuning them, then running into the control room and adjusting levels before telling us to play. We'd replay the whole song, this time recording it. He'd make more adjustments, we'd do another take, he'd make more adjustments, we'd do another take, and eventually he'd say that's enough. That Thursday we did four versions of "John Henry" and five of "Take a Sniff on Me."

'It takes a long time, doesn't it,' Owen said at the end of the day. We were both tired and sick of playing those two songs.

'It'll be worth it at the end,' Steve said. 'You hear all these albums coming out that could sound ten times better if the guy recording it knew what he was doing. Plus, it'd be longer if we were putting it together track by track rather than live, which will also sound better, anyway.' He got very animated when he spoke, waving his hands in front of his chest like a football referee signaling false start. Steve had produced the first Kid Tiger album, too, one of my favorite albums, so I was willing to listen to anything he said and do whatever he told us. After putting away our guitars, we went to a bar around the corner for a drink and then went home where we found a letter from Washington, D.C.

Congressman Jack Noone
9th District, California
Rayburn HOB
Washington, D.C. 20515

Mr. Owen Noone
352 King Street
Los Angeles, CA 90010

October 28, 1997

Dear Mr. Noone:

I received your hostile letter and am taking the time to respond personally. I find your allegations perplexing, mainly because I have no recollection of their occurrence nor do I believe that I know who you are.

Mr. Noone, we may indeed share a surname but there our similarities end. That you copied your far-flung allegations to two prominent newspapers suggests to me that you are simply a publicity-hungry individual looking to boost his career and make a name for himself. I believe that should you decide to continue forward with what you call your 'independent public campaign' against my election, you will find yourself dealing with matters far beyond your knowledge and control. I say this simply for your benefit, Mr. Noone. National politics is a serious matter. Indeed, one of the most serious matters of our national lives and it should not be made trivial and ridiculous by would-be media stars such as yourself. I urge you to consider your actions carefully before you irreparably harm the campaign for me, for my counterparts and for yourself.

Sincerely,

Congressman Jack Noone
9th District, California

The letter trembled in Owen's hands as he read it, once to himself and then twice more aloud. We stood around the kitchen, Owen leaning forward on the table and glaring at the paper as though he could divine some secret between the lines if he just stared at it hard enough. Anna and I stood leaning against the counter on either side of the sink. I hoisted myself to a sitting position. Nobody said anything for a couple minutes. The name Congressman Jack Noone stuck in my ear, repeating itself over and over until it was meaningless, just sound.

'What does he mean?' Anna broke the silence.

Owen looked up, scowling. 'What do you mean, "What does he mean?" He means he's a fucking prick.'

'But how can he say those things in a letter? It makes it more official, like it's evidence or something. If the truth comes out publicly, here he is officially denying it. I mean, isn't this the kind of thing that comes back to haunt these guys?'

Owen continued to glare. 'What are you saying? That he's not lying? That I'm making this up?' His voice rose in a crescendo to a full shout. 'You think this is all just some kind of fiction in my fucking head? Goddamn it! I thought at least you, Anna, would trust me on this.' He turned to me. 'What about you? Who are you siding with?'

'Owen,' I said as calmly as I could. 'Nobody's said anything about not believing you. We're just baffled. Trying to figure out what it all means.'

'So you don't believe me, either. Fuck you. Fuck you both.' He jammed the letter into his pocket and marched out of the kitchen. We heard the front door open and then slam behind him.

'That's not what I said.' Anna's arms were wrapped around her. She shook her head slowly back and forth. 'That's not what I said at all.' I could see that she was trying to keep the tears from rising in her eyes and spilling over. 'He doesn't listen sometimes. He doesn't listen at all.'

I felt useless. There was nothing I could say except yeah, or don't worry, it'll be all right, or just give him some time to think about it, none of which were intelligent things to say. I slid down from the countertop, my bare feet slapping the linoleum quietly, and stretched my hand out to touch Anna's shoulder. She turned and started to cry. I put my arms around her and hugged, not saying anything because I didn't know what to say.

'Do you want to go to the beach?' Anna said, raising her arm to wipe her eyes.

I let my arms drop and took a step back. The beach. It sounded strange for some reason. The word, the concept, the beach. We'd been living in Los Angeles for more than two months, been to New York City and North Carolina, but I'd never been to the beach, or seen the ocean. I remembered going with my parents to Michigan City once when I was little and playing on the beach, looking out across Lake Michigan. The horizon was water and it seemed as big as the ocean, although Lake Michigan wasn't even close to the same size. Looking in another direction I could see the skyscrapers of Chicago poking up from the shoreline, ruining the illusion. That was the biggest body of water I'd ever seen. I hadn't even thought of going to the beach in all the time we'd been in Los Angeles.

We walked down to Dockweiler Beach, shading our eyes against the burning pink of the setting sun. The beach was right near the airport and every couple of minutes a plane would land, filling the air with a roar, getting bigger and bigger, silhouetted against the sun until it passed over our heads, the landing gear sticking down from the belly. I thought of the rhyme, 'red sky at night, sailor's delight.'

'Do you think there's any truth to it?' I thought out loud.

'To what?' Anna turned and squinted at me.

'Red sky at night, sailor's delight. And does pink count as red?'

Anna shrugged. 'I grew up on a farm. I don't know.'

'Maybe pink is just less than red, like if red sky is delight, pink is just contentment or mild amusement, and then if it's morning, it's not so much warning as, I don't know, caution. Or maybe I'm just talking nonsense.'

We came to the edge of the beach, and I took off my shoes and stepped barefoot into the sand, feeling it ooze up between my toes. The sun had almost set and it spread a widening column of shimmering pink across the water. The waves weren't as big as I thought they'd be, but they pushed towards the beach, crawling up the sand until they retreated suddenly, curling back under themselves and creeping back into the ocean until the next wave piled over the top. I wanted to stand in it and get my feet wet, so we walked closer to the water.

'What do you think of all this?' Anna said.

'It's amazing,' I said, 'So big and beautiful.'

'No, I mean about Owen and his father and everything.'

'Oh.' I felt embarrassed. A wave rolled up and around my ankles. 'Jesus! It's fucking cold!' I was avoiding the answer. 'I don't know. I don't understand – can't understand, really, but I think he's getting carried away. At least right now. It'd probably be better if he just concentrated on making the album.' We started walking along the edge of the water, skipping to the side when the waves rolled near our feet. 'That's what I want to do, not this politics crap. I mean, the guy's been in Congress for ages and Owen's never done anything, so why now? I just want to make the album, play music. We can't really change anything. I don't know, maybe I'm being selfish.'

'No, I understand. He's just so intense about everything. He needs to relax a little. You're right, he can't control this election thing. I don't know what he hopes he can get out of it, what he thinks he can achieve. Knocking down his father, I guess. Whatever good that will do. I don't think it'll make him feel any better.'

'He needs to realize that not everything is about him.'

'Exactly. And not take it out on us.'

Anna stopped. I turned towards her. She was looking into my eyes. I felt myself leaning in and shifting my feet so our bodies were closer and I put my hands on her elbows. She was still watching me. Our faces moved closer. Our noses touched. Anna's arms wrapped around my torso and she turned her head away, pressing it into my shoulder as she cleared her throat. 'No,' she said quietly into my T-shirt, and I could feel the word vibrate against me.

We separated and started walking again. I don't know why I tried to kiss her. Maybe I wanted to know what it was like to kiss her, what it was like to be Owen.

'Sorry,' I muttered, my eyes on the ground.

'Don't say sorry.' She took my hand in hers and squeezed it gently.

It was nearly dark now. We could see someone walking down the beach towards us. When I realized it was Owen I let go of Anna and shoved my hands into my pockets. It seemed to take a long time for our paths to finally meet, and I felt restless not knowing what to say to him, if there even was anything to say. I didn't want him to be there.

'Hi,' Owen said. 'Look, I owe you both an apology. I'm sorry. I got carried away. So,' he spread his arms to the side and let them fall against his thighs. 'I'm sorry.'

That's okay, thank you, fuck off and I understand all presented themselves as possible responses, but none of them felt real. I dug my toe into the sand.

'Owen,' Anna said, 'Why don't you just forget about it for a little while and get this album made. You're not going to accomplish anything with this right now anyway. Let it go for a while. You can't control everything.'

'I know. But it would be nice, wouldn't it, if I could? For me, anyway.' Owen put a hand on each of our shoulders. 'Let's go home.'

The next morning we were back in the studio, and as Owen and I got more comfortable with the whole process, it started going much more smoothly. By the end of the next week we had recorded the fourteen songs we wanted for the album plus four more. Owen and I started waking up early because we were so eager to get started. We'd get to the studio before anyone, waiting outside the door until someone arrived with a key, and then sit among the equipment fiddling with our guitars, chattering stupidly to each other until somebody knocked on the glass partition between the recording room and the engineering room, which housed the massive mixing board and reels of tape. On Wednesday, Anna came in and we made a version of 'Careless Love' with her singing along like at the Neptune gig. When we finished two days later we took the whole group – Steve, an assistant engineer, a couple staff from the studio – to a nearby bar and Owen bought everybody drinks. Music, once again, was everything. The only thing we really cared about, thought about, the only thing we actually did. Dave Ferris called to tell us congratulations on finishing and that they were planning a small promotional tour. He mentioned some cities, but we weren't really paying attention. It didn't really matter to us. We'd finished an album, our album, and we felt the same excitement, the same shot of energy in our chests that we felt when we first played in Peoria, at Fuzzy's and at CBGB's. Rock 'n' roll was feeling again like what it was supposed to feel like – the greatest thing to be doing in the world.

WHO ARE OWEN NOONE AND THE MARAUDER?

With the growing success of the *Yankee Doodle* EP, *CMJ* decided it was high time to figure out who, exactly, Owen Noone and the Marauder are. *Kate Litman* spoke to Mr. Owen Noone himself to get the lowdown.

KL: So, it's just two of you in the band?
ON: Yes, just me and the Marauder.
KL: How long have you been together?
ON: About two years.
KL: Where did you guys first get together?
ON: Peoria, Illinois.
KL: Have either of you played in other bands?
ON: No.
KL: What other jobs have you had?
ON: Professional baseball player.
KL: Really?
ON: Yes.
KL: Who are your biggest influences?
ON: There's too many to mention.

KL: When can we expect a full-length album from Owen
     Noone and the Marauder?
ON: I don't know.
KL: Soon, I hope?
ON: I don't know.
KL: Finally, what do you hope to accomplish?
ON: Change the world.
KL: Really?
ON: Yes.

After a little research, *CMJ* discovered that one Owen
Noone did indeed play professional baseball for the
Peoria Chiefs and the Iowa Cubs. The Marauder was
unavailable for comment, and we've been unable to coax
any information about him from his label. A full-length
album is expected in November or December. *Yankee
Doodle* is available now and is number seven on this
month's *CMJ* chart.

Dave Ferris sent a copy of the magazine. Neither of us was
pleased.

'They make me sound like I'm incapable of putting
together a sentence, like I'm some kind of Neanderthal.' As
usual, we were sitting around the kitchen.

'What's this crap about unavailable for comment? I was
right here – ' I stamped the ground – 'and available. I chose
not to comment. There's a fucking difference.'

'And why the hell do they have to go weaseling around
to see if we're telling the truth? Like it's impossible that I
was a professional baseball player, and what do they expect
to find about you? That you went to Bradley? That you're
from Indiana? What does any of that crap matter?'

Anna laughed. 'You guys are too uptight. Why do you
even care what they say? It's all publicity. It's not like
they're libeling you or anything. You're number seven on
the chart. Don't worry about it.'

'The *CMJ* chart,' I said, my expertise from being a DJ coming through, 'Hardly makes any difference, except to a few college radio losers.'

'Were you not one of those losers yourself once?'

'Shut up, Owen.'

'But you were.'

'Shut up, Owen.'

'And did it matter to you then?'

'Yeah, I guess.'

'So it'll help us sell records.'

'A few.'

'Then I guess we won't sweat it. Nobody actually reads this thing anyway, do they?'

'Just losers like me who buy our records.'

The same day, Jack Noone came back into our lives, or rather, we let him in. Owen got a phonecall from the *San Francisco Examiner*.

'Mr. Noone, we've done some checking and it sounds like you're telling the truth,' said the reporter, a guy named Paul Danielson. 'We want to use your story but not without your consent, and we want to wait until it might have its biggest effect. Could we set up a meeting?'

Paul Danielson came down from San Francisco two days later and had an hour-long meeting with Owen in our living room. He was a middle-aged guy, not quite as old as my parents, with light brown hair and a bald spot at the back. Even though he wore a suit, he gave the impression of being sloppily dressed – tie askew, ill-fitting jacket. He was a nice enough guy, though, and seemed sincere. Anna and I weren't supposed to be in on the meeting, so we spied from the kitchen. Paul sat on the edge of the sofa holding a notebook and facing Owen, who sat opposite, sunk into the cushions of an easy chair. Paul also had a tape recorder, which he balanced on his knee.

'Owen, you understand that we, the *Examiner*, can't pay you for this story.'

'Paul, I don't need money. I don't want money. If I were doing this for money I would have gone somewhere else, and some other time. This has nothing to do with money.'

'Okay, good. You haven't been contacted by the *LA Times* have you? Purely so I know where we stand.'

'No. If I had, I wouldn't be wasting both of our time, and I won't be wasting their time if they do phone.'

'Now, Owen, what is it exactly you're alleging?'

'I'm not alleging anything. I'm saying that Jack Noone is my father, and all I'm asking is that, if he's going to run this campaign about family values and the corruption of our children and all this bullshit —' Paul Danielson's eyebrows raised when Owen said bullshit. Not so much at the word, but at the increasing volume in Owen's voice. ' — if he's going to claim to be the great crusader, upholding these virtues, then he ought to be held accountable, shouldn't he?'

'What do you mean by accountable, Owen?'

'Simply that he should acknowledge his role in the corruption of youth, if that's what he wants to call it. He should be made to acknowledge that he's spent his entire life ignoring his only child, denying me this supposedly wonderful and virtuous nuclear family life he claims to defend. He can talk about music and movies and everything, but to be honest, if it weren't for things like music and movies, I'd probably be delinquent due to his complete lack of responsibility and his total self-interest when it comes to the duties of being a father.'

'And what about your mother, Owen?'

'What about her?'

'Where does she fit into this? Is she backing you up in these allegations?'

Owen leaned forward to the edge of the chair, grasping the armrests. 'Look, I told you before, there's no alleging involved. This is simple fact.'

Paul Danielson raised his hands and waved them defensively. 'Yes, I know, Owen, but there's certain language journalists have to use to keep ourselves out of court battles. Could we return to the question about your mother?'

Owen pointed at the tape recorder. 'Only if you turn that off. My mother remains, as you would say, "off the record".' Paul shut off the tape recorder. 'My mother remarried and she lives abroad. Whatever problems I may or may not have with her are completely separate from this. It's none of her business and I would ask that you respect my wishes and her privacy and keep her completely out of this.'

Paul looked Owen directly in the eyes. 'You have my word, Owen.' He turned the tape recorder back on. 'What do you remember of your father?'

'That's just it, Paul – nothing. My father left when I was two, I mean, my parents divorced, he didn't just run out. I've tried to see him once since then, on my sixteenth birthday, but he was too busy. He was expecting me. He had a gift for me. But he wouldn't come see me. I drove all the way to Washington and all he had to do was walk down a hallway, but he wouldn't do it. He sent some lackey. I wanted to meet my father – I wasn't asking for anything else. I wanted him to be proud of his son and all he wanted was to get rid of me as painlessly as possible – for him.'

'What was the gift?'

146

Owen leaned back and laced his fingers behind his head. 'A guitar.'

'Do you still have the guitar?'

Owen's smile straightened. 'No. No, I don't.'

Then Paul asked Owen about the band. 'I understand you're in a rock band?'

'Yeah, so?'

'Well, this is a bit delicate, Owen, but there's some concern among my editors that perhaps your intentions aren't entirely pure.'

'I don't follow.'

'To put it bluntly, they're concerned that you're using this opportunity to promote your music career.'

Again Owen leaned forward to the edge of his chair. 'Then I'll put it just as bluntly, Paul.' He pointed at the tape recorder. 'And you can play this for your fucking editors, okay? This has nothing to do with my fucking band. My fucking band is not my fucking band to begin with. There's two of us and it's our band, and frankly I'm insulted by, to use your term, such an allegation. Our music career is going quite well without any shameless publicity. If I could, I would keep the two separate. But I can't. That's not my problem. We don't need a completely unrelated article in a fucking newspaper to further our careers. You and your fucking editors can just keep all mention of my band out of your fucking article. Got it?'

Paul Danielson's tape ran out just after Owen finished. The click seemed to reverberate around the room. 'I understand, Owen, but I had to ask. Thanks for your time. I'll give you a couple days' notice before we run the story, and will send you a copy.'

Two weeks later Pulley held a record release party for

us in Los Angeles. Dave Ferris flew out from New York and rented a bar where they played the album about a thousand times and everybody got drunk. There were tons of people there, most of whom we didn't know – industry people I guess, a few bands, some music journalists, the odd low-grade celebrity. We'd hoped that Steve Wood would be there, but he'd already left for Chicago to record an album for somebody else. Owen and Anna and I hung around together near the bar, a way of kind of defending ourselves against the swarms of strangers. Occasionally we'd see someone point towards us and lean towards someone else, talking into his or her ear. Then both would come over to us and introduce themselves. It happened at least a dozen times:

'Hi, I'm So-and-So, nice to meet you.' We'd exchange handshakes. 'So, uh, congratulations on the album. It's really great.' We'd say thanks. A silence, followed by the jangle and roar of Owen Noone and the Marauder. 'Well, it was nice meeting you guys. See you later.' They'd shuffle away.

When "Old Smokey" started playing for what must have been the tenth time, a small group – six people, maybe – started a drunken waltz, which only sort of worked, partly because there was no drumbeat and partly because we only kind of played it in 3/4 time, Owen singing in the right time signature, but the guitars basically keeping sloppy 4/4, my arpeggios constantly adding or dropping notes to try to stay in rhythm. A woman who I recognized as a movie actress came over to where we stood. She was slightly taller than me, but shorter than Owen and had chin-length, shiny black hair. She wore a low cut, sleeveless blue-sequined dress and was, by far, the most overdressed person there.

'Hi,' she said, looking straight at Owen. 'I'm Ellen

Trelaine. I love the album. Just love it. Would you like to dance?'

Owen looked at Anna, then back at Ellen. The second verse, 'For meetin' is pleasure / And partin' is grief,' was just beginning. 'No, I don't think so.'

'Aww, Come on.' Ellen tried to look pouty, as though she were Bette Davis or Marilyn Monroe and not a soon to be forgotten B-list actress. Then she turned to me. 'What about you, Marauder?'

There's a scene in a movie where Ellen Trelaine dances with a rich guy at a swanky dinner party hosted by another rich guy, and I have to admit, I'd imagined myself dancing with her in that scene at least a couple of times. There wasn't any chance I was going to say no. She took my hand and led me out to where the others were dancing, and we began to stumble through a waltzlike pattern. Everybody else was dancing poorly too, so it didn't matter, I was living out a minor fantasy. Towards the end of the song Ellen leaned towards me.

'Who's the girl?'

'What girl?'

'Owen's date.' She cocked her head in their direction.

'Anna?' It struck me, suddenly, what the word for Anna was. 'Anna is Owen's wife.'

A look of disappointment spread across her face. 'Oh. Well, thanks for the dance.' She kissed the air next to my cheek and I paralleled this gesture automatically, not quite knowing why. I made my way back to the bar and got another drink.

'Lucky boy,' Anna said. 'What'd you two talk about?'

I had a large glass of whiskey and took a huge slug from it, feeling the burn spread through my mouth, across

149

my chest and down into my stomach. 'She wanted to know who Owen's date was.'

Anna and Owen both started laughing. 'What did you tell her?' Owen asked.

'The truth.' I finished my whiskey.

Rolling Stone, November 11, 1997:

Owen Noone and the Marauder
Owen Noone and the Marauder
(Pulley)
****

Since the appearance of the Yankee Doodle EP the reputation of Owen Noone and the Marauder has been growing, and with the release of this, their first full-length album, the duo are sure to firmly secure a spot in the current indie-rock limelight. With a formula so simple it defies logic, the two guitarists plough, stumble and churn their way through fourteen folk songs, taking control and breathing new, if sacrilegious (one imagines John Lomax rolling in his grave) life into them. Most of the songs follow the same basic pattern: jangly-guitar verses explode at the choruses when Noone's guitar leaps into a feedback-laden ecstasy juxtaposed with the continuing strumming and arpeggios of his counterpart. Off-key, sometimes screaming vocals add to the sense of an impending train-wreck, a catastrophe that, while seeming always to be just around the corner, never actually happens. Particular joys are the opener, "John Henry," and the more subdued "Big Rock Candy Mountains," as well as the furiously-paced Leadbelly tunes, "The Midnight Special" and "Green Corn." The biggest surprise of the album is "Careless Love," which, as if to highlight the duo's innate dissonance, features beautiful, floating female vocals (credited to previously unknown Anna Penatio), a conceit that works like a charm. Whether drumless, discordant folk playing has any potential for a sustained career is another matter, but for now, Owen

Noone and the Marauder are a fresh and very welcome presence.

CHARLIE WHEELER

The *Rolling Stone* review pushed us into more mainstream attention, and the album started selling very soon after it appeared. Our small promotional tour suddenly expanded and instead of playing five East Coast gigs, we were booked to an eleven-city tour, covering the entire country in just over two weeks. We'd start in New York City at CBGB's, where we'd played our first real gig and where we'd met Dave Ferris, then to Boston, Washington, D.C., Cleveland, Detroit, Chicago, Milwaukee, Seattle, Portland and San Francisco, and end with two gigs back in Los Angeles. For the final concert we were to be the second of three bands at a New Year's Eve party. On December 7 we packed up the truck and started driving for New York City, the reverse trip of the one we'd made in August, heading up Interstate 15 to Barstow where, instead of continuing up to Las Vegas, we switched to I-40 and took a more southerly route through Arizona, New Mexico, the panhandle and beyond, new territory for us until Tennessee, where we would retrace some of the miles that had taken us to Charlotte, a time and place that seemed far away. The space between events in our lives was shrinking, pushing them deeper into our memory banks, further away from who we were and who we were becoming.

There's a belief about the romance of driving the American road: the carefree life, the landscape hauling by with the wind. But it's not true. Once you've crossed the mountains and deserts of Arizona and New Mexico, there are few things more boring than crossing into Texas, a sign welcoming you to THE LONE STAR STATE with the famous admonition against littering, and the flat, arid prairie unrolling all the way into and across Oklahoma, until finally the terrain changes to the rolling river valleys of Arkansas. It's a lot less Jack Kerouac's great unfolding American Continent and a lot more Woody Guthrie's Dust Bowl ballads.

After three long, tedious days we crossed into the city of Memphis and knew immediately where we had to go.

There's not much point in describing Graceland. It's a money-monument, not only to Elvis, but also to wretched taste. I couldn't even laugh at the tackiness. The heart-shaped chair in the Annex, the suits, the purple upholstery. The Meditation Garden in which I can hardly imagine anyone finding inner peace, with its white ionic columns, stained-glass windows, fountain and, around the graves, flowers flowers flowers, arranged in variously shaped wreaths. Only the music room is completely plain. It's just a small, white room with a grand piano, as though Elvis didn't want distraction when he sat down and sang.

But the amazing thing about visiting Graceland isn't the place itself. It's the fans, which is hardly the right word to call them. They're more like devotees or followers. There's some kind of fervent religious quality to their behavior. Women old and young wearing black T-shirts with airbrushed pictures of the King weep over his grave, blotting their mascara with wads of Kleenex then stumble off into their husbands' or boyfriends' arms. We shambled around for an hour or so looking at Elvis's kitchen, where he made peanut butter and banana sandwiches, his jungle-themed living room, his bedroom with its massive bed, his misspelled gravestone, but not, disappointingly, the toilet upon which he popped his last pill and croaked out his last syllable. Still, I guess we shouldn't have expected to see it; that's not Elvis for those T-shirt wearing ladies. Their god was not supposed to have died such an unglorious death. Seeing it would only remind them and point out there wasn't any resurrection, videos of that last show in Hawaii, twenty bucks in the gift shop, notwithstanding.

We spent the night in Memphis and the next morning were back on the interstate, heading east for the Smoky Mountains. There we changed direction northward to the Appalachians and then the Alleghenies, eventually leaving these low, sprawling mountain ranges to cross Pennsylvania into New Jersey. Six days after leaving Los Angeles and three after Memphis we were crossing underneath the Hudson River, through the Holland Tunnel and out into Manhattan. Although we'd lived there for only a week, it was the source, the beginning of our success in a lot of ways. Coming to New York was like coming home. More so than Charlotte or Peoria. We went straight to CBGB's, where our lives had taken their biggest turn, and where in three hours we would be playing again as the headliners, the band people were paying to see, the band whose name was on the posters, the one whose T-shirts they wanted to buy, whose songs they wanted to hear and sing along with.

Village Voice, December 16, 1997:

OWEN NOONE
AND THE MARAUDER
CBGB December 12

Two guys sporting Telecasters strum the chords to the folk song "John Henry," and they're almost playing together. One guy is singing, or yelping – not really in tune with anything.

Then the singer stomps on a distortion pedal and a shriek of feedback and adrenaline slams across the room, his voice getting louder and coarser, his arm pumping across the strings of his guitar like he's beating the shit out of it. The other guy stands there playing his jangly chords, a seemingly oblivious counterpoint to his wailing bacchanalian friend. Meanwhile, the noise of the two guitars seems to be getting more out of sync.

Ladies and gentlemen, this is Owen Noone and the Marauder, the most unlikely punk band ever. There's no drums, no bass, just these two guys cranking out songs written seventy years before they were born. And the kids in the audience love it, bouncing along screaming, especially on the show closer, "Yankee Doodle," this year's unlikely college radio darling. Unlikely is the word for the whole experience. It's absolute genius.

Dave Ferris was there and Anna sang with us on "Careless Love." The whole thing felt even better than it had that very first night in August, four months before, because everybody there was there for us. We were the main act, the feature presentation, the reason that people paid. The opening act was some New Jersey punk band, and people seemed to like them, but after their gear had been cleared off the stage and ours brought on, microphones tested, guitars tuned, people started getting excited. Some whistled, others called out the occasional 'Yeah.' I suddenly realized there's some sort of fake tension before a band comes out, at the edge of the stage just hidden from the view of the audience, as though there's a chance that the band might not come out. It's both the anticipation and that you can't really be sure until they actually appear, and pick up their guitars and start.

It was time. I walked out onstage first and a few people, presumably those who'd seen us play here before, recognized me and cheered. Then Owen came out and a few more cheered. As I was lifting my guitar strap over my shoulder, Owen put his hand on top of the microphone stand, leaned in and said, 'Hello, everybody. I'm Owen Noone and that there is the Marauder. Are you ready for a little music?' It was the cheesiest line possible, but it didn't fail to get its response. The entire audience clapped and whistled. Owen strapped on his guitar and we played.

Before we left New York City to drive up to Boston the next day we went for breakfast at the same place we'd eaten after our first gig in New York. The same place where we'd read about Jack Noone. It was a strange feeling walking in there, remembering that sentence in the newspaper and how it had changed things, wondering briefly if it had been for the better. After all, our lives were moving in the right direction. We wouldn't be living in warm L.A., I thought, if it weren't for that. We'd be stuck here in the gray, cold winter of the East Coast. It had probably helped to give us focus, always wanting to get things done before Owen's energies turned to other plans.

Pasted in the window of the café was a poster advertising the gig from last night. OWEN NOONE AND THE MARAUDER was written huge at the top and PLUS SPECIAL GUEST small underneath. I couldn't remember the name of the special guest. While we ate our eggs and bacon silently, waiting for the coffee to work its magic, a teenage boy came over to our table.

'Excuse me,' we heard, and looked up. He stood shifting his weight from foot to foot, his finger rubbing a pimple on the side of his nose. 'Aren't you guys, um –' he exhaled a nervous sputter of whispered laughter. 'I mean, aren't you Owen Noone? And the Marauder? Could I – I mean, I saw the show last night. It was great. Great. The best show I saw all year. Do you think, I mean, could I please, could you please sign my CD booklet?' He produced the CD from his backpack and placed it on the table next to Owen's plate. I noticed that he was wearing our T-shirt – Dave Ferris had ordered some, navy blue ones with orange writing that said our name in typewriter letters on the front and on the back were printed the words to the chorus of "Yankee Doodle:"

> *Yankee Doodle, keep it up,*
> *Yankee Doodle Dandy,*
> *Mind the music and the step*
> *And with the girls be handy.*

Owen signed his name across the front of the booklet and passed it across the table to me.

'What's your name?' I asked.

The kid made his laugh again. 'Oh, it's, uh, Ed.'

I wrote, "To Ed, thanks for buying our record, Marauder."

'Have you eaten, Ed?' Anna asked.

Again he did the nervous laugh. 'No.'

'Why don't you sit down, then?' She waved her hand towards the empty seat next to me.

So we ate breakfast with Ed and asked him what bands he liked, where he went to school, what he wanted to do when he finished. He played guitar, too, but not in a band. He didn't know anybody else who liked the same kind of music. He was trying to get a scholarship for the film program at NYU.

'You could direct our video, if we ever make one,' Owen said.

Ed laughed – he seemed to laugh all the time and it cracked us up. We all started laughing. Then Owen stopped. 'No, seriously, though. You could. You must know what you're doing.'

'Well, sort of, I guess.'

'Here –' Owen wrote down our address and phone number on a napkin and put it in front of Ed. 'Write us a postcard with your address, Ed. You'll be the first person we call.'

Ed took the napkin and smiled without laughing. 'Thanks. Are you serious?'

Everybody was looking at Owen and I thought about that bar in Peoria, when he'd chatted me deaf, and then the next day when he'd been waiting outside my dorm with the bag of books, and then over a year later when he'd shown up to start the band. I knew he was serious.

He nodded. 'Your T-shirt has my name on it,' he said.

It was fun playing in Boston and there were lots of college students. While we played, I could hear people singing along, people who'd bought the album, who'd listened to it and liked it. After Boston we had an eight-hour drive to Washington, D.C. We left Sunday morning, getting there in the afternoon with plenty of time to kill before our Monday night gig. Neither Anna nor I had ever been to Washington, and Owen had only been there once, to see his father, he said. We wanted to see the White House, the Capitol Building, the monuments, so we spent most of the day sightseeing, haphazardly wandering from one thing to the next. Owen got hyper on the steps of the Capitol.

'Right here,' he said, hopping from one foot to the other. 'I smashed that fucking guitar. That was the best thing I could've done. I only wish he'd watched me do it.'

It was cloudy and windy, and Anna and I stood a few steps below him, shivering against the cold.

'Okay,' Anna said, 'You're going to tell us right now what this is all about.'

Owen had been smiling, but now the corners of his mouth dropped and he crossed his arms over his chest. He sighed. 'When I was sixteen my mother told me about my father. About his being a congressman. I'd never really known much about him, and hadn't ever really cared, or thought about him, either. She and my stepdad bought me a plane ticket and told me to go to Washington to see him, that this had always been the plan, when I was sixteen I could meet him so he could explain the divorce to me, and why he and my mother – why he and I – never spoke.' Owen, having just gotten his driver's license, insisted on taking the car. They acquiesced. 'I felt like an adult, like a real, mature person, driving up to Washington through North Carolina and Virginia, on my own for the first time. It was great. I drove up there in one day and got a hotel room. I wanted to spend that first night alone, then find my father at the Capitol the next day.' He got up early the next morning and drove straight there. 'I had this baseball bat with me, my mom gave it to me on my birthday, it had been my father's, she said, a gift for his sixteenth birthday. I was going to show it to him, tell him how good a base-ball player I was, varsity, when I was just a sophomore and everything, but they took it away from me at the security check. I tried to explain but they didn't care. Then, after I told them I was Jack Noone's son, they phoned his office. "He wants to know what your name is," the security guy said. He was a big guy, football-player-sized, and bald, but with a big brown mustache. "Owen Noone," I said. I felt proud. It sounds stupid, but I did, being the son of Jack Noone, Republican Congressman. The security guy repeated it into the phone, then listened, and looked up at me a couple of times before saying, "Okay" into the phone and hanging up. "Just wait here a minute," he said.

'There were people filing in through the metal detectors, showing identification and walking down the corridors to work. After a while this aide came walking towards us. He must have been a college kid or something, he didn't really look much older than me, but he was smiling, wearing a suit, red tie, and carrying a small guitar case. I swear I suddenly felt like I was in a movie, like he was going to flip that thing open and start shooting everybody or something. He walked up to me and said, "Owen? Congressman Noone can't see you. He asked me to give you this, and to say Happy Birthday and have a safe trip back to Charlotte." He handed me the case and turned and walked away. I just stood there, watching him until he disappeared around a corner. Nobody seemed to pay any attention.'

Owen was speaking very evenly, very controlled, as though he'd rehearsed the story a hundred times. 'I turned and looked at the security guy, but he was busy. I walked out of the Capitol and opened the guitar case. It had a brand new Martin acoustic guitar inside. I took it out and smashed it on the steps. Then I started crying.'

That was it. He'd never known his father anyway, and this insult was proof that he wasn't worth knowing. It didn't mean he didn't care, though. Angry, he drove back to Charlotte, wondering if his mom had known what was going to happen or whether she wasn't to blame at all. But when he got home, he didn't confront her. 'My mom was smiling, asking how it went, and I started to think maybe she knew all along, like that smile was just a sinister one. But I didn't know, and I didn't want to tell her, so I smiled back and said it was fine, we'd had lunch, and left it at that.'

Whenever Owen talked about his father I felt silent and empty. They were emotions that I couldn't understand, and which were somehow absurd. It made me feel guilty to think they were absurd, because it made Owen seem absurd, and I didn't want to think that, especially because I knew how serious he was. I hated thinking that my best friend – my only friend other than Anna – was absurd. So I never said anything.

'We should send him a ticket.' Owen clapped his hands together. 'Do you think he'd come?'

'Do you want him to?' Anna asked.

'Oh yes, definitely. I'd sing every song right at him, so he'd know.'

'Know what?' She walked up two steps, halving the distance between them.

'That I'm somebody. He wanted me to be nothing. When I came to see him that day to tell him that I was a baseball star, I thought he'd be excited, show an interest, but all he did was give me some shitty guitar that I never wanted without ever saying a single word. He didn't care. And now he just writes a letter because he knows the truth can hurt him. I want to look him in the eyes from that stage and step down on that fuzz pedal and just keep staring at him, letting him know that I've made it despite him. That he's nothing to me.'

Owen sent the ticket, but Jack Noone didn't come. It was a small club, and we could see everybody in the audience. He wasn't there. We played lousy because we were just going through the motions, but people seemed enthusiastic nonetheless. The only thing we did well was the encore.

After we'd put down our guitars and walked off the stage, we stood behind the wall listening to the claps and shouts, and I said to Owen, 'Let's just go out there and play.'

'I know,' he said, and I knew what he meant. When we got out onstage and people were shouting and clapping more loudly, Owen leaned towards the microphone. I picked up my guitar but he didn't. He said, 'Thank you. There's a guy who lives in Washington who we know, and we gave him a free ticket, but he didn't come. Do you think that's fair?' People started booing in response. 'His name is Jack, and he's a Congressman, and this song is for him.'

I knew what Owen had in mind. I started banging down the chord, my guitar out of tune, and he started singing, hoarsely, 'Ding-Dong, the witch is dead,' and on 'Which old witch?' the crowd, without missing a beat, shouted, 'The wicked witch!' On the last chord the A-string snapped, curling back to the head and then drooping towards the floor. I took off the guitar and picked up Owen's, and we played "Yankee Doodle" with just one guitar but both of us still playing; I strummed the chords and Owen, while singing, played air guitar, stepping on the pedal before and after the choruses and looking a little like Joe Cocker at Woodstock. It was weird to hear my own chords distorted and to have the change disembodied by an action beyond my control. Still, it worked, and we salvaged something from the show.

We took two days to drive to Cleveland, cutting across the southwest corner of Pennsylvania and spending the night in Pittsburgh before continuing the final three hours. Dave Ferris had phoned us in our hotel in Pittsburgh and told us that the *Plain Dealer* had requested an interview. We spent an hour before the concert eating burgers and answering music critic Frank Newlun's questions.

NO SENTIMENTAL LIES

Plain Dealer music critic Frank Newlun talks to Owen Noone and the Marauder.

Owen Noone and the Marauder are the most unlikely phenomenon in rock, as much as they would be in folk music if they'd started playing in the Appalachians instead of the Midwest. Sans drummer, they blaze through a back catalog of folk songs straight from the work of John and Alan Lomax as though the Carter Family suddenly got their forks stuck in the toaster. The simple formula has turned them into darlings of college radio almost overnight and now, on a short national tour, they seem on the brink of breaking into the mainstream.

I stroll into McDonald's, the place they insisted on meeting. "It's not like we always eat here or anything," Noone, tall and scruffy-haired, explains. They've got a limited amount of time, he continues, and McDonald's is purely a pragmatic choice. "I don't even really like their burgers."

Noone does most – actually, all – of the talking. The Marauder is the smaller of the two and seems content to let his partner field all of the questions, drinking a strawberry milkshake and occasionally brushing his curly black hair from his face. I ask him where he grew up and Noone answers for him: "Indiana." Noone himself grew up in Charlotte, North Carolina, but the duo met, improbably, in Peoria, Illinois. Noone also tells me that he was a professional baseball player. I don't believe him at first, but he insists, eventually pulling out a statistics chart clipped from a newspaper with his name on it.

Did either of them listen to folk music as kids? No. "Really, we just wanted to start a band and found this book with all these songs in it, and they were easy to play, easy to learn." So, you weren't in any bands before this? "No. Neither of us could actually play."

How do you explain the popularity of "Yankee Doodle" and the new album? "Everybody knows "Yankee Doodle," that's the thing. They can sing along and feel like they're part of it. The rest of them are good songs, that's why we're popular. People like simple, good songs played by real people, not this electronic, tuneless stuff you hear." Noone launches into a discourse about electronic music, sounding something like an old fogey. I tell him so, and he laughs. "I just like my music to be made by real people."

Do you think these songs have a relevance to today, to modern audiences? "Not really. They're fun. They're noisy. But relevant? No. They just make people happy. That's why we do it." Is that true of rock music in general? "Yes. I think so. You can't change the world with rock music, can you? Nobody has." What about John Lennon? "He's dead, isn't he? And he wrote lousy songs, anyway. "War is Over," "Imagine there's no heaven," blah blah blah. If there's one good thing about the songs we play, it's that they're not sappy, drivelly lies like that."

I'm about to say that a lot of his fans would disagree with his opinion of the late Beatle when a girl roughly the same age as the duo comes over to the table. Noone introduces her as his wife, and although I'm skeptical – I don't see any rings – I keep it to myself, lest he pull out a copy of the marriage certificate. She says it's time to get ready for the gig, and the Marauder picks up the trays of burger wrappers. Noone thanks me and they walk across the street and into the club, unrecognized by the line of fans waiting to get in.

After Wednesday in Cleveland we had three gigs in three days in three different cities, Detroit on Thursday, Chicago and then Milwaukee, after which we had almost a week to get to Seattle. We left Milwaukee Sunday morning. I was driving and Owen sat next to me, looking at the map.

'We could go to Iowa City.'

'Isn't it out of the way?'

'So what? We could go and say hello to Miss Kitty and go to Fuzzy's for a drink. Show Anna where we really got started. We've got plenty of time.'

I began to get nervous when we got to the edge of Iowa City. About what, I'm not sure. The familiar but long-forgotten buildings made me feel exposed. Unlike everywhere else we went, they somehow knew that we were nothing special, just a couple of guys who played songs in a student bar. I grew more nervous as we drove down Gilbert Street and closer to Miss Kitty's.

But when we got there, Miss Kitty's house was gone. There was just an empty lot and dirt ringing the open foundation – the basement we'd practiced in, now surrounded by orange plastic fencing. A cardboard sign that said FOR SALE in large, red letters stood at the edge of the property. We walked over to the orange fencing. Little brown clumps of dirt clung to the overgrown but now dead and brown grass. The fence was too flimsy to support any weight, but I held onto it anyway and peered down into the empty hole that used to be the basement. The walls were streaked from the rain and small piles of windblown dirt stacked up against the far wall – all that was left of the boxes and broken chairs that had filled the room. We knocked on the neighbor's door – the one whose house we'd also painted – and asked what happened.

'Oh, boys,' he said, hitching his jeans up to his belly, 'Nobody told you? I suppose nobody thought of it, or knew where you were. Well, Miss Kitty died, you see, about June, watching baseball on the television one Saturday. That traveling salesman was sitting right next to her and said she just kind of sputtered and quit breathing. She was dead when the ambulance came. So the nephew inherited the house, and everything kept on going just like before only without the old lady. Then in September, it was, I come home from the grocery store one day and there's two cop cars outside the place. You know how that nephew was always leaving the house every morning, but never worked or nothing? Apparently he was dealing drugs and the cops nailed him for it. House was sold at auction and whoever bought it just knocked it down – you boys know the state that place was in – and put it on the market. Hey, you boys here overnight? You need a place to stay?'

Hearing that Miss Kitty died made us sadder than we could have expected. Mr. Simmons, the neighbor, showed us the spare room, which had a double bed, and got out a folding cot. Then he gave us a spare key and told us not to worry about how late we got in. It felt like staying at your favorite uncle's house. After drinking a cup of coffee with

Mr. Simmons and swapping a couple of Miss Kitty stories, we went off to Fuzzy's to say hello to Mike. It felt good to be going someplace so familiar. Iowa City was our first home, where we'd practiced all day every day, where we'd gone from a couple of guys who played at an open-mic night in Peoria to the regular band at a bar. Like New York City, it represented a big step in our progress; unlike New York City, it felt worn in and comfortable; everything wasn't constantly racing forward to something else. In Iowa City we could breathe, relax, without expecting something else to happen.

Fuzzy's looked exactly the same, which shouldn't have been a surprise. I don't know why we'd expected it to look any different, we'd only been away for eight months, but a lot had changed for us in that time, and I guess we expected that everything else would be different, too. We stood in the doorway for a moment, blinking as our eyes adjusted to the light, then went to the bar where Mike had his back to us, loading bottles of beer into the refrigerator.

'Could we get some service anytime soon?' Owen said.

Mike turned around, and as he recognized us the glare in his eyes shifted to disbelief, then happiness. 'What are you guys doing here?' he said, grinning and shaking our hands. Owen introduced Anna and he shook her hand, too, and put three bottles of beer on the bar. Mike wouldn't take our money. 'Aren't you guys rockstars now? What are you doing in Iowa City? You're not playing here tonight, are you? I haven't seen any posters around.'

'No, we're just passing through,' I said, 'On our way West. We're doing a tour to promote our record.'

'Yeah, I saw the review in *Rolling Stone*. Haven't had a chance to buy it yet, though.'

'Here,' Owen said, pulling a CD out of his jacket pocket, 'I brought you one.'

Mike took it and asked if we'd mind if he put it on. It was strange, as always, to hear our sound. 'What are you guys doing tonight?'

We both shrugged.

'I couldn't con you into playing here, could I? I've got nothing going on, and I could probably get the word spread fast enough to pull in a decent crowd. I'll give you everything we pull in from the door.'

Owen, Anna and I exchanged glances. 'Yeah, we'll play. But no money,' Owen said. 'We don't want it. Playing here is like playing in our own living room.'

We went back and got the truck, and by the time we returned Mike had made some telephone calls and had a huge, hand-painted sign in the window that said in massive black letters: TONIGHT ONLY. IOWA CITY'S OWN, OWEN NOONE & THE MARAUDER. 9 PM. NO COVER.

By nine o'clock the bar was over capacity. We started playing at quarter past with "John Henry," and played every single song we knew for two hours without stopping, finishing, of course, with "Yankee Doodle." It didn't occur to me until after we'd finished how exhausted I was, and then I thought of how nervous I'd been the first time we'd played on that stage. This time it was just fun, and I don't think we'd ever played so well as we did that night. It was like a baseball team playing on its home field in the playoffs, when the familiar surroundings and support of the crowd pull out the best performance. After we played a lot of people came up to us and told us how much they liked it, and how much they liked us, and it was weird, because it was the first time in my life that girls wanted to talk to me, and looked at me as though I were interesting. I guess that's what it means to be a rockstar, I remember thinking, and I remember also realizing that even with the easy opportunities stardom could offer – sex, really – I was still too shy to do anything other than mumble nervously and look at the floor.

Next morning, after Mr. Simmons had insisted on cooking us a huge breakfast of pancakes, sausage, bacon and toast, we started for Seattle. Aside from being tired, I felt heavy leaving the comfort and familiarity of Iowa City. But we had to move on and so, after four days of driving across the boring, windy plains of South Dakota, Wyoming and Montana, and then climbing over the Rockies and Cascades, we got to Seattle. After playing a lackluster – we were exhausted from all the driving, sleeping in hotels and eating junk – but well-received show, we drove down to Portland where we went through the motions again before crossing the border back into California and down to San Francisco. We had a day to recover before playing our last gig until Los Angeles, where we could sleep in our own beds in our own house and not have anywhere to drive.

We'd driven around the day before to find the place we were playing in, so we'd know where it was, and not get lost when the time came. Christmas decorations had been up everywhere since Thanksgiving, so we didn't even notice them anymore and it didn't occur to us until we got to the hotel, and the girl at the reception desk wished us a Merry Christmas, what day it was. Nothing was open in the area, so we got out the Yellow Pages and phoned a Chinese place that delivered, and had Christmas dinner of egg rolls, chow mein and fortune cookies. We all got the same fortune: 'Pets are for life, not just Christmas,' it said, listing the phone number and address of the local humane society.

As we drove to the club on the night of the gig – December 26 – Anna said, 'It'd be cool if you guys could play the Filmore.'

'Home of fucking hippie music,' I said, my college rock DJ personality rising up unchecked. 'No thanks.'

'Fucking right,' Owen said. 'I wouldn't play there even if it were possible.'

'Jerks.' Anna slumped deeper into the seat, the safety belt scraping along her chin. 'Snobs.'

Neither of us had time to retort, however, because we had arrived at the club, and the scene outside was beyond anything we'd seen before. A line of people wrapped around the building and a little way down the block, and there were reporters holding microphones in front of TV cameras standing right outside the door. Photographers as well. It looked like one of those scenes you see on courtroom dramas after the verdict, when the defendant is trying to get through a scrum of journalists on the courthouse steps. We drove around to the back entrance and began unloading our gear.

'What's going on outside?' I asked the manager.

'You oughta know.' He nodded at Owen. 'He's the one who gave the interview.'

Owen looked for a second like he was going to drop the amp he was carrying. Still holding it, he stopped walking and said, 'The *Examiner*? Shit. He said he was going to tell us before he ran it.'

'Well, he ran it,' the manager said, 'Whether he told you or not. Front page on Christmas Eve.'

After the opening band had finished and their equipment was being carried off, we got ready to go on. Owen turned to me and said, 'Do you think I should say something about it? About the article – about my father?'

'We don't even know what it says. It doesn't have anything to do with the music, anyway. That's not why people are here. Don't say anything you wouldn't otherwise. That's what I think.'

Owen didn't say anything about his father, and we didn't play "Ding-Dong the Witch Is Dead." At one point someone in the audience yelled, 'Fuck Jack Noone,' but Owen ignored it and immediately started playing the next song. We took our time packing up the truck when the gig was over, and when we left the club the street was empty. The television crews had gone home with nothing to report, or at least with nothing new to report about us, about Owen. Wanting to get home as fast as we could, we left early the next morning for Los Angeles. We were worn out, we'd lost track of time and at least in Los Angeles we could just play, and have fun. We'd forgotten, somewhere on the highway between New York City and San Francisco, that we were supposed to be having fun, remembering only for a couple hours in Iowa City.

12/20/97

Owen,

I tried phoning several times to inform you that we're going to run the story. I convinced my editors to hold it a couple extra

days so I could give you notice, but they want it to appear
before the holiday, so unfortunately, unless you get this before
then, it'll be in print before you know. My apologies. I'll keep
phoning until I get in touch. A copy of the article is attached.
I hope you approve.

Yours,
Paul Danielson

NOONE DISHONESTY
ON FAMILY VALUES

by *Examiner* investigative reporter Paul Danielson

The *Examiner* can exclusively reveal that, despite his high rhetoric about family values, Congressman and would-be Senator Jack Noone has been less than open and honest about his own personal approach to the issue. Owen Noone of Los Angeles has stepped forward claiming to be the Congressman's son from a first marriage, a claim corroborated by a birth certificate from the files of a hospital in Charlotte, North Carolina. According to Owen Noone, the Congressman, then a successful North Carolina lawyer, and his mother divorced two years after his birth, and the two Mr. Noones have never met since, despite the efforts of the son. According to Mr. Noone, his attempts to contact his father have been either ignored or met with derision and denial of parentage.

"I want people to be aware," says Mr. Noone, a musician, "that when this man preaches about family values, he should acknowledge his role in the corruption of youth, if that's what he wants to call it." According to Mr. Noone, at the age of sixteen he traveled to Washington to see his father, who was by that time in his current position representing the 9th District of California. He was turned away and at no time in the years that followed has the Congressman made any effort to contact his son, although a letter sent to the Congressman, seen by the *Examiner,* prompted a written denial.

In this letter, Congressman Noone claims to have "no recollection" of being the father of Owen Noone, and further claims, "nor do I believe that I know who you are." Efforts made by the *Examiner* to contact Congressman Noone received no reply, save for the standard "no comment."

"He cannot continue to blame movies and television and rock music for the degradation of American children," says Mr. Noone. "He's got to realize that he can't just go around blaming others for problems that he creates personally, not through legislation, but through his own behavior and lack of responsibility. People like this don't deserve to be making laws for our country if they don't admit their own contributions to the degradation of others' lives." [. . .]

The article covered most of the front page and there was a big picture of Jack Noone. It didn't really say much because all that Paul Danielson had to go on was the interview with Owen and the birth certificate. There weren't any other relatives and Jack Noone's office wasn't saying anything. Now that the truth was out in the public domain, Jack Noone would have to respond. There would be no way around it.

The *Los Angeles Times* phoned the morning after we got home, asking for an interview. 'Sorry,' Owen said. 'I've done my one interview about it. You had your chance.'

Ten minutes later, the phone rang again. I answered. It was the *Los Angeles Times* rock critic, asking for an interview with Owen. 'You're joking,' I said, and covered the phone. 'Owen, the *LA Times* wants to do a rock 'n' roll interview.'

'Right,' he said. 'Why don't you do it, then?'

I uncovered the phone. 'Owen's not here, but I can do the interview.'

There was a long pause. 'Yes, okay,' the guy said. He asked me who our biggest influences were, how we liked working with Steve Wood and what were our long-term plans for the band. Finally, at the end, he said, 'I don't, uh, suppose you could, um, comment on the, uh, Congressman, could you?'

'What Congressman?'

'Uh, you know, Congressman Noone.'

'Oh, him. Yeah, sure. He's Owen's father, you know.'

'Yes.' A long silence followed. 'So, could you, uh, comment?'

'I thought I just did,' I said and hung up. I felt bad for the guy; he'd obviously been put up to it, but there was no way, if Owen wasn't going to say anything more about it, that I was. Needless to say, the interview never made it into the paper.

New Year's Eve finally came. The telephone wouldn't stop ringing. Every newspaper in California wanted to follow up on the *Examiner* story, and so did every television and radio station. Owen refused to answer the phone after the third call, and Anna and I started pretending they'd reached the wrong number. We didn't even look at our guitars until the day before the gig, when we sat down to strum through the songs we were going to play and remind our fingers where to go. As we were loading the truck to leave, the phone rang. It was Anna's turn to answer, and she came out to the door, calling for Owen.

'Tell them I'm not here.' He pushed an amplifier to the back of the cargo bed.

'It's your father's office.'

Owen walked up the lawn to the house, and I followed. He picked up the phone and said hello. 'I'm sorry,' he said after a pause, 'Can't the Congressman himself phone?' There was another pause. 'Too busy? It seems that this should command his personal attention. I'm sure he's busy trying to squeeze his hypocritical ass into a tuxedo right now, but frankly, I don't have my minions phone him, and I don't think it's very respectful for him to pawn this duty off on someone else. Tell him if he has anything to say, he can phone himself, and not on New Year's Eve. I've got better things to do tonight.' He dropped the phone back into its cradle and picked up the other amp, which was sitting next to the sofa, and carried it out to the truck without saying another word.

There were supposed to be three bands, Neptune, us, and another Pulley band called Customer. But Customer had to cancel because two of their members had the flu. We were suddenly the main act and had to play a longer set to keep the gig going until midnight, when there would be a short break for the countdown, and then play another half hour after that. We added several more songs to the list – almost everything we knew. The show got underway around eight-thirty with Neptune, the band for which we'd opened a few months earlier. We watched from backstage for a while, then went to the back of the audience to get in front of the speakers and hear better.

'What's up, guys?' I turned towards the voice and immediately recognized Stuart Means, the Pacific A&R guy. 'Congratulations on the album. It's really great, I really like it.' He grinned, shifting his eyes from Owen to me and back without bothering to look at Anna. 'Oh, Owen, I don't think we've actually met. I'm Stuart Means. I do A&R for Pacific. I met your partner here a few months ago.' He stuck out his hand, but Owen just kept looking at him without moving. 'We're still very interested in you guys and would love to bring you onto our team.'

'What do you mean, "team?"' Owen asked. He had to

shout to be heard. 'Isn't it more of a company?'

'Well, we like to think of it more as a team, you know? Everybody working together towards a goal.'

'What's the goal?'

'Good music. Quality music for our consu – for rock fans.'

'How much will you pay us?' Owen asked, and Anna and I both turned our heads towards him. I could see my grimace reflected in Anna's scowl. He'd said before this wasn't his or my band, it was our band and we'd do these things together.

Stuart pushed his hand through his hair. 'Well, I'm sure we can work out something amenable, if you're interested. More than your current employer is giving you, and more investment and loyalty, too.'

'What the hell do you mean, loyalty?' I blurted out. 'You're not in any position to be questioning our label's commitment, you dick.'

'Hey, whoah.' Stuart waved his hands defensively. 'I'm not doing anything like that, man. I'm just saying, you know? Remember the last time we met? It was here, and you were opening for this band, the same one that's opening for you guys now. What makes you think that in a few months time, when sales have pretty much dried up – which they will, because indie albums never sell more than five or very low six figures anyway – what makes you think you won't go from flavor of the month to warm-up act for the next big thing? That won't happen at Pacific. We've got more to invest to keep your sales and popularity going, and once you're headlining, you'll stay that way.' Stuart clapped a hand on each of our shoulders. I felt my muscles tighten. 'Listen, I know you guys want to get ready for the gig –

I'm looking forward to it myself – so I'll leave you alone. But I really do want to get you on board and give you the support you deserve. Think about it, guys. I know what I'd do in your situation.' He wished us good luck and walked away. I noticed the back of his T-shirt as he turned. It was blue with the orange chorus of "Yankee Doodle" on the back. He was wearing our shirt.

'Why are you asking him about money?' I demanded as we walked back through the crowd to the backstage area.

'I was just curious, you know? Just to see what he'd say. I wasn't going to sign up or anything. Calm down about it.'

I inhaled deeply and looked out at Neptune. Their arms were a blur as they pumped back and forth over the guitar strings. 'Okay,' I said. 'I just wanted to know.' Neptune's last chord rang out and in a few minutes it would be our turn.

Los Angeles Times, January 2, 1998:

OWEN NOONE AND THE MARAUDER
Roxy, December 31, 1997

This Midwestern duo has become pretty well known to Southern California since they relocated to Los Angeles at the end of the summer, and with the added publicity of the Congressman Noone allegations, what few tickets remained for this New Year's Eve show were quickly snapped up. Half-hearted fans were curious to see what if anything might be added to the scandal over the course of a rock show, which in the end turned out to be nothing except for good music.

Owen Noone and the Marauder seem intent on starting every concert with the same song, "John Henry." A good decision since it sends a high octane blast into the air that some of their other songs, missing the grounding that percussion would provide, can't deliver. There is no question of delivery in this nearly two-hour-long set, however; even the normally reserved Marauder flails at his guitar like a man under demonic possession, and for the first time the visual experience of seeing the band live matches the off-beat punk ethic of their music. Even more sedate songs like "The Big Rock Candy Mountains" and the lullaby, "Hush Little Baby," take on a breath of fresh air, and on several songs the Marauder leans close enough to Owen Noone's microphone for his backing vocals – hitherto a nonexistent element of the band's performance – to be heard.

The set threatened to self-destruct when, after taking a timeout to ring in the New Year, they restarted with "Ground-hog." An ominous crackle and buzz could be heard from Noone's guitar, and he had to stop the song halfway through to fix a problem with his amp, accompanied by the Marauder's improvised lounge-music chords. The electricity harnessed, they launched back in from the top and powered through the rest of their set with fresh energy as if claiming rock 'n' roll ownership of the New Year, leading the audience through a rendition of "Yankee Doodle" that had everyone feeling like they, too, could be "macaroni".

So we started a new year with electricity pulsing through our fingers and out of our guitars. I must have run, walked and jumped about a mile during that show, roaming the stage like a confused Frankenstein, slamming my guitar strings harder than I ever had. I was irritated about Stuart Means, I was sick of being in a truck and driving thousands of miles and I was sick of anything that wasn't music. I poured all the energy I had into that show. Usually I stood pretty still when I played, just watching my hands make the chords, looking out into the audience, at Owen, at my feet, but now I felt unlocked, like it didn't matter what I did as long as the chords came out right and people liked it. I didn't have to pretend to be myself because I wasn't myself and nobody knew who I was. I was just the Marauder, a ridiculous name. I could do anything, be anyone and get away with it.

Our first royalty checks came from Pulley in mid-January, and even though it was just a couple hundred bucks each, I felt like I'd earned something. It was a validation of what we were doing, of our lives. Any guilt I might have felt about ditching the job in Peoria and living off of someone else's money for almost two years disappeared as I held the check in my hand and looked at the amount, and my name, printed on the piece of paper.

On the same day, Jack Noone phoned. Jack Noone himself. I answered and told Owen, asking him if he wanted me to leave for a while. He said no, he wanted me to be there. I sat on the sofa watching Owen talk. Anna had gone out jogging.

'Hello, this is Owen,' he said, pretending not to know who it was. 'Wait a second – have you got me on speaker phone?' There was a brief pause. 'Well take the fucking thing off. I'm not talking to everybody in your goddamn office.' Another pause. 'I won't calm down. Who the fuck are you to tell me to anyway? This doesn't have anything to do with those people. Turn it off.' A longer pause followed, and I could see the muscles in Owen's jaw tightening and pushing against his skin. 'Okay, then hold on.' He took the phone away from his ear and covered the mouthpiece with his hand. 'Go get a tape recorder,' he said to me. I went upstairs and got the four-track – it was the first tape recorder I thought of, although we had two smaller ones –

and dragged it and a microphone downstairs, plugged them in, and handed the microphone to Owen. 'Hold on,' he said, 'I'm just going to put you on speaker phone.' I'd never even realized we had a speaker phone. Owen pressed the button and put down the receiver, then nodded at me. I pressed record and he put the microphone next to the telephone. 'Now,' he said to Jack Noone, 'What was it you wanted to discuss?'

'Owen, take off the speaker phone.'

'No. I insist on a level playing field. Who else are we talking to?'

'Nobody.'

'Bullshit. I can hear them breathing.'

There was a silence. I watched the tape heads rotating inside the machine. 'Two of my personal assistants are here, Owen, but that's nothing unusual. Who do you have there?'

'Just the Marauder, sir. My wife is out at the minute, unfortunately.'

'Wife?'

'There's a lot of things you never bothered to learn about me. What do you want to talk about?'

'Well, Owen, you might have seen the article in the *San Francisco Examiner* —'

'I may have even been quoted in it.'

'Yes, well, that's what concerns us — concerns me. I think you've got a false impression of me, of where I stand on some of the campaign issues, and I think we can clear some things up, and hopefully allow the electoral process to continue as it should.'

'Do you ever talk like a human being? Do you ever listen to yourself? You sound like a fucking robot.'

'Um, Owen, I don't think —'

'Just tell me what you want.'

'Owen, I don't want people – I don't want you – to have the wrong impression of me. I'm not the demon you make me out to be. I have a family, you know, and they're very hurt by these things.'

'That's not my fault, is it? You're the one in the driver's seat here, pal. You're the one who's been ignoring me for twenty years, not the other way around. Don't tell me about hurt families. I never asked for very much, did I? Recognition from my father, that's all I asked. You won't even give it now, will you? You won't do the honest thing.'

'I don't think it's a question of honesty, Owen, I –'

'Like hell it isn't! That's all it's about – your dishonesty. Do you really think I care about whether you send me a birthday present every year or any of that shit? I just don't think someone as morally bankrupt as yourself deserves to be preaching to a bunch of people about how they should live their lives and what kids should watch on TV or listen to on their stereos, when the real problem is assholes like you who think their kids can be bought off –'

'Owen, it isn't like that. It was a long time ago, and while I may have, in retrospect, made some mistakes, I don't think that gives you the right to publicly slander and demonize me.'

'There's no slander about it, though, is there? I haven't seen any lawsuits. You must be the most dim-headed person ever. Do you even realize how offensive you are? How disrespectful? You may think that I'm the one being obnoxious but that's because you have no idea what it's like to see your father turn up in the newspapers preaching against the very things that, in your experience, he embodies. Don't tell me about mistakes, Congressman, because if you really regretted it then you'd have done something by now. And I don't mean giving me some shitty guitar on my sixteenth birthday. You can't buy off a kid's love, Congressman, any more than you can turn him into a delinquent by letting him listen to rock 'n' roll.'

Owen stopped talking. He was breathing hard. There was the sound of a pen being tapped against a desk. Then Jack Noone sighed.

'Owen, I'm sorry. I truly am. You obviously don't believe me. I have good intentions, Owen, and I know what this country needs a lot more than you do. I'm asking you to stay out of this election for the benefit of the nation. It's not right for you to get some smug satisfaction out of attacking my character for your own pride, or career, or for whatever reasons you have. There are things bigger than you, Owen, and I'd ask you to respect and consider that, and decide what is worth destroying and what isn't. I hope we can talk this through a little more rationally sometime.' There was a click, followed by the dial tone.

'I fucking hate that guy!' Owen yelled, his voice dissipating into the walls. He picked up the phone and slammed it back down on the table. The microphone rolled off and hit the floor, and I saw the needles jump across the dial on the machine.

Anna came in out of breath, headphones in her ears. She looked back and forth across the room, at Owen standing, his jaw looking like it would explode through his skin, his eyes big and dilated. 'What's going on in here?' she said loudly, before turning off her music.

Owen clenched his hands into fists. 'Can we go for a walk?' he said to Anna, very quietly. 'I need to go for a walk.'

Anna looked at me. 'Let's go,' she said, holding her arm towards Owen. He walked across the room and they left. I watched them walk across the lawn, Anna's hand slowly rubbing Owen's back. There was a loud click as the tape ran out.

I sat on the floor next to the four-track for a long time, not thinking, not feeling, just staring out the door, my entire mind blank. Which is a lie because I started thinking about my father, to whom I hadn't spoken since the day after graduation when I'd called from the phone booth in Iowa City. It seemed like a long time ago. It was a long time ago. It occurred to me that my parents didn't know where I was, what I was doing or who I was anymore. I wanted to phone them, but I didn't know what I could say. So I just stayed there on the floor rubbing my hand back and forth across a patch of the carpet, tracing patterns in the shag.

I sat there for at least an hour until Anna and Owen came back. Owen walked through the open door and said, 'Good, it's still out. Let's record some songs.' Anna came in behind him carrying a grocery bag. Owen pointed at it. 'We have beer.'

There was nothing else I wanted more than to record. We dragged the amps and guitars and microphones down to the living room and while Owen plugged everything in, I rummaged around my room for the Alan Lomax book. 'Only new songs,' Owen said, 'Nothing we've played before.' I found it under a pile of magazines and old newspapers. The library return slip was still pasted to the inside. FEB 23 1995, it said. I grabbed a tape, too, and went back downstairs.

Owen opened the book and started flipping through it and I picked up my guitar and strummed a couple chords, just to hear the sound. We hadn't played anything since New Year's Eve, and it felt good to hear the hum of the amps and the crisp sound of an electric guitar. I began strumming "Yankee Doodle," but Owen told me to stop.

'Nothing old,' he said.

'But we haven't actually started yet.'

'Nothing old. Here –' he tossed the book to me – 'Pick a couple of songs. I've got "The Dying British Sergeant" and "Will You Wear Red?" You've got to pick by title alone.'

I chose "Weary of the Railway" and "Wanderin'" and then we both agreed on "The Titanic," "Rye Whiskey" and "Fare Thee Well, O Honey." Anna tossed us each a can of beer and flopped into the easy chair. We set the book on the sofa so we could both see it and opened to the first song, "The Dying British Sergeant."

We played a couple of verses to figure out how it went and then, after taking a few sips of beer, pressed down the record button. We both played really hard, as if we were out to break every string, but Owen didn't use the fuzz pedal until the fourth verse. I wasn't paying attention. I had my eyes closed just listening to the sound when he stepped on it and the burst of noise shot my eyelids open. 'But to our sad and sore surprise,' Owen growled, his voice growing in volume and getting hoarse, 'We saw men like grasshoppers rise, / "Freedom or death" was all their cry, / Indeed, they were not feared to die.' As soon as the verse ended he stepped on the pedal again, and the room seemed quiet even though we were both still playing. Owen stopped strumming on the last words of the first line, and I continued until halfway through the third, when I stopped, letting the chord ring and fade until Owen stepped on his pedal and

183

played alone and loud, shouting over the thick distortion. 'Whilst I lie dead in Amerikee.' His guitar was out of tune and the textured notes clashed against each other, the vibrations skidding through the room until they dissipated. Everything was silence.

'I think that was pretty good,' Owen said, pressing stop on the four-track. 'I like that one.'

After a couple hours we'd recorded six songs and drunk all the beer. Sometime during the past year we'd acquired a tambourine, and Anna picked it up and played along, the results barely audible on the tape. We'd picked seven songs and intended to record all of them. The last one was 'Wanderin'.' We were tired and half drunk, but we wanted to finish.

Owen turned to me. 'You sing this one.'

'No.'

'Why not? You never sing for real, but I always hear you when we're playing. Make this one yours.'

'No, I can't sing.'

'Neither can I.'

I sighed. I didn't want to sing for people. But it was just for an audience of two, so it didn't matter. 'Okay.'

Owen pressed record and I started to play and sing the slow, sad song. Owen didn't play until the chorus, where it picks up, and as I sang, 'And it looks like I ain't never gonna cease my wanderin',' Owen played a single, quiet, distorted note, striking the string on every syllable until the last, when he came down across all the strings for the C-chord that finishes the phrase. It sounded ghostlike, and everything faded together until once again the room was quiet, and we were finished.

We made a couple copies of the tape and sent one to

Dave Ferris the next morning to encourage him to book us studio time. After getting ground down by the touring and the Jack Noone stuff, we were starting to feel on a roll again, and we wanted to keep it going. It kept us level, unlike the touring, which after the first few days just got boring and aggravating, even though we were supposedly doing what we wanted. Otherwise, we could go back to our previous lives, Owen playing minor league baseball and me writing internal newsletters for a tractor company. Of course, I never actually had that previous life. It was something I'd renounced before I'd even gotten it, and I didn't want to have to find out what it was I'd given up.

We got a postcard from Ed with his address on it. We'd forgotten about Ed.

> *Guys,*
> *I hope you were serious about writing. It was fun meeting you*
> *and I really would like to make a video for you, if you meant*
> *it. –Ed*

'Do you think we could get Dave to finance a video?' Owen was looking at the postcard, a night-time picture of the New York City skyline.

'I doubt it. I don't think they really have the money for that. Or the distribution, or whatever it takes to get it on MTV.'

'But it wouldn't cost much, would it? I mean, depending on what we did, but we wouldn't have to pay Ed that much.'

'Except to fly him out here and then feed him and all that, plus all the video and stuff – do you think he even knows how to make a music video? Do we even have an idea for a music video? Do we even want to make one?'

'Yeah, why not?'

'Have you ever seen a good one?'

'Good point.' Owen looked up from the postcard and I could tell from his face that he had a bad idea. 'But we could make it political – against my father. This could be our best weapon.'

'Owen, no. I don't want to start mixing these two things any more than we have.'

'What are you talking about? It's no different than what we did in Washington or what we should've done in San Francisco. We should be using our position more.'

'Don't you remember what you said to Paul Danielson? That our band has nothing to do with it?'

'But it does – not that way, though. We've got a platform is the point. Kids listen to everything we say. Or they will listen to anything we say. We're not getting popular because of Jack Noone, but we should be using our popularity to do the right thing.'

We were in the kitchen, and Anna was standing in the doorway. 'Are you sure you're doing the right thing?' she said.

Owen turned. 'Are you against me, too?'

'Haven't we been through this before?' she said.

Owen raised his hand to his cheek then pumped it slowly in front of his chest, twice, like he was trying to snap his fingers in slow-motion. 'Yeah. I guess we have. Okay. But I still think we should do something. I want you guys to understand. We have to be political. We should be.'

'Why?' I said.

'I think – we just should. That's what rock is for, that's what these songs we play are for, aren't they? Not all of them, but look – "Yankee Doodle" and "Dying British

Sergeant" and other ones, too. They're political songs, revolutionary songs. It's in the spirit of what we're doing.' He sat down. 'It's not just because he's my father. That's part of it, a big part of it, but it's the whole way these things are done in this country. We just know about this one case because he happens to be my asshole father. But they're all assholes. We can make an example of him and change things.'

I started walking along the edge of the kitchen, tracing my hand along the countertops. 'What's to change, Owen? Look at us. We have it good. This isn't the sixties, when there was something to protest. We've got money and not much to complain about. I don't want us to turn it into a circus.'

'Don't you see,' he said, 'This is why we have to do this, why we have to demand changes. We've got it so good, we've got to complain about shit like Jack Noone. Now or never. You can't change things like that when there's war. So when it's going good, the little hypocrisies should be changed. We can't just sit still.'

'Owen, I guess I just don't know what you want to do. And I don't want to get involved in things that are going to pull us away from being a band, from making music. That's what we started this for, isn't it? I'm living this fantasy, and I don't want to lose it.'

'That's just it,' he said. 'What good is the fantasy if you don't use it for something? If it's just this one-dimensional dream, and one day you wake up? Because we won't last forever. Remember when we were at Graceland? We're not like that. We'll get old and fat and nobody will care about us anymore. Nobody's going to come crying to this house to see where it all happened. Nobody will give a shit. We

187

might as well take advantage of everything we have now before it falls apart and we're working in McDonald's and talking about how great we were. Look, I've been thinking about this for a long time. We've got one chance to make things better. At the end of my life I don't want to sit around realizing that everything I did was – at best – negligible.'

I didn't want to be negligible either. I guess I'd never thought about much except myself and how much everybody else owed me, from the people I went to college with – the ones I envied and hated at the same time – to my parents, who when I spoke to them from the phone booth, were only being selfish from my point of view, telling me to take a job I didn't want because they wanted to have a son to be proud of. It never occurred to me that they wanted happiness, comfort, safety and success for me. They just defined it in their own terms. I'd been bad at everything I did, a bad poet, a bad son, a bad, self-centered person. I'd never looked beyond the moment I was living in, never seen anything behind or ahead of me. As I stood in the kitchen replaying Owen's words in my head I thought maybe now was the time to start doing something that mattered, something I believed in. Of course, I didn't know what I believed in. But I started to think I did. At least I wanted to.

Dave Ferris phoned when he got our tape. He liked it. A lot.

'Can we get in the studio again soon then?' I asked him.

I could hear the soft sound of his breathing, then a sigh. 'Well, I don't know. It's – it may not be my decision.'

'What do you mean?'

'I've been given an offer to license your albums to a major label. To Pacific.'

'Pacific?' I practically yelled into the phone. 'Pacific,'

188

I said more quietly. 'Don't we have any say in this? We don't want to be on Pacific.'

'Yeah, of course you do, of course. You can say no. But look: this isn't a big company, Pulley, and the royalty rate they've offered me is more than decent. I need it.'

'But Dave – what about us?'

'Don't worry. You'll be better off if that's what you're worried about.'

Was it? I wasn't sure what I was worried about. I'd gotten comfortable with Pulley and having control of just about everything we did. I knew that wouldn't happen with Pacific. Pacific had more resources, bigger marketing budgets, more to spend on us, and that could help. But it wasn't what I had in mind when I thought back to our first night at CBGB's, when I'd signed that piece of paper back-stage while Owen searched for Anna, Kid Tiger self-destructed and our rock 'n' roll career began.

'They've heard the new tape,' Dave said, 'And they love it. I'm sure they'll get you in the studio as fast as you want to.'

'Yeah,' I said, not really listening to what he was saying but just hearing the vague shapes of the sounds.

'Anyway, this isn't just good for me. It's good for you guys. I can send you the contracts and you can look them over. But I've got to tell you, it's the best thing. For me and for you.'

I told him to send the paperwork. Then I told Owen, unsure about how he'd react.

'Pacific? But this is great! Now we can do it, now we'll have the money.'

'To do what?'

'The video. Everything. Anything. I mean, I like Dave

Ferris, but they don't exactly have the resources that Pacific has. This is it for us. We'll really mean something once we get this new album made – and sell a million copies of it. This is the best thing that's happened to us. What's that look for?'

My mouth was wide open. I wasn't sure how Owen would take the news, but I didn't think he'd be so excited. Usually when decisions were made without him, he got angry. He always wanted control. And even though Dave said we had a choice, really we didn't. But then, maybe this choice, in Owen's mind was so good that it didn't matter whether he'd made it or not.

A couple of days after we'd signed the agreement we got a phone call from our new friend Stuart Means. 'I just wanted to welcome you to the team,' he said. We had him on speaker phone. 'We've all heard the demo and really like it.'

'Who's we?' Owen asked.

'The team,' said Stuart Means. 'Everybody here. Even the president of the company. Anyway, my job is to see that you guys are happy and that you have everything you need.'

'When can we get in the studio?'

'Soon. Soon. We just need to find a place and a producer. Meanwhile –'

'What about Steve?' I asked. It was the first I'd spoken.

'Oh, hi, you're there too. Steve who?'

'Steve Wood. He did our last album.'

'Oh, him. Yes, well, I think we can get someone better. A bigger name.'

'Better? But he –'

'The truth is, guys, we don't really use him. He did some work for us in the past, and it didn't go well. We've

190

got a lot of other people in mind who will do a better job, don't worry. I'll let you know as soon as we get it worked out. Meanwhile –'

'What do you mean, didn't go well?' I didn't like the sound of what Stuart Means was saying. It seemed like he was keeping something from us. Besides, I liked Steve Wood and I doubted there was anybody who was better.

'Nothing, really, nothing to worry about,' said Stuart Means. 'Meanwhile, we'd like you to do a show, just a one-time thing, to promote the label change.'

'Where do you want to do it?'

'Here in L.A.'

The gig was on the last day of February at the same place we'd played on New Year's Eve. It'd been two months since we'd been in front of people, and we had seven new songs in our repertoire and a new record label. Everything felt new, fresh, like we were just starting out. Pacific had given away a bunch of tickets and there had been a couple of radio station contests. The rest had quickly sold out. There had been a small paragraph about our label change in *Rolling Stone* that generated more publicity, positive and negative. We'd even received letters from fans accusing us of selling out. Meanwhile, Pacific was doing a marketing offensive with posters advertising us and the phrase, "New Album Out Soon" in record stores. But Stuart Means hadn't gotten us a producer yet and no studio time, either. We were getting antsy. We wanted to do something more than sit around the house answering the telephone. Also, he'd told us not to do any interviews until the album was finished. We didn't understand why, but apparently some clause in our contract prohibited it even if the interview had nothing to do with the band, which meant no talking about Jack Noone either.

We'd asked to have Neptune as the opening act, but Pacific had insisted on having one of their lesser-known bands, Krux, do it. They had three guitarists, a bassist and a drummer. Two of the guitarists did vocals and the whole set was full of noise. Two guitars churned tightly distorted power chords along with the overloud bassist and the third guitar played frenetic lead parts that sounded straight from Iron Maiden albums while the drummer tried to keep up. Owen and I stood backstage watching and wondering who thought this would go together. The audience didn't seem impressed, either, and politely clapped after each song. They weren't there to see Krux. They were there to see us.

They finished and it was finally our turn. Roadies pulled their gear off the stage and set up our amps and guitars, and even tuned them. We felt uncomfortable with this, not seeing why we couldn't tune our guitars ourselves. Stuart Means told us to just go with it. Why bother tuning them ourselves when we could afford to have somebody else do it? We weren't sure who was paying, but we didn't seem to have much choice. The guys finished setting up and put our guitars on stands in front of the amps. The crowd started cheering, whistles rising up from the applause and shouts.

'Let's go,' I said to Owen.

'No, wait a little,' Stuart Means said. 'Let them get more worked up. It's part of the showmanship.'

'Let's go,' Owen said, and we walked out onstage to the rising cheers of our fans. We picked up our guitars and heard the crackle and hum as we switched on our amps. I tested out the sound, strumming a couple of quick chords, and Owen did the same, stepping on his pedal a few times. This business made people cheer louder. Owen looked at me and I nodded. He stepped up to the microphone. 'I'm Owen Noone and that's the Marauder,' he said, pointing to me. 'We'd like to thank Krux for starting things tonight. This is a song about hard work.' Then he began belting, 'Jaaaaaaaaaaaaaawwwwwwwwwnnnnnnnnnnnn,' and on 'Henry' I let loose, banging on the C-chord, and we were rolling, the crowd clapping and singing along, everything else blocked away, only music, the disjointed chords from our guitars and the singing of both Owen and the crowd mixing into some kind of off-kilter, happy union.

At that moment music was the only thing we cared about. Owen and I kept looking at each other, smiling. Anna came out near the end to sing "Careless Love," after which we played "Will You Wear Red?," one of the new songs we'd put on the demo. People liked it even though they couldn't sing along, and the cheers increased when we finished. Then we played "Erie Canal," one of our first songs, after which it was my turn to sing on the set closer, "Wanderin'."

Owen picked up the microphone stand and moved it closer to me. I grabbed it with one shaking hand to make sure it was actually there and to steady myself. I felt like I was going to fall over. I looked out over the faces in the first couple rows where people were staring, some leaning and talking to the person next to them, waiting to hear the Marauder sing. I cleared my throat and said, 'This is another new song from the new album, if we ever record it.' Then I started strumming and singing, croakily,

> *I been wanderin' early,*
> *I been wanderin' late*
> *From New York City*

To the Golden Gate.
And it looks like
I ain't never gonna cease my wanderin'.

And Owen played as he had before, a single note through the two lines of the chorus, ending with the final C-chord, the vibrations of his distorted notes seeming to shatter the clean notes of my own guitar. The audience, I could see, was completely still, all of them silent and listening to my quiet voice, my quiet guitar, and Owen's notes drifting across the space between us. When we came to the last chorus, I let the last notes ring out and then thanked the crowd. The audience clapped and cheered loudly as we took off our guitars, set them in the stands, and walked off the stage.

Stuart Means greeted us. 'Nice show guys, nice show. But do me a favor.' He put his hand on my shoulder, giving me his approximation of buddy-buddy sincerity. 'Don't play any of these new songs and don't talk about the new album until we actually have it ready. It's not good business.'

The crowd was still clapping and cheering. Owen and I exchanged glances. 'Are you in the band?' Owen asked.

'What?' said Stuart Means.

'I asked if you're in the band. Because the last time I reviewed the situation, we were Owen Noone and the Marauder. Not Owen Noone and the Marauder and Stuart Means.'

'What do you mean, Owen?' He was still doing his sincere look but had added slightly puzzled to the mix and taken his hand from my shoulder.

'We'll play the songs we want to.' He turned to me. 'Let's go.'

We went back onstage and the cheers rose. Owen nodded into the crowd and then voices came out of the sound system. After a few seconds I realized what it was. 'Well, Owen, you might have seen the article in the *San Fransisco Examiner* –' It was the tape I'd made of his phone conversation with Jack Noone. I looked over at Owen as I picked up my guitar and mouthed 'What the hell?' He just smiled – 'I don't think it's a question of honesty, Owen, I – ' and Owen stepped to the mic. As he spoke it became a surreal mix of Jack Noone, Owen Noone and Owen Noone talking.

'I got an interesting phone call the other day,' he said, 'and I thought I'd share it with you.' There was no reaction from the crowd. 'Anyway, we'd like to thank our new label, Pacific, for putting this together, and also Dave Ferris. There's a guy named Stuart Means who works for Pacific Records, and he thinks he's our boss. He told us not to play this song, so we'll dedicate it to him, and to Jack Noone. It's called "The Dying British Sergeant."' We started playing as, on the tape, Owen's voice said, 'You can't buy off a kid's love, Congressman.' We played it slowly but deliberately, hitting each new chord change hard, lending a percussive element as each new vibration slammed into the magnets of the pickups. Owen sang loudly, hoarsely, his voice cracking right down to the final line, 'Whilst I lie dead in Amerikee.' The two guitars rang, one clean, one distorted, and before they'd finished Owen had started singing "Ding-Dong the Witch is Dead." He'd looped the tape of the phone conversation so it replayed in the background as I strummed aimlessly along, not stopping at the end but picking up the pace into "Yankee Doodle." The crowd joined in, the chorus rising louder and louder until I couldn't hear the tape anymore, just voices and guitars, everybody sharing this patriotic song that no longer seemed patriotic but was simply a song that everybody knew and never thought about understanding. And called it macaroni.

Stuart Means was furious when we got backstage. 'What the hell was that all about?' he demanded. His face was crimson and I thought his eyes might fly out of his face. 'You two have some things to learn if you expect to get anywhere in this business. I will not have you trashing the company in the middle of a gig.'

'Actually, Stuart,' Owen said evenly, 'we thanked the company. It was you we trashed. Really, I can't imagine how irate you'd be if you'd realized that.'

'Very funny, Owen,' he said, his face darkening.

Anna came over and kissed Owen on the cheek. 'Great show,' she said, then saw Stuart Means's face. 'Jesus, are you choking?'

Stuart Means opened his mouth to say something, then closed it, breathing deeply through his nose. 'No. I'm fine. We were just – discussing a couple of business points.'

'Business?' Anna said, crumpling her brow at Stuart Means then turning to Owen. 'You don't know anything about business, do you?' She turned back to Stuart Means. 'They were great, though, weren't they? You've made a good investment with this product, Mr. Means.' She laughed and Owen smiled. I bit my lip to keep from laughing.

Stuart Means grunted and walked away.

'Get us in the studio, Stuart,' I called after him. 'Soon.'

We treated Stuart Means badly, but we felt justified. After all, we'd never asked for him to be hanging around all the time, and we'd been doing just fine without him. We didn't need him laying out commandments about when to go onstage, what to play, and certainly what to say and not to say. It was our forum. We had the floor. When we were performing we had two hours in which the world was ours and we were all that mattered. Anything about money, business, Jack Noone – everything – disappeared for two hours for us and for our audience, our fans, watching two people who were just like them do something special, create an atmosphere, hold them captive, put music into the air and make it the most important thing in the world. That was why they paid and why we played and why we would be there even if there was no money involved.

A couple of days later Stuart Means called. 'I think I owe you guys an apology,' he said. 'I was too pushy the other night. I hope you don't take it personally. I just want our bands to succeed, and I get overanxious. So, I'm sorry about upsetting you guys.' I think he expected us to say that's okay, but we didn't and there was a long silence. 'Oh, and another thing,' he said finally. 'Can you guys come down here to the office tomorrow afternoon? There's some people who want to talk to you about doing a commercial.'

We went to Pacific's headquarters, which was two floors in a massive office building downtown. We had to drive there and park the truck in a parking garage for three dollars an hour and walk two blocks to the building. When I was about ten my parents took me to Chicago, and I remember there was a building that curved inwards, away from the sidewalk, which made it look, if you stood at the very base, like it was leaning over you, about to fall, an effect aided by the clouds pushing through the air above it. I spent five minutes gazing at it, until my father grabbed my hand and said, Come on, and we walked down the street to the Mercantile Exchange to watch the traders with their colored jackets and silly hand signals.

The building that housed Pacific wasn't like that. There were no clouds for one, so when I looked up there was nothing moving to contrast with the stillness of the building. It was merely stationary, offering no opportunity to fool the senses, the mind, into thinking that a building could lean and fall over in the middle of the afternoon. We had to tell a security guard that we had an appointment, and he confirmed it before pointing us to the elevator. On the fifteenth floor the doors opened and we were greeted by Stuart Means.

'Welcome to HQ,' he said.

Stuart Means led us along a corridor and past cubicles where people sat in front of computers or talked on the telephone or did nothing at all. Aside from hushed murmurs it was very quiet, which seemed strange for a record company. It occurred to me that I'd expected to hear music, Pacific recording artists being pumped through the building, but there was no music, no noise except for the murmurs and the air conditioning.

Stuart Means led us to a conference room, knocked lightly on the door, and went in without waiting for a response. There were three men seated at one end of a large oval table and two pitchers of water. They all stood as we came in and Stuart introduced: the head of A&R for Pacific, an account manager from an advertising agency and a marketing executive from Arroyo Trousers. They all seemed about the same age – mid-thirties – and were all wearing gray suits. It finally struck me that Stuart Means was wearing a suit, too. It was the first time I'd seen him in anything other than rock-fan gear. Owen wore his orange Fuzzy's T-shirt and shorts; I was wearing jeans, sandals and a Bradley T-shirt. After introducing us Stuart Means sat down, and so did everyone else.

The account manager started talking. 'I assume you've seen our current campaign for Arroyo Corduroys,' he said, staring at a pile of papers on the table in front of him.

'No,' Owen said.

'No problem.' The account manager picked up a remote control and aimed it at a television on a cart at the other end of the table. 'Watch these.' A video started playing. A famous actor stood in a white room wearing brown corduroy pants and a black T-shirt and holding a tambourine. He started playing the tambourine, singing, 'Old MacDonald had a farm, ee-eye-ee-eye-oh, and on that farm he had a cow, ee-eye-ee-eye-oh,' dancing around in a circle as he sang. At the end of the verse he stopped, looked at the camera, and said, "This is simple." Then a yellow circle with the word ARROYO in the middle appeared on the screen. Another one started playing after that, with Ellen Trelaine, the actress who had been at our record release party, playing something incomprehensible on a recorder while wearing corduroys and a white blouse. After half a minute she stopped and repeated the actor's phrase, "This is simple," then disappeared into the Arroyo logo. The account manager stopped the tape.

'So you want the two of us to wear corduroy pants and Arroyo T-shirts and play some shitty song, then say, "This is simple."?' Owen asked.

The Arroyo executive scratched his temple. 'Well, I wouldn't say shitty –'

'How much are you going to pay us?'

'We have a figure in mind,' he said, 'But we can negotiate. How much do you want?'

'Why us?' Everybody turned and looked at me. 'The other two are actors – why do you want a small-time rock band?'

The Pacific guy jumped in. 'Not small-time. You guys are definitely not small-time. I think everybody here feels that you have the right image, the credibility. We think it can be a mutually beneficial relationship.'

'Yes,' said the account manager. 'We've heard your "Yankee Doodle" song. We'd like to use that one. It fits right in, it's a song everybody knows – whether or not they're familiar with your version – and you guys look good. You're young, our audience can identify with you. What do you think?'

'How much money?' Owen asked again.

The executive named an amount.

'All that is for us, right?' said Owen. He wagged his finger back and forth between Stuart Means and his boss. 'None of it goes to these two clowns.'

Stuart leaned forward. 'Owen, I'd appreciate it if –'

'Stuart, I think we've had this discussion. Have you gotten us studio time yet? Have you done anything, actually?' Owen returned his attention to the advertising duo. 'Now, is all that for us?'

'Absolutely,' said the executive.

Owen slapped his palms flat on the table. 'Could you gentleman just leave us here for a couple minutes, so we can discuss this?'

Stuart Means opened his mouth and inhaled, then decided not to say anything. The three businessmen stood and left and Stuart Means followed behind.

Owen turned to me. 'Well?'

'It's a lot of money,' I said.

'We could use it to turn the living room into a proper studio.'

'We'd have to buy the house first.'

'We could do that, too.'

'I'll do it.'

'We shouldn't let them get their whole way, though. We should make them concede something.'

'Like what?'

Owen shrugged. 'I don't know. We should choose the song ourselves, not let them choose.'

'What would you choose?'

''Yankee Doodle.''

'Me too.' We both started laughing.

We asked the businessmen back in and Owen told them we'd do it. All four started smiling and the Arroyo executive shook our hands. 'Wonderful,' he said. 'We're very happy to have you on board. We think you'll enjoy it.'

'One thing,' Owen said. 'We'd like it to say something about the song being available on our Pulley Records album. Just in small letters, or something.'

Stuart said, 'Owen, I don't think –'

The Arroyo executive smiled and waved a hand. 'No, no, Stuart, that's okay. Sure, Owen, I understand. I think that's reasonable. We can do that.' The account manager slid some papers in front of him. 'Now, if you just sign these contracts.'

'Not until it includes the clause about our record,' Owen said. I hadn't thought of that and was already starting to reach for the paper. 'Just add it in and send them to us. We'll sign it, don't worry.'

The meeting ended. Stuart Means walked us back to the elevator. While we waited for it to arrive, he said, 'You know, guys, I really don't think it's fair the way you treated me in there. Have I wronged you? Have I treated you badly? I think you owe me a little more respect.'

'Stuart,' Owen said, shaking his head like a disappointed mother, 'How many times do we have to make this clear to you? We don't want you. We didn't hire you and you didn't hire us, okay? I know you tried, and maybe in your head we're your little success story, but keep in mind that all you did was buy out a contract. We can get along just fine without you. Your one job, as far as we're concerned, is to get us into a studio, and soon. This is what we get paid for, and it's what you get paid for – to make sure our record gets made. So do it, okay? And leave the singing, playing, and decisions to us. We're not children, and you're not our mother.' The elevator bell rang a single ding. 'Just do your job, please.' We got on the elevator and watched as the doors closed, slicing away our view of Stuart Means, who stood mute in the corridor.

Los Angeles Times, March 11, 1998:

NOONE MAKES IT OFFICIAL

ORANGE COUNTY – Congressman Jack Noone, Republican representative for the 9th District, became the official Republican candidate for the U.S. Senate yesterday, winning the primary election after running unopposed.

Congressman Noone's spokeswoman said, "We are very happy to have passed this milestone, and look forward to a positive, issues-based campaign." Congressman Noone first made his positions clear in a speech in Washington last October, when he attacked the morals of both the entertainment industry and the Democrats. His remarks on family values were followed in December by allegations of hypocrisy made by a Mr. Owen Noone, who has claimed to be the Congressman's estranged son and is calling for the Congressman to acknowledge his part in corrupting family values.

The motives of Owen

Noone, a musician, remain unclear, and Congressman Noone has yet to address the allegations in any specific way. Asked to make a statement on the issue, the Congressman's spokeswoman said only, "We are concerned about these allegations, particularly the way in which they could damage any real debate on issues of integrity and reform in the upcoming campaign."

Attempts to reach Owen Noone were unsuccessful.

Spin, May 1998:

YANKEE DOODLE DANDIES

Owen Noone and the Marauder fill us in on good music, politics and leprechauns

With their appearance in an Arroyo Corduroys commercial, Owen Noone and the Marauder have gone from cult indie-rock band to mainstream recognition overnight. The song they play in the commercial, "Yankee Doodle," has become a Top Ten single, invading the territory dominated by R&B, hip-hop and dance. Their eponymous album has become the best-selling indie-label release of all time, selling 500,000 copies. Now under contract with major label Pacific, the boys took time out from their busy schedule to talk about success, failure and the upcoming elections.

I meet the duo at their home in west Los Angeles, a two-story brick house near the airport. Airplanes seem to pass over constantly, and I comment, pointing to the various pieces of musical and recording equipment lying around the living room, that it's odd for a band to live and practice in such a noisy place.

"You have to live somewhere," Owen Noone, tall, sandy-haired, athletic, says. "Besides, it's close to the beach."

From the beginning of the interview, it's obvious that Owen is going to do most of the talking. Even when questions are directed at the Marauder – whose real name remains something of a mystery – Owen jumps in. The Marauder doesn't complain, seeming to enjoy his role as Harpo to Owen's Groucho. They sit at opposite ends of the sofa. I ask them about their repetoire, why they only play folk songs.

"They're the only songs we know," says Owen. "We've got a book of them, and we learn them. Besides, they're good songs, interesting songs, real songs written by real people about how they really feel. None of this shit that people write now or in the last thirty years. All that is old, sentimental crap. And now, it's all just cover versions with new, boring drumbeats. We've got to throw them all away, burn them up and do something new."

I point out that their songs are old – old folk songs.

"But they're songs nobody listens to anymore, nobody understands. People would be a lot better off listening to these songs and taking them to heart. They're real. Not these fake, over-sentimental, manufactured myths that come out of the music industry. Nobody would ever write a song like "Wild Mizzourye" anymore, with that kind of power and imagery and emotion all together. There's no cliché in these songs. Everything else is cliché, and it's boring."

Why don't they have a drummer?

The two guitarists exchange glances. "Do we need one?" This is one of the only times the Marauder speaks. "What could a drummer do for us?" Owen adds. "There's only two of us, and we both play guitar." Couldn't they hire a drummer? "If we wanted to. I don't know what we'd do with him, though, and it's our band. When other people start getting involved, it becomes a problem. This is just our experience." I ask what experience he means exactly, but he doesn't answer.

They don't feel that they've betrayed anything or anyone by advertising for Arroyo. "They came to us and offered us a bunch of money. There didn't seem to be any reason not to. It was a lot of money." How much? "A lot." But some fans have accused them of selling out. "Look, people who say things like that have no idea what they're talking about. First, if they were offered similar amounts of money, they'd probably whore themselves, too, and we did everything on our own terms. Plus, I don't know who these people think they are. They buy our records because they like our music. We haven't ever told them anything else. We don't tell them what clothes to wear, we don't tell them to stay off drugs or stay in school or who to vote for. We don't ask them to like us, or to be like us. We play music. We're not spokesmen for a generation or any of that shit. Let somebody else do it. We just want to make good, meaningful music."

Doesn't meaningful imply a certain ethic that an Arroyo ad would seem to go against?

"No. Meaningful is a lot of things, but it doesn't mean a political or social stance on anything. Except for two songs, there aren't any we play that have any sort of political message or context." Which two? "Listen to the goddamn album."

I point out that in fact, Owen Noone and the Marauder have told people who to vote for, or at least who not to vote for, in the form of Owen's public allegations against California Senatorial candidate Jack Noone.

"I haven't told anyone to vote for or against him," Owen says quietly, with more control than I expected. "I've told him to be honest. That's not too much to ask. If fans accuse us of selling out for doing Arroyo ads, at least we're honest about it – we advertised pants because they paid us a ridiculous amount of money to do it. Do we actually wear them? I think I have a pair somewhere. But never have we insisted people wear them. This guy, my father, insists people live this way or that way. He makes laws about it. He accuses others of things and he wants to dictate how people make art, and here he is, ignoring the facts of his life, ignoring his son and pretending like I don't exist. That's dishonest. The only thing I ever asked out of him is honesty and nothing else. People can vote for him if they want to, I just want them to know who they're voting for. He doesn't want them to know. He just wants the power, the glory."

What makes Owen think that people will listen to him?

"The same reason they get mad when we advertise corduroy pants."

Meaning?

"Because I'm a rockstar. People listen to rockstars. Lord knows it's stupid, but that's the situation. They believe in rockstars."

What does that mean?

The Marauder leans forward from his crosslegged position and provides the final words of the interview. "If he said they believe in leprechauns, would you ask what that means?"

No.

"Okay, then."

The publicity created by the Arroyo ad – particularly the *Spin* cover story – finally convinced Stuart Means to do something for us. He phoned a week after the magazine appeared to tell us he'd hired a producer and a studio. On the first of June Owen, Anna and I were sitting in Station Studios in Chicago waiting for Vic Reems to show up. Anna had done some waitressing in L.A. but she didn't have a steady job, so she'd come along. I'd suggested that she'd get bored watching us in the studio every day. Owen said that there were museums and other things to keep her entertained if that was the case. I think the real reason she came is because she and Owen couldn't have been apart for that long.

Vic Reems was one of the best-known producers in the business, having done some ridiculous number of gold and platinum albums and winning a few Grammy awards along the way. Stuart tried to impress all of this upon us, counting off the names of the many bands who had successfully worked with Vic Reems, many of them multiple times. These facts didn't really excite us. We didn't like any of Vic Reems's bands, we'd wanted to work with Steve Wood again, and we didn't want to leave Los Angeles to make an album. Plus Vic Reems was late, so his already low stock was plummeting fast. He didn't help himself when he finally showed up.

'Hi, guys,' he said, shaking our hands and looking around the studio. He was dark-haired and had a closely trimmed goatee. Despite the outside heat he wore black pants and a black turtleneck. 'Where's the rest?'

'The rest of what?' I asked.

'The band.'

'There's only two of us.'

'Yeah, right, I know. I listened to the demo and everything.' He patted his slicked-back hair. 'But your guy at Pacific, Stuart, said they were hiring some session guys.'

This was news. I didn't bother looking at Owen. I knew his face would look exactly like mine felt: tight and red. Vic Reems's expression slowly changed from a broad smile to an open-mouthed gaze of incomprehension. 'What?'

'Excuse me,' Owen said. 'I need to make a phone call.'

Owen was gone for twenty minutes while I stood in the studio with Vic Reems and Anna. Nobody spoke. The two session musicians arrived together, both chattering until they walked in. The obvious tension cut off their conversation and they both stood against the wall silently until Owen came back.

'You're the two session guys?' he said, striding into the room.

'Yeah.'

Owen jammed his thumb at the door. 'Out. We don't need you.'

'But —'

'Out. You'll be paid.'

Vic Reems stepped in. 'Owen, let's just do a few takes with these guys and see —'

'Vic,' Owen said, and I could feel what was coming.

'I'm going to tell you exactly what I just told Stuart Means, and that's the last I want to hear from you, other than when you're tuning instruments and placing microphones and actually recording this album, okay? This band is called Owen Noone and the Marauder. I'm Owen Noone. That's the Marauder. "And" is a little word that joins us. There isn't anybody else in the fucking band. No session musicians. No drums, no bass, just Owen Noone – that's me – and the Marauder – that's him. Stuart has a hard time understanding this concept. I hope you won't because it'll be a long two weeks if you do.'

'What about the chick?' Vic Reems said, pointing at Anna. 'She the tambourine player?'

Owen raised a finger. 'Vic –'

'Fuck you, asshole.' Everyone turned towards Anna. She took two steps towards Vic Reems. 'Don't even start. You're not the boss here. You've been hired to work for these two, so what these two say is what goes, not whatever stupid comments pop out of your mouth. And I'm his wife. You can deal with me if you have any problems, and you'd better watch your trap.'

Vic smiled with one side of his mouth, so it looked like a sneer. 'Whatever, Yoko. Let's get started, guys.'

Owen had Vic Reems against the wall so quickly I couldn't even register what was happening. One arm was across Vic's neck, pushing up on his chin, his other planted on Vic's chest. He'd lifted Vic off the floor.

'That's my wife,' Owen hissed. 'If you say another fucking thing –'

'Owen.' I was surprised to hear my own voice. Owen turned his head, and Vic Reems's eyes shifted towards me. 'Let's just get to work.'

Owen let go. Vic Reems lost his balance and almost fell. He rubbed his throat and coughed twice, then moved to the other side of the small room.

I turned to the session musicians. 'Sorry guys.' They shuffled out and it was just the four of us. Owen still stood by the wall, Vic on the adjacent side, closer to me. Anna stood by the door. Her face was gray.

'So,' Vic said, his voice hoarse. 'Maybe we should just start tomorrow?'

'I think that's best,' I said. 'We'll come in at nine, re-introduce ourselves and get down to business.'

'Jesus, Owen,' I said when we were out on the street.

'What? The guy was a dick.'

'Yeah, but there's other –'

'Look, just forget about it. I did what I did.'

'I'm not going to forget about it,' I said, turning to Anna, but she was staring down the road, her back to us. 'It scared me.'

Owen rolled his eyes. 'Calm down. I wasn't going to kill the guy or anything. I didn't even hurt him.'

'You looked like you were going to hurt him.'

Owen gave a short laugh through his nose. 'Get over it.' He tapped Anna's shoulder. 'It's not a big deal, right?'

She turned. 'I'd say it's a big deal, Owen.'

'No it wasn't.'

'Owen, it scared both of us.'

'I was looking out for you.'

'That's great. I don't need Mr. Macho to go around for me.'

Owen sighed. 'But –'

'No "but", Owen! I'm not a child, and I'm not some weak little girl who just follows you around and needs you to protect me.' Her voice changed to a mock little-girl voice, but it wasn't funny. '"Ooh, Owen, protect me from the man with the goatee."' Give me a fucking break. I can think for myself. I'd already stood up for myself.'

'I was just trying –'

'No! Owen!' Anna turned to me. 'Look, I'm sorry. But I think he and I need to discuss this somewhere else. Alone.'

I walked up the street to the El station without saying anything and spent the rest of the day wandering around downtown Chicago. I sat on the beach for a couple of hours. The air was warm, but because it was so early in the summer the water was still cold and not many people were swimming. Some were playing volleyball and others were throwing Frisbees. Owen had scared the shit out of me, so I didn't want to be near him anyway. I'd seen him act like an asshole before a few times, but never anything like that. Nothing violent. I wondered if Anna had seen him like that. They argued occasionally, but not any more than other people probably, and they were never horrible arguments. I couldn't imagine him doing anything like that to her, but that must've been what scared her. It was what scared me most.

The worst two weeks of our music lives were those two spent in Chicago with Vic Reems. He seemed to forget the fact that Owen had almost choked him, and was obnoxious the whole time, constantly talking about what he'd done with this band or that and how well it had worked, but never actually talking about us, the guys he was working with, recording, and supposedly thinking about. He kept trying to get Owen to use different effects pedals and he tried running my guitar through a whole series of chorus, compression, octave blah blah blah pedals. We refused every suggestion. Vic Reems didn't seem to know much about tuning a guitar, either. Steve Wood had personally retuned our guitars before every take, sometimes stopping mid-song to retune if he didn't like what he heard. Owen and I tuned our own guitars with Vic Reems and when we stopped mid-take, it was because of something we heard, not because of Vic. He'd give us an astonished look, then ask what was wrong. Also, he never really touched anything. He had three assistants who fiddled with all the knobs, set the microphones, adjusted levels. Vic Reems just stood behind the mixing board stroking his goatee with his thumb and index finger, nodding and telling us about the Grammy-winning heavy metal band he'd produced.

It was emotionally wearing, too, because Owen and Anna were obviously unhappy. The three of us only went out together once during the entire two weeks. The rest of the time they were by themselves 'discussing things,' as Owen put it one day. So I was on my own in my hotel room for two weeks, watching movies and sports on TV and feeling sorry for myself. Occasionally I went to the hotel bar, but it was boring watching groups of businessmen in suits drinking and laughing. I resented being left on my own all the time. I didn't say so but I let Owen and Anna know by the way I acted. Owen and I didn't talk to each other much in the studio, only saying what was necessesary to get the job done. Other than Good Morning I probably didn't say more than three sentences to Anna, who sat in the control room during the sessions, either staring through the window into the live room or reading magazines. By the time we'd finished recording the fourteen songs we never wanted to see that studio or Vic Reems again, and he was probably sick of us whining at him, too.

We flew back to Los Angeles the same day that we

finished recording, leaving Vic Reems and whoever he hired to do the mixing. We'd written down the order in which we wanted the songs to go and left. It wasn't our album anymore, if it ever had been. Nothing we said or did changed the way Vic Reems and his minions went about their business. We'd just been a necessary nuisance to them.

Back home we spent the whole first week sitting around the house doing nothing but listening to music and opening mail. We'd started getting fan letters and after two weeks, they'd piled up. We read them and tried to respond, but usually there was nothing to say, which made it hard. We'd send postcards with one sentence and our signatures on them. If they asked us questions, we'd try to answer them. The fan letters just made me lonelier. I didn't have any real friends apart from Owen and Anna, and although after a few days at home we were all acting more or less normally, there was still some tension among us. All these kids – and not all of them were kids, a lot were around the same age as us – wrote telling us how much they loved us and I honestly started thinking about writing to some of these girls and giving them my phone number. I was twenty-four years old and I'd never had a girlfriend. The more I thought about it the lousier it made me feel, and I was too embarrassed to talk about it with Owen or Anna. Especially Anna. And the more I thought about writing to one of these girls, the more I felt like a pervert.

Stuart Means phoned us in the middle of the next week. He'd gotten the master copies of the album. 'They sound great. Great,' he said with his usual overenthusiasm. 'We're going to put it out August 4th,' he said.

The release party on August 3rd was the first time we heard it. Pacific set the whole thing up, renting out a room in a fancy hotel and inviting a bunch of people we didn't know – top celebrities, movie stars, journalists and what seemed like a swarm of Pacific employees. Owen invited Jack Noone, who didn't come even though we knew he was in California campaigning. Vic Reems was there, dressed in the same uniform that he'd worn every day of the recording sessions – black pants and black turtleneck.

Anna didn't come to the party. She'd flown to New York two days before because her father had fallen off a ladder and broken his leg, and they needed help on the farm. So Owen and I were alone in this sea of people who didn't know us and didn't care, getting free drinks and networking or gossiping for their articles.

After an hour or so of schmoozing Stuart Means came over to the bar where Owen and I stood watching people and drinking to tell us they were going to play our album. 'If that's okay with you guys,' he said. It was the first he'd spoken to us all night, and he said it tentatively, expecting, I suppose, the usual outburst from one or the other of us.

'Sure,' Owen said. 'It's your party.'

Stuart smiled nervously. 'Your party. Your party.' He started to reach his hand towards Owen's shoulder but stopped and just pointed at each of us with his thumb. 'Your party.'

'I hope it's good,' Owen called as Stuart walked away.

It wasn't. The songs themselves – our part – were fine, good, better, in fact, than our first album, simply because we could play better, and we knew what we were doing. The production was terrible, though. There were no dynamics – every song was exactly the same volume from start to finish, even "Wanderin'," which was supposed to have pronounced changes and definite shapes to each verse and chorus. On most of the songs they'd overlapped multiple guitar tracks, so it sounded like four or five players instead of just two. We stood against the bar watching people nod their heads to the music, watching people, most of whom we didn't know, turn to look at us and smile, wave and give us the thumbs up. I ordered two double whiskeys. Owen and I toasted each other and drank them in one.

'You guys have done it again.' I turned from the bar where I'd just set my glass to see who it was, blinking several times to clear the blur from the whiskey burn. It was Ellen Trelaine. 'Great album,' she said, winking at Owen. The sequins on her blue dress – the same dress she'd worn to the last party – flashed under the lights.

'We think it's shit,' I said.

'No, no – it's good.' She swept her hand towards the middle of the room. 'Look at all those people. They like it. They're dancing.' They were. It was true.

'But we don't like it,' I said, 'And that's the important thing.'

Ellen looked at the empty space next to Owen. 'Where's –' She waved her hand in small rotations.

'Anna?' Owen said. 'She had to go to New York.'

Ellen rocked back on her heels. 'Anna, right. She wouldn't grudge me a dance, would she?'

'Excuse me,' I said. 'I have to piss.' Ellen Trelaine shot me a look of disgust. I wove through the crowd and some people told me how good the album was as I passed. They were playing the album very loudly, and the notes, deadened by the closed door, pushed their way into the toilet stalls. I tried to block it out by pissing as loudly as I could straight into the water of the toilet bowl. It mostly worked, though not completely. I washed my hands slowly, making the water as hot as I could so that it stung my hands.

"Will You Wear Red?" was just finishing as I jostled my way back across the room. Owen was dancing with Ellen Trelaine and I saw her lean towards him and kiss him on the mouth. I turned away and went to the bar and ordered another double whiskey, drank it, and went out to where Owen was just finishing kissing Ellen Trelaine.

'Home,' I said, pulling Owen's shoulder away from Ellen Trelaine, 'We're going home.'

Owen turned towards me with his mouth open, the pink lipstick imprinted on its corner. 'I – ' he looked at Ellen, then turned back to me. 'Yes. Home.' He turned to Ellen again. 'I have to go home now.'

She half-squinted and smiled, placing her hand on his chest. 'Can I come with you?'

Owen turned to me, then back to Ellen. 'No. We have to go.'

'Just one more dance? C'mon.'

Owen took a step back. 'Yeah, okay, one more. Just one more.'

Leaving Owen behind with Ellen, I pushed through the crowd and left the hotel. I should've dragged him with me. But I didn't want to. I wanted Owen to fuck up just once, even though I knew it would hurt Anna. It seemed as though he never did anything wrong. Even throttling Vic Reems hadn't been wrong. He'd gotten away with it. The spotlight always shined brightly on him. I just stood on the edge and got what was left, which was – what? He had a wife, a movie star, and took and did what he wanted. I just reacted to whatever came my way or ran from it. Or followed Owen Noone. Well, fuck Owen Noone.

It was a hot summer night. Pacific had rented us a limousine, and it stood shining and black under a streetlight at the end of the sidewalk. I walked past it and hailed a cab, crawled into the back seat, and read and reread the Passengers' Bill of Rights until I got home.

Rolling Stone, August 4, 1998:

Owen Noone and the Marauder
Wanderin'
(Pacific)
*

Between their last album and this release, Owen Noone and the Marauder have been busy going from six-figure selling indie darlings to a major label, recording a commercial for Arroyo Corduroys and keeping themselves in the papers with paternity claims. All this success, it seems, has ruined the once-potent mixture of energy, good songs and inability to play that was their hallmark and their charm. For this is a charmless album. Gone is the stripped-bare, two-guitar howling style that thrilled on their first album, replaced by the multiple-track layering techniques of producer Vic Reems whose talents, it seems, are put to better use in service of the hard rock and metal acts with whom he made his name. The sense of spontaneity and disjointed playing that marked the first album are gone too. While technically well-played, every track lacks the energy and fun that ran through their previous effort. Even the title track, featuring the vocals of the usually mute Marauder, is flat, despite, or perhaps because of its minimum of, five guitar tracks. At least they didn't try to add bass and drums, a move that would surely have pushed them over the edge into absurdity. Where the previous album replicated with great accuracy the spontaneity and energy of their live act, this effort wallows in its own production values, which render the music mundane and spiritless.

CHARLIE WHEELER

Anna came back a few days later. Owen was on the phone with Stuart Means discussing the details of our forthcoming promotional tour when she came in, dragging her large brown suitcase behind her and trying to blow strands of hair from her face. In her other hand was a newspaper. She pulled the suitcase violently through the door, leaving it on its side in the entryway, then marched to where Owen stood and, without saying a word, hit him several times with the rolled-up newspaper before throwing it on the sofa and racing up the stairs.

'Hold on a minute, Stuart,' Owen said, and let the phone drop. 'What was that?' he asked me.

I reached across the sofa and picked up the newspaper. It was the *National Enquirer*. I started flipping through its pages, stopping when I saw what was on page five. 'Oh,' I said, staring at it. 'Oh. This,' I said, opening the paper and holding it towards Owen, 'is what.'

National Enquirer, August 4, 1998:

WHEN OWEN MET ELLEN!

Enquirer cameras snapped these pictures of alternative rocker Owen Noone and up-and-coming movie starlet Ellen Trelaine at the star-studded Los Angeles release party for Owen's band's new album, "Wanderin".'

It all suggests that the two are quickly becoming more than friends. Several of the party guests confirmed that the two were "very friendly" and spent a good deal of the night together, most of it on the dance floor. One source confirmed that they left the party "about the same time," although it was unclear whether they left together.

Rocker Owen, whose star status has been climbing ever since his appearance with side-kick Marauder – real name unknown – in the recent Arroyo advertising campaign, was seen talking with Ms. Trelaine and his angry – or perhaps jealous? – cohort, who then left alone. Owen and Ms. Trelaine continued to dance, and stayed at the party for several more hours.

His record label, Pacific, could not confirm that the two are now an item, but a spokesman told the *Enquirer*, "Owen Noone and the Marauder are rising stars, so of course they're spending more of their time with other celebrities."

Could it be love for the hunky rocker and beautiful actress? The *Enquirer* hopes so!

Owen set the phone back on its cradle without saying a word. He stared at the open pages of the newspaper. There were two pictures, one of Owen and Ellen Trelaine talking with their arms around each other, and another of them kissing. He took the paper from my hands, folded it over and read the article, muttering unintelligibly with each sentence. When he finished, he looked up and our eyes met. He seemed to be asking me for something, silently pleading for advice.

Suddenly I felt sorry for him. 'I don't know, Owen.' I took the paper and looked at the pictures and article again. 'I don't know. Be honest.'

He nodded and walked upstairs. I heard him knock on the door and say Anna's name and then, after a minute or so, try the doorknob, which rattled in place. He knocked, and said her name again, waiting. The floor creaked as he paced the hallway. I heard him knock again and picked up the paper, brushing the pictures with my fingertips as if they would wipe away with my touch. As Owen said Anna's name I remembered when she first heard us play and he sang "The Wild Mizzourye" for her. I thought of those words now:

Farewell my dear, I'm bound to leave you,
Away, you rolling river,
O Shenandoah, I'll not deceive you,
Away, I'm bound to go,
'cross the wild Mizzourye.

Taking the paper with me, I left and walked down to the beach, squinting against the afternoon sun. It was hot and the beach was crowded with children digging in the sand with bright plastic shovels, filling buckets and turning them over to make sand castles while their mothers watched or read books. Over the ocean, an airplane made a slow, wide circle before beginning its descent, the engines getting louder and louder as it came in to land. I followed the plane's progress, watching until it was directly above, rolling my eyes back until it disappeared behind me. I dropped the newspaper and it flopped open to expose the pictures of Owen and Ellen Trelaine. I kicked a little sand over it, then picked it up and walked to the hard, wet sand at the edge of the ocean. I dipped the edge of the newspaper in the water and watched as the wetness crept up the edge, darkening the paper and blurring the words. Letting it fall, I pushed it under the water and held it there as though I were drowning it, pushing the air from it.

Somebody nearby turned on a portable stereo and a sudden burst of jangly guitar escaped across the beach. The song was "Will You Wear Red?" and the band was Owen Noone and the Marauder.

O will you wear blue, O my dear, O my dear?
Will you wear blue, Jennie Jenkins?
I won't wear blue, for I won't be true,

I'll buy me a twirley-whirley, sookey-lookey,
Sally-Katty, double-lolly,
Roll-the-find-me, roll, Jennie Jenkins, roll.

A kid in diapers started dancing without moving his feet, just wiggling his hips back and forth and playing his shovel like a guitar. A few smiled and laughed while the song played, verse-chorus-verse-chorus rolling out of the stereo across the sand and into the ocean until the noise of a landing airplane drowned it out completely.

As I was walking home I saw Owen walking in the opposite direction, his hands thrust into the pockets of his corduroy pants, his eyes fixed on the concrete. I watched him pass by, waiting to see if he'd look up. He didn't. I continued towards home, looking once over my shoulder at his slouching figure as he shuffled further away. It was almost sunset, and my shadow extended in front of me, thin and long across the sidewalk. I thought of the fairy tale in which a man sells his shadow to the devil and nobody will go near him because he doesn't seem human without it. It occurred to me that since Owen was walking in the opposite direction he couldn't see his shadow stretching out behind him.

I stopped at a convenience store and bought a case of the cheapest beer, then went home and opened a can. The house was empty and quiet. I sat on the sofa drinking beer in the silence, too lazy to put on the radio. Occasionally I could hear a car go past. I heard the rattle of glass bottles in a shopping cart as a homeless man passed on his usual route.

It was dark when Owen came home. He fumbled with his keys before realizing that the door was unlocked. I'd had three and a half cans of beer and was still sitting on the sofa with the lights off, a lump among the shadows.

'Hi,' I said as Owen closed and locked the door. 'Want a beer?'

He flipped the wall switch and I shut my eyes hard to cut away the sting of the light. 'Yeah,' he said, taking a can. 'Yeah.' He sat on the easy chair, opened his beer and took a long drink. 'She's gone.'

'I know.'

'For good, I mean.'

I finished my fourth beer. 'I know.'

We sat looking at each other in silence, each of us sipping our beers. 'I went to the beach,' Owen said after finishing one beer and taking another, 'And sat right at the edge of the water, about two feet away. I kept watching the airplanes come in and others leave, listening to the sound they make. I hoped that Anna would come and sit down next to me, and we'd let the water run closer and closer until it came to the tips of our toes, and then made our legs wet. We'd sit in the ocean until we were too cold and then come home and lie in bed together, keeping each other warm while we dried. But I knew she wasn't going to come to the beach.' Owen wiped the sleeve of his T-shirt across his eyes. 'So when I felt the water at my feet, I got up and walked back.'

'Did you do it?'

'Do what?'

'With Ellen Trelaine?'

Owen leaned forward. 'Did I – ?' He slumped back and just stared at me. After several seconds he said, 'How could you ask that?'

''Cause it's important.'

Owen sipped his beer and stared. 'But it isn't your business.'

'It is my business. Anna's my friend.'

'So am I. And she's my wife, and that's a difference.'

I knew he was right. I wasn't asking because I wanted to help. I was asking because I was jealous. And because I loved Owen and I loved Anna and even though I shouldn't I felt like I had a right to know everything about what went on. I didn't want to accept that there were things between them that were private, things that weren't for me to know.

We met Stuart Means the next afternoon to go over the plans for our tour. We'd drunk the whole case of beer and both looked and felt ill and fragile. Stuart Means was not the person we wanted to see; we didn't want to see anyone, really. But we had to go to Pacific headquarters to learn about the tour bus they were hiring for us, and about all of its deluxe features.

'But there's only two of us. Wouldn't it save money to just use our own truck?'

Stuart looked at me. 'You won't have to worry about driving this way. Plus it saves on hotel rooms, so no, it won't save money. And you've got to have a tour manager on board to coordinate everything and make sure things run smoothly, plus the roadies for your gear. I know you guys hate that idea, but it's company policy, so it's out of all our hands. I've got a manager you'll like. Besides, you guys are big now. National news. Stars. You deserve to travel in style.'

'What national news?' Owen said.

'An article in the *National Enquirer* for one.' Stuart smiled. 'And despite an unfair review in *Rolling Stone*, your sales figures will have your album in the Top Ten by the

222

end of next week.' He paused and shifted his attention between the two of us. 'Great stuff, huh?'

'Great stuff, Stuart,' Owen said. 'Fuck you.'

Stuart raised his hands like a waiter holding a tray at a cocktail party. 'What? I don't get it. What did I possibly say wrong this time?'

'You just don't get it, do you? You never pay attention to anything except record sales and profits. You don't know anything about us and don't care as long as we're in the Top Ten. You didn't think for one second that maybe that article in the *National Enquirer* wasn't such a good thing, that maybe it had, I don't know, adverse effects on my personal life, that maybe there's other things going on in this world that I care about beyond selling records.'

'Owen, selling records is my job. It's your job. Maybe you think I'm crass, but I don't really give a shit about your personal life if it doesn't have anything to do with my job. Whatever bad things happen to you because your picture appears in a tabloid, that's not my problem. It's yours. You did it, not me. You're a rockstar whether you like it or not, and I think you do like it. There's certain things that go along with rock stardom, with fame and celebrity, and one of them is having your picture in the newspaper on terms that you don't necessarily want. It's all well and good to go do interviews about Congressmen, isn't it, when there's nothing for you to lose? But suddenly when the tables are turned and you've got something to lose, it's a problem. Welcome to the real world, Owen, where everything doesn't go your way and you can't blame it on asshole Stuart Means because he had nothing to do with it. If you want to go around fucking movie stars, you've got to accept the consequences.'

The three of us stood there in the conference room and didn't say anything for a couple minutes. Owen was staring at the table, as though he could bore holes into it with his eyes. I shifted my weight from one foot to the other and looked at different spots on the wall. Stuart was breathing hard and shaking. He'd probably wanted to rant at Owen for months now.

'Okay,' Owen said. 'We'll go in a tour bus.'

By the end of the week we'd sold one million copies of 'Wanderin'.' Or rather, record stores had sold one million copies; we hadn't sold anything. We'd been sitting around our house since the record came out, reading the newspaper, listening to the radio and occasionally picking up our guitars and practicing a couple songs. The tour was to start with gigs on August 29 and 30 in Los Angeles and then work its way across the country until the end of the year, with two-night stops in the biggest cities. After Los Angeles we would go down to San Diego, then to Phoenix, Tucson, Albuquerque, Dallas, Austin, New Orleans, Atlanta, Charlotte, Washington, Baltimore, New York City, Boston, Buffalo, Pittsburgh, Cleveland, Detroit, Chicago, Milwaukee, Madison, Minneapolis, Lawrence, Denver, Boise, Seattle, Portland, San Francisco and back to Los Angeles for New Year's Eve. We met Ron Midland, our tour manager, who, we insisted, wouldn't actually start until after the L.A. gigs. We were also told that the roadies would be taking a separate bus, which seemed a ludicrous expense – and one that we'd no doubt be paying for – but was another of those things that Stuart described as "out of our hands." Meanwhile, he wanted us to make a video to help push record sales even higher. We insisted on doing it our own way, so we wrote to Ed in New York City, telling him not to buy tickets for our gigs there and to make sure he had a video camera and lots of film. The single from the album was "Will You Wear Red?" and that was the song for which we were told to make the video. Given a choice, we would have done "Yankee Doodle" or "John Henry," but those weren't on the album.

By the time the 29th came around, we were ready to quit sitting around the house all day and start playing. It was strange and empty-feeling in the house without Anna, but neither of us spoke about it. Owen hardly spoke at all, unless we were practicing or I asked him a question. At night we would sift through the fan letters – which were arriving in even bigger piles than before – and answer a few. Teenage girls would write professing their undying love for Owen – and on occasion for me – and teenage boys would write telling us which songs were their favorites, and how they knew how we felt when we sang "East Virginia" or "Will You Wear Red?" or "Fare Thee Well, O Honey." We only got a few letters from people who weren't teenagers.

The telephone woke us on the morning of the 29th. It was Jack Noone. Jack Noone himself. Owen was still in bed and I tried to get him out but he refused.

'But it's your father.'

'I don't care. I do care, but I'm not getting out of bed for that prick.'

'What should I tell him?'

'That I'm not getting out of bed for him. And that he's a prick. Use your judgment. Take a message.'

I told Jack Noone that Owen couldn't come to the phone, but I didn't say why.

'Tell him that I said thank you for sending me concert tickets, but unfortunately I'll be unable to attend,' he said.

'And tell him also that I'll be holding a press conference early this afternoon at my headquarters here in Los Angeles, and I think he'll be interested. I've personally added his name to the list of approved non-press invitees. I hope he'll attend.'

The press conference was at two o'clock in the afternoon. We got there at quarter to two so we didn't miss anything. The security agents and policemen were surprisingly accommodating when we arrived, considering we had no official badges or anything. Owen just told them who he was and that he'd been personally invited by Congressman Noone, and they called over one of the campaign workers and asked him to show us to the press room. This campaign worker, who looked about eighteen, chattered away about how excited everybody was about the press conference.

The press room wasn't very big, just a small conference room like the one in Pacific's headquarters. There were a few rows of folding chairs and a one-foot platform with a podium, on top of which were clustered several microphones. The room was almost full with reporters testing dictaphones, scribbling notes and talking to each other. The campaign worker pointed to two empty seats in the back corner.

'Those are reserved for you,' he said. 'I've got to get back to work.' He spun around on his heel and walked out of the room, almost at a run.

The reporters around us turned and greeted us with nods and fake smiles. They clearly didn't care who we were, except that we weren't one of them, and they didn't really want to talk to anybody who wasn't one of their own, unless it was the Congressman himself. Owen and I sat silently in the middle of the buzz of reporters waiting for the press conference to start, wondering what to expect and how to react – or at least, I was wondering how Owen would react, depending on what the Congressman said.

Jack Noone came into the room from a side door at ten minutes past two. The noise of the talking reporters dissipated as he entered. He stepped behind the podium and surveyed the room. I wondered if he was looking for Owen. His eyes stopped briefly on us, and I thought I saw him make a small smile.

'Prick,' muttered Owen.

Jack Noone reached into his shirt pocket and put on a pair of reading glasses, then reached into his jacket pocket and took out a piece of paper. These movements were supposed to seem natural, but they had an air of acting about them. I imagined his press secretary or somebody telling him how many seconds to count as he reached, and how many seconds in between putting on the glasses and taking out the paper. 'Sorry to keep you all waiting,' he said after looking at the piece of paper for a few seconds. 'I'll keep this as short as possible, and then take questions for a few minutes at the end.

'Ladies and gentlemen of the press. Last December certain allegations surfaced in a San Francisco newspaper regarding my personal life. As you are no doubt aware, allegations of paternity and claims of hypocrisy and other slurs were made against me by a then little-known rock musician named Owen Noone.'

I glanced at Owen and saw the ball of his jaw muscle tighten.

'I would like to address these allegations today, both the specific paternity claim and the more vague, uncorrob-

227

orated slurs that have been made and repeated in the press over the last several months.' Jack Noone paused, and his Adam's apple rose and fell as he swallowed. 'At this time I would like to state publicly and officially that Owen Noone is in fact my son from my first marriage, which terminated two years after Owen's birth.'

A murmur spread like a slow wave across the room.

'At no time, however, have I acted illegally in any way towards Owen. I provided monetary support to both him and his mother until she remarried, and I continued to provide financial support for Owen until he turned eighteen.

'Owen himself was not, I don't think, made aware of these arrangements by his mother and stepfather, and so continued to believe that his biological father had abandoned him completely, an unfortunate and erroneous viewpoint that led to his public outburst, but one that I do not hold against him.'

Owen started mumbling something quietly, too quietly for me to tell what he was saying, and he stared at his father.

'What I find particularly unfortunate, however, is the timing of Owen's misguided campaign against me. He could have broached this subject privately with me at any time but he did not see fit to do so. Instead, he has used me and my public standing as a tool to boost his own career.'

Owen's mumbling was getting louder, and I started to understand.

'At the time he made the allegations, he was a largely unknown musician. Riding the back of the publicity he created through his exploitation of me, however, he is currently to be heard on every rock radio station in America, a fact that I hardly see as coincidence.'

Hearing Owen, a few of the reporters around us began

to turn to see what the disturbance was. Owen's voice grew louder, but not loud enough to reach the podium.

'The cynicism exhibited by my son in exploiting this situation reflects exactly the reality of the entertainment industry against which I have positioned myself during the course of this campaign, a reality that exploits the most sacred bonds we have in this nation, the God-given bonds of family, of parent and child.'

Owen stood, and his mumble, having grown to conversation pitch, now erupted into a shout that threatened the supremacy of Jack Noone's amplified voice. Jack Noone heard him and stopped speaking. Every reporter in the room turned to the back to see the source of the song.

Owen was singing. Or shouting, rather, but he was shouting a song – "Yankee Doodle." His voice filled the room, his face almost purple with strain, a vein pulsing out against his skin at his temple.

> There was Captain Washington
> Upon a slapping stallion,
> A-giving orders to his men,
> I guess it was a million.

As Owen began the chorus his voice rose even louder. Jack Noone tried to regain his composure. 'I'm sorry, ladies and gentlemen. Owen, please don't act like a child.' He stared at Owen. 'Don't act like a child.'

But Owen wasn't going to stop. He kept singing:

> The troopers they would gallop up,
> And fire right in our faces,

It scared me almost half to death
To see them run such races.
Yankee Doodle, keep it up,
Yankee Doodle Dandy,
Mind the music and the step
And with the girls be handy.

Jack Noone was getting frustrated. 'I have a few more comments to make, if you'd please be quiet. Act like an adult, please, so we can have a proper, civilized discussion here.' Nobody was listening to him. Owen's spectacle had the full attention of every person in the room. Some of the reporters were scribbling on their notepads and the television cameras were pointing their lights at Owen, his eyes wide and staring, unblinking, trained on Jack Noone who by this point had lost control of the press conference and his patience entirely. 'Michael,' he said, looking over his glasses at the back door, 'Could you please do something about this?'

I turned to the back door and saw a private security agent and a policeman walking towards Owen. I wanted to say something to him but I knew it wouldn't matter, it was too late, and letting Owen do what he thought he had to do was the only thing I could do. The policeman and security agent each touched one of Owen's shoulders. He didn't even flinch, and kept singing as though they weren't even there.

The policeman looked down at me. 'Tell him to stop.'

'I'm not his mother.'

'Don't be a smartass,' he snarled. 'I'll arrest him right now if he doesn't stop.'

I could feel my blood pumping adrenaline in my chest

and in my neck and in my temples, making everything seem sharp and defined. I stood. 'Officer,' I said, 'I can't tell him to do anything any more than you can, and to be honest, I don't want to.'

'I'll have you arrested,' the policeman said. 'I'll have you arrested along with him.'

'You can't.'

He clenched his jaw and squinted, then turned on his heel and nodded to the security agent. 'Give me a hand with this, Michael.' He grabbed Owen's shoulder and pulled the folding chair away with his other arm. 'Come on, son, let's get out of here.'

Owen tried to throw off the policeman's arm, but the security agent had his other shoulder and caught his arm, pinning it behind his back. 'Ow!' Owen yelled, then picked up his singing without missing a beat. The policeman and security agent pulled him along, and Owen went slack, his feet dragging along the ground, his voice getting hoarse as he shouted the last verse:

> Yankee Doodle is the tune
> Americans delight in,
> 'Twill do to whistle, sing or play
> And just the thing for fightin'.

He grabbed onto the doorframe, and I heard his wrists slam against the wood, but it was to no effect, and his voice began to fade as they dragged him down the hallway, the last words, 'And with the girls be handy,' repeating over and over, as though he were a scratched record, repeating and repeating until it was just a fading noise.

The entire room had turned to stare at the door. I stood

in front of my chair, next to the empty space where Owen had been. Eyes turned towards me, the room silent, even Jack Noone's gaze bearing down on me. I could feel my pulse and took deep, slow breaths to try to slow it down. It was clear that everyone expected me to say something. I felt their eyes pressing on me, felt their will trying to drag words from me. But there was nothing to say. Nothing. He wasn't my father. What would I say if he was? What would I say to my own father? The last thing I had said to him had been, 'I've moved to Iowa City to start a rock 'n' roll band.' I've moved to Iowa City to start a rock 'n' roll band. And he'd said Oh, son, over and over. I've moved to Iowa City. To start a rock 'n' roll band.

'What – ' the microphone emitted treble feedback as Jack Noone started to speak again. 'What does that mean?'

My arms were slack against my sides, and I felt paralyzed. 'What does what mean?' I said.

'I've moved to Iowa City,' Jack Noone said.

'You've moved to – ' My lungs deflated audibly, like a balloon hissing. I didn't realize I'd said it aloud. But it didn't matter. I shrugged. 'It means,' I said. 'It means – ' I shook my head. 'It means something. Nothing.' I turned and walked out of the room, down the hallway, through the door, across the campaign office where the workers looked away from the television to stare after me as I stepped out onto the sidewalk and into the hot afternoon, squinting against the sunlight.

I didn't know where to go or what to do. I didn't know where Owen was. Arrested, presumably, but they could have taken him to any number of police stations. I walked down the street, making space between myself and the press conference. There were only a few hours before the gig and we had to be there soon and I had no idea where to go or what to do. So I hailed a taxi and went home.

I expected, or hoped, actually, to find Anna sitting on the sofa, or leaning against the kitchen counter with a cup of coffee reading a newspaper. But she wasn't there. She was gone.

When I got home the telephone was ringing and I could tell, somehow, that it had been ringing for a while.

'What the hell is going on? Is Owen with you?'

'Stuart,' I said. 'No.' I stared out the open front door. 'He was arrested.'

'I saw. Everybody saw. Where is he though?'

'I don't know.'

'You don't know?'

'I haven't heard. I don't know. He was arrested.'

'Okay, listen. Just stay there and hopefully he'll phone you. I'll get in touch with the management and make sure they know you'll be there, but that you might be late. How are you getting there?'

'Where?'

'To the gig. Are you listening to me?'

'Oh. Yeah. Driving. We're driving over. In the truck.'

'Just don't leave until you hear from Owen.'

Stuart Means hung up, but I continued to hold the phone to my ear until it played the dial tone. I sat down sideways in the easy chair with my legs hanging over the armrest and stared out the door at the houses across the street. The shadows were creeping down their front lawns, threatening the sidewalks. The phone rang.

'They decided not to charge me with anything,' Owen said. 'There's nothing to charge, actually. Do you have any money? I've got to get a cab home.'

To keep myself occupied I started loading the equipment into the truck while I waited for him. When the taxi pulled up, I'd just put the crate of cables into the back and closed it. I walked down to the street and gave the driver money.

'Are you famous, too?' he said as he counted the bills. 'He was on TV this afternoon.'

'No,' I said. 'I'm not.'

The taxi drove away and Owen walked into the house. I followed him and asked what happened.

'It wasn't a big deal. They took me to the police station and I sang "Yankee Doodle" all the way. It drove them nuts. When we got there they took off the handcuffs and gave me a lecture about disturbing the peace and the democratic process and all that crap and then they let me go. On my way out some cop gave me a pen and told me his kid was a big fan and asked if I'd sign an autograph, so I did.' Owen was calm, no hint of the anger in his face or voice.

'Why didn't they press charges?'

'I think my father told them not to. He doesn't want any more publicity for me. He knows I'll do it again. I think he thinks he's won the war. Fuck him.'

Los Angeles Times, August 30, 1998:

OWEN NOONE AND THE MARAUDER
Hollywood Palladium, August 28, 1998

By the time the show started everybody in the audience had seen or heard about what happened on television a few hours before, so there was a strange and excited buzz as this packed house waited for Owen Noone and the Marauder to take the stage for the inaugural show of their *Wanderin'* tour. Rumors circulated that Owen Noone wasn't going to show at all, that he'd been arrested and was sitting in a Los Angeles jail.

The rumors proved to be just that, however, and when Owen and his sidekick the Marauder finally took the stage the buzz became positively electric, unharnessing itself into an ovation that lasted for a full three minutes of nonstop applause, cheering and whistling. Noone stood silent before the adulation like the rock god he has indubitably become, while the Marauder tentatively tested a couple of chords.

When the applause finally died down, Noone, without acknowledging his audience, opened his mouth and released the most coarse and chilling opening to "John Henry" of any performance, his hoarse voice breaking and sputtering into the microphone on the elongated "John" before turning to a growl for "Henry," the cacophony of guitars – Noone's resolutely distorted throughout the song, the Marauder's its typically glorious barely-tuned jangle – raining down like a monsoon.

And this was just the beginning. The performance Owen Noone and the Marauder gave their fans tonight was surely the greatest, most inspired of their career. Each song crackled with life and energy from the opener right through, even the quiet, slower songs like "Old Smokey," "Fare Thee Well, O Honey" and "Wanderin'," the latter rendered particularly powerful by the Marauder's whispered vocals, Noone's expert guitar playing and, on the final chorus, Noone's voice adding an extra layer to the sound, floating in unison with the single notes of his electric guitar. The only disappointment was that they didn't play "Careless Love," the male-female duet that always lends an odd element of beauty to their set.

Given the day's events, it's safe to say the audience had been waiting for "Yankee Doodle" all night. So it was some surprise when, at the end of the set, Noone announced, "There won't be an encore this evening." He clicked his distortion pedal on and off a few times, trying out a chord as though he wasn't sure the guitar worked anymore. Then he said, "You may have seen our new video for this on TV this afternoon. I know Jack Noone saw it." The audience responded with an exuberant cheer, then stopped abruptly as Noone raised his hand like one giving an oath. "Sing," he said. With this word, the Marauder began playing the first strains of "Yankee Doodle," the crowd began singing and whether or not Noone even bothered to sing one word, I don't think anybody knows. A one-thousand-voice chorus accompanied by two guitars brought a fitting end to one of the best nights of live rock music Los Angeles has seen in a long time, if ever. Dandy.

Like the newspaper said, it was the best show we'd ever played. We drove home in complete silence and went to sleep without saying a word to each other. By the time I woke up the next day, it was already afternoon and the sun was cutting across my bedroom. I watched the dust falling through the blade of light that split through the half-drawn curtains before getting up and taking a shower.

When I got downstairs Owen had made a breakfast of overcooked bacon, undercooked eggs and perfectly fried potatoes. I made coffee and we sat down and ate, stirring the runny eggs into the potatoes, the only noise that of our forks scraping the plate and the slurping sound as we sipped the hot coffee. The newspaper sat folded on the edge of the table, but I hadn't looked at it and didn't know if Owen had. It was almost certain what the headline would be, and it didn't even seem worth looking at it. I knew that however it was reported, it wouldn't be the truth. At best it would be a half-truth. At worst, outright lies. I had no idea what went on after I left the press conference, what the question and answer session was like, or whether they even continued, but I was sure that the whole thing was slanted against us, against Owen.

'Did you look at it?' I asked, tapping the newspaper with my fingertips.

'No. I know what happened.' Owen picked up a piece of blackened bacon and bit into it, his teeth grinding it with a sound that was like walking across gravel. 'I don't need to see what lies they wrote or what he said to make himself look good. I tried to show how he really is, who he really is, but I guess I don't have enough power to actually make a difference. I don't have a speechwriter, a press secretary and a storefront office packed with volunteers.'

'You've got a guitar,' I said, feeling stupid as I listened to myself.

'Yeah, so what? Nobody wants to hear a preacher with a guitar. They want the music, for whatever reasons they have, not whatever reasons I have, we have. The notes die out, the music stops, people go home, talk about how good it was and then they go to sleep and forget about it. I have no control over that.'

'What about the album? That's permanent.'

'Yeah, and it's not ours. Some guy we didn't know and didn't like recorded it, took away whatever control we had over it, and you know what? I don't even care. Albums, so what? Before, that's all I wanted, an album, a piece of immortality, but now I'd rather just stand up in front of people and play. It's like when I played baseball. When I was making a play or up at the plate, all the attention was on me. I was the focus, and I was focused. It's the same playing a show, only better because we're actually making a difference to people. Just by playing. Making them happy, or whatever. I don't care about the rest of it now. This tour will be the best thing we've ever done.'

Owen was leaning halfway across the table and his eyes

were serious and staring, his jaw clenched. It wasn't until later that I wondered whether his look of determination was because he believed what he was saying, or was determined to convince himself that he believed it. I'm still not sure. At that moment, though, I knew exactly what we wanted to do and who we were. I picked up the newspaper and shook it open.

NOONE COMES CLEAN
Congressman acknowledges paternity and faces down strange verbal assault

I turned to the back to find our review.

'Do you think she'll come back?' Owen was staring at the review, tracing his finger across one line, over and over.

I knew which line it was without looking any closer. 'Only if she wants to.' If I'd been honest I would have said no.

'I wish I could go and tell her what – ' Owen pushed his coffee mug from one hand to the other. 'I'd tell her that when I saw her on that street corner in New York I wanted to think of something to say to her, like in a movie, something that would be funny and make her want to have a coffee with me. And how, when she came home that day with the newspaper, if I could have found something to say I would have, but it wasn't until then, when I knew that she was leaving, that I realized I wasn't the same without her.' He looked straight into my eyes. 'Every night I put on "Careless Love" and listen to it over and over and the only thing I hear on that recording is her voice. That's the only reason the song is any good, because of Anna, and it's the only thing I can hear anymore. I fall asleep listening to her voice.' He started rubbing the words again. 'I don't think I can ever play that song again.'

We stood backstage watching the warm-up band, a trio that played instrumentals. We were going to get on our tour bus and start driving for San Diego as soon as we finished our set. Stuart Means stood next to Owen, leaning against a wall and nodding his head along with the music, and Ron was there, too. We'd had two tickets sent to Jack Noone's office, but hadn't seen him anywhere. We sent the tickets because it was the only thing we could do. It was the only way we could say he hadn't won. The only way to show we were still in charge.

Stuart Means introduced us. He hadn't the night before – nobody had; nobody usually did. But he wanted to introduce us because this show was being recorded for a radio broadcast, and it was our send-off, he said, for the tour. As we stood in the wings, Stuart Means walked out to the microphone. Our guitars stood in stands behind him. A smattering of applause and whistling greeted him.

'Hi, I'm Stuart Means from Pacific Records,' he said and paused. There was no reaction. 'Tonight's headliners are just about to head off on a tour that will take them across the country and back, ending up right here in L.A. for New Year's Eve. There's no need to tell you who they are – they've got a Top Ten album and they've been all over the newspapers and television the last two days – so please welcome L.A.'s own Owen Noone and the Marauder.'

The noise from the audience filled the entire room. We passed Stuart as we took the stage, and he said something to us, but we couldn't hear, the audience noise rising a few decibels higher when they saw us. We picked up our guitars and switched on the amps, Owen and I both testing out our guitars to make sure they were more or less in tune and that everything was working. Then we stepped to the microphones and I looked over at Owen, waiting for my cue.

'Thanks, everybody,' he said. 'Somewhere at the back, Jack Noone is watching.' A mixture of boos and cheers – nobody knew how to react – rose in the air. 'So if you see him, be nice. Buy him a drink or something and try to convince him that rock 'n' roll isn't ruining the youth of today.' Owen gave me a sideways glance and nodded to indicate he was going to start: 'Jaaaaaaaaaawwwwwwwnnn Henry –' My arm pumped across the guitar strings and the crowd began shouting, some of them singing along. Owen Noone and the Marauder were in command.

What Owen said at breakfast was right. For that hour and a half we were making a difference to people, more of a difference than anything else we did. Attacking Jack Noone seemed like sport in comparison. It didn't do anything. It was a sideshow that nobody took seriously except for us, except for Owen. This was what people wanted: two clanging guitars and a pile of songs so, for a little while, they could forget everything else or remember what they wanted to, feeling for a short time that little bit of joy at watching and hearing something that extended through them, something simple that they understood or that they didn't need to understand. It was about believing in the two people onstage, in their – in our – ability to make nothing else matter. Owen asked the crowd to sing extra loudly for Jack Noone when we got to 'Yankee Doodle," and while they sang, while we played, it was the most important thing in the world for a thousand people, but it didn't mean anything beyond those five minutes of the song. When people got home the next morning and told their friends about the great show, something would already be lost in the telling, and when they put on their CDs and listened to 'Yankee Doodle," they'd recapture a thread of it again, but only a thread. Then they'd get older and have bills to pay and kids to chase, and eventually they'd find Owen Noone and the Marauder at the bottom of a stack of CDs and put it on, and that little strand of memory would almost find its way back. And they'd smile and remember how fun it was when they were younger.

We didn't see Jack Noone. I don't know if he was even there. I imagined him standing at the back in a suit, shifting from foot to foot, wondering why he had even bothered. But this is just what I imagined. He wasn't really there. When the show was over we got onto the tour bus, stopping to sign autographs for the handful of people who'd waited by the back door for an hour, but we didn't talk to them. It was midnight and our bus was heading down the highway towards San Diego. Our four months of traveling and playing had begun. It was the worst four months of my life.

I think things started falling apart when we got to Charlotte. Maybe it was inevitable that it would go bad in Charlotte, or maybe it just seems that way now. All across the Southwest and into the Southeast, the tour was great. We'd arrive in a town, and sometimes we'd walk around during the day. It was getting hard to do that, though, in some towns like San Diego and Dallas, because a lot of people had seen the press conference and recognized Owen. But we were happy to be out of Los Angeles with nothing to think about except playing songs. When we finished playing, we got back on the bus and were driven to the next city, the next concert hall filled with people who had paid twenty dollars to see us play.

We arrived in Charlotte three weeks after the press conference and the start of our tour. We hadn't really lived in Charlotte for very long, but it still felt like a homecoming of sorts. Not as much as going to Iowa City did and not like when we drove through Peoria, but somewhere in between. We'd played in every bar in Charlotte, it seemed. It's where we'd sent out demos, doubled our repertoire and played countless games of pool. The only reason we'd left was the hurricane.

So it was pleasant, almost calming to see the familiar streets, the familiar buildings and parks as our bus drove across Charlotte to the university, where we were playing that night. It was close to noon, the sun at the top of the sky, the shadows short along the ground.

'I can't decide,' Owen said as the bus arrived at the field house, 'whether or not I want to go by the house.'

I'd been thinking about this, too. Of course it meant more to Owen than to me, but I'd been thinking about what it must look like, whether the lawn was overgrown, the shutters falling off, or whether it looked like people still lived there. I don't know why Owen hadn't sold it. Maybe he wanted to move back there eventually, or maybe he couldn't sell it, maybe the papers weren't actually in his name. I thought of when we'd opened the basement door and the water was halfway up the stairs, the book bumping against the step, and knew that I didn't want to see it again. 'I don't.'

'You're right. Neither do I.'

A kid from the university radio station wanted to interview us. Owen didn't want to do it, but I made him. I remembered when I was doing my show at WCBU and how much I would have liked to interview the bands that came to Bradley.

'Aren't we kind of above this now?' Owen said as we walked across the campus to the building that housed the radio station.

'No. No way. Never.'

'But we're like one of the top ten bands in the country. We shouldn't have to do these little college stations.'

'We don't have to. We want to.'

'No. I don't.'

'Yes you do, Owen. When we first started, when "Yankee Doodle" came out, who played it? Not K-rock and shit like that. College stations. Kids like this guy who wants to interview us. Kids like me. They're the people who actually care about this music, who think it matters whether or not anyone else does and whether or not it's in the Top Ten, the top one hundred, or nowhere at all. We wouldn't be riding around the country in a bus playing songs for people if it weren't for the likes of this kid. So we want to do it.'

'Okay. But if Stuart Means had told us to do it, we wouldn't have.'

'Stuart Means is an asshole. And he's not asking. I am. I'm not some executive, I'm not some A&R guy. I'm your friend. There's a difference.'

'Okay. Okay.'

The radio studio was in the basement of the student union, a small series of three windowless rooms that looked like its architect's original intention was for it to be a deluxe broom closet. Our interviewer, a junior named Josh Givens, led us down a corridor to the studio, the walls of which were covered with posters of various bands. I pointed at the Owen Noone and the Marauder poster, which was the same photograph as our album cover, a picture Anna had taken of Owen's broken-down Bronco before we'd left it behind in Colorado.

'Did you put that up for our benefit?'

It was supposed to be a joke, but Josh's mouth fell open. 'No – it's been – we've had it up for – for ages. Really.'

I smiled and told him I was just kidding. He laughed nervously and pushed his hand through his hair before showing us into the studio where a girl was playing a Velvet Underground song. Microphones were set up for us, and we sat down. The girl who was DJing stayed at the control board and when the Velvet Underground finished she put on "Will You Wear Red?". As it finished, she told Josh she was turning on the microphones. A few seconds later he began talking.

'This is WNCC, North Carolina-Charlotte Radio. I'm Josh Givens and with me here in the studio are Owen Noone and the Marauder, who are playing on campus tonight. That last song you heard was their single, "Will You Wear Red?," from their album, 'Wanderin',' which is number one on the *CMJ* chart and in the *Billboard* Top Ten, too.' He looked towards us. 'Guys, you've had an incredible amount of success since the release of your first record with Pulley last year, and now this new album is on a major label. How has this success changed things for you?'

'It hasn't changed much of anything for us,' I said.

Owen jumped in. 'Well, it has, some things. We have to do things we don't want to now, and we didn't before.'

'Like what?' Josh asked.

'Oh, you know, work with people we don't like, be nice to horrible celebrities, go wherever our label tells us to go, that kind of thing.'

'Isn't it worth it, though? I mean, you guys are living a dream, aren't you? People all over the country listen to your music, read interviews with you in magazines, put your posters on their walls, wear your T-shirts.'

'The thing is,' Owen said, 'That's all nice and everything, I mean we're not exactly complaining, but these people don't really know us, and I don't get why they want to read about us or be like us. We just play music, you know? That's all I want, people to like my music. Our music.'

'Some people have complained that it's costing too much to like your music with concert tickets costing twenty bucks.'

'Yeah, I don't get that. We don't set the prices. It's not our fault. We used to play for three dollars when we first started, and we set that price. But so many of these decisions – they're not ours, you know? We're not rich from this, and neither is our record label, yet. They give us money to make an album, and then everything else is theirs, until they make it back. We can't play for three dollars and eat. Besides, if it's too much, people don't have to come.'

'But they want to. Because they like your music. I'm not trying to accuse you of anything. I'm just asking for your opinion.'

'Yeah, yeah, I know. We get all the blame for these things. But really, we're just as powerless in it as anyone. We used to drive ourselves around when we toured last year. But now, they make us have a bus and a tour manager, and another bus just for the roadies. So we have all that. For two people. It's ridiculous. But it's how things are done, so we do them.'

'You were recently in the news all across the country for your actions at your father's press conference. What were you trying to say?'

Owen inhaled slowly, then let the air creep out for several seconds before he answered. 'Imagine if it were you,' he said. 'How would you feel? What would you do?'

'A lot of people say that you were just doing it as a publicity stunt.'

'Fuck those people.' Josh's face turned to a look of horror when Owen said fuck. 'Oh, sorry. I can't say that on radio, can I? Sorry. But those people have no idea. It's not something I want to talk about anymore.'

'Okay,' Josh said. 'I've got just one more question. Anna Penatio sang on "Careless Love" on your first album and at most of your gigs, and this was one of the real crowd-pleasers, one of your defining songs. But she's not on this tour. Who is she, and why is she gone?'

I felt my whole body go rigid and opened my mouth to speak, but couldn't think of anything to say.

Owen was silent for several seconds. Then he started talking, leaning very close to the microphone. 'That's not something either of us is prepared to talk about, Josh.'

Josh's face went pale. 'Ss-sorry.'

Owen waved his hand. 'Don't be sorry. It's just an unresolved private issue and we don't feel it would be appropriate to speak about it.'

'Well, thank you very much Owen Noone and, um, the Marauder for coming in to talk to us. They're playing tonight at the University of North Carolina-Charlotte and it's sold out, but you might be able to get a ticket from a scalper or something –'

'We've got two tickets we can give to the first person who calls and tells us the names of the two bands we played with the last time we played at this university,' Owen said.

Josh's face crumpled in confusion before growing into

a grin. 'Yeah – okay. So there you go, two free tickets for that. Call now. This next song is another by our guests. The title track from their current album, 'Wanderin'.' The girl at the control board turned off the microphones and our song began to play, my off-key voice rising above the soft guitar.

'Where was the gig?' asked Josh.

'It was some springtime outdoor party or something,' I said, 'And we lied that we were students. It was in a field on campus. A couple years ago. But what were those other bands called?'

'I don't remember,' Owen said. 'That's the point.' He waved his hand at Josh. 'Just give them to the first person who calls. We'll put their names on the guest list.'

By the end of the next week our bus was driving through the Holland Tunnel and we were back in New York City. It was our twelfth city in three and a half weeks and already we felt like going home and just sitting around the house, doing nothing. There wasn't anything exciting or fun about playing anymore. We didn't think about the songs, we just went out and played them, and the people watching and listening didn't matter to us like they used to. The crowd reaction was the thrill of playing live, when the energy level out in front of the stage lifted, lifting us with it. We used to vary things, play the songs a little differently each time, but now it was just another night, another city, another venue filled with another several hundred people, and we felt like we were just there to do a job, and we did it with all the enthusiasm of workers in a canning factory. We didn't even care about the attention, about the boys and girls who hung around in the parking lots waiting to talk to us and trying to sleep with us. It had never mattered to me that much before, but it had been flattering. Now it was just irritating and I found myself wanting to tell them all to fuck off.

But New York City was different. It seemed like nothing bad could happen in that city, the place where we'd stumbled into our first real gig and our first record contract. That's how it felt, anyway, and when we came out of the tunnel and into Manhattan, we were like kids on vacation, pressing our hands to the windows to look at the passing landscape. New York City was going to be different. We were playing at CBGB's, we'd insisted on it, and Ed was going to film the whole second night for our video. So we had a new energy. We felt a little like we were making a fresh start, and it felt good.

We met with Ed a few hours before the gig to discuss the video. The idea was simple, just a bunch of live footage with the song playing over it. We wanted it to look as cheap as possible and to achieve this we agreed that we'd just do it as cheaply as possible: Ed had one camera, and he would walk around the stage filming whatever he wanted to. Pacific had given us a ridiculously large budget, all of which we gave to Ed. He was starting NYU next year and the money we gave him was enough to pay his tuition at least twice.

We'd put Dave Ferris on the guest list, and he came backstage to talk to us while the opening act was playing. It made me think of when I'd met him after we'd opened for Kid Tiger. While they were self-destructing onstage I'd signed the memo that had started our career. I started wishing that we'd stayed with Pulley, with Dave Ferris, in New York. But that was out of our hands. It hadn't really been our decision – we couldn't have denied Dave the money he needed – and a lot of other things wouldn't have happened if we'd stayed. There wasn't any point in thinking about what might have happened and what didn't happen. We were living the lives we wanted to live. We just had to accept that there were things that went along with that lifestyle that we couldn't control.

We were introduced by a DJ from the radio station that was cosponsoring the show, and as we walked out to pick up our guitars, Ed's camera followed behind. Owen put his hand on my shoulder. 'Hold on a second,' he said. I turned. The crowd was still cheering and clapping, and I leaned towards Owen to hear him. 'We have to play our best tonight.'

'Right,' I said.

'No, I mean it. We really have to concentrate and play like we mean it, like it's the only time we'll ever play again.'

I didn't like his choice of words. 'Okay, sure.'

'Because I put Anna on the guest list,' he said. 'Do you think she'll come?'

I exhaled upward, my breath blowing my hair. 'I don't know. How would she know?'

'Because she'd see it advertised, and when she couldn't get a ticket maybe she'd hope that I'd thought of her.'

'Owen, I think –'

He squeezed my shoulder, hard. 'But we'll play like she can hear.'

'Okay.' I walked across to my guitar and picked it up and the crowd got even louder.

Ed was right in front of the stage, his camera pointed up. I tested my guitar and Owen did the same. The crowd was still cheering with all its energy. I looked at Owen and then at the camera and then out at the dark shapes of the people who were cheering, and started strumming the C-chord that begins "John Henry" very slowly, just dragging the pick across the strings once every two seconds or so, slow enough that each individual note of the chord could be heard separately. After a few strums the crowd started clapping in time so there was a clap and a strum almost in unison. Little by little the clapping started getting faster and I followed it, gradually quickening my pace until, after a couple of minutes, the clapping was a thunder of applause and whistling and cheering and my arm was pumping as fast as it could across the strings. Owen stood still and silent behind his microphone and when I looked over at him I saw that his eyes were closed and his head was moving in a shallow nod. My arm was sore from moving so fast and I changed the pace of my strumming, just hitting down on the strings once a second instead of churning back and forth across them. I looked over at Owen again and he opened his eyes, returned my look, nodded once, smiled and faced the crowd, and screamed into the microphone: 'Jaaaaaaaaaaawwwwwwwwwwwwwnnnnnnnnnn Henry.' And we were off.

We stood backstage listening to the applause that was trying to coax us back for a second encore. We'd just played "Yankee Doodle," the song we always ended with. But the house lights hadn't been turned back on and everyone was clapping and shouting and whistling and waiting for us to come back and play something else. Owen and I stood next to each other, catching our breath and staring out at the empty stage and the darkness beyond it. We had to go back out and play something.

'Come on.' Owen started walking and I followed him out, deafened by the noise. We picked up our guitars and I made sure mine was more or less in tune. I had no idea what song we were going to play. It didn't seem right to end with something other than "Yankee Doodle," but it also seemed stupid to play it again. We stood, side by side, looking at the faces in the front row and at Ed and his camera.

'This is the only city where we'll play this song,' Owen said, then added after a pause, 'Until further notice.' People cheered, although I don't think they knew what song was coming. I knew. 'This is for Anna, who might be here, and might not be here.' Owen closed his eyes and sang, and I watched. His guitar just hung in front of him, the head angled towards the floor, and his voice started cracking as he got to the fourth verse:

> *I cried last night and the night before,*
> *I cried last night and the night before,*
> *I cried last night and the night before,*
> *I'll cry tonight and cry no more.*

The last three words were almost inaudible, and as we returned to the chorus, I leaned towards my microphone and started singing, keeping my eye on Owen. My voice gave him some reassurance, and he wiped the corner of his eye with the heel of his hand and kept singing, his voice regaining a little strength. I continued singing with him, trying with moderate success to harmonize, but neither of us could really sing, so it didn't make much difference either way. We sang on into the fifth verse:

> *Lord, I wish that train would come,*
> *Lord, I wish that train would come,*
> *How I wish that train would come*
> *And take me back where I come from.*

As though he'd just remembered that he had it, Owen started playing his guitar on the next chorus and when we got to the sixth verse he stepped on his pedal, pushing the volume up but singing just as quietly as before until we'd gotten to the chorus, when we both began to crescendo to end the song, both of us playing our guitars hard, Owen's neck straining as he howled, his eyes closed, on his toes as though he was trying to lift himself into the air. We let the last chord ring and stood together on the stage. I placed my hand on his shoulder, both of us oblivious to the noise being made by the audience and oblivious to the camera, which was two feet in front of us and four feet below.

We met Ed the next morning for breakfast at the only café we'd ever been to in New York City, the only café we knew. Ron sat on the other side so he wasn't in the way. In fact, Ron spent most of his time on the tour being not in the way, which suited us fine. Ed brought his camera along because he wanted to do some kind of interview to go either at the very beginning or very end of the video. He sat across from Owen and me with the camera on his shoulder, asking us questions. We liked Ed. He was genuine, we trusted him, and so we told him he could ask us anything he wanted as long as we had final say about what went in the video. He started by asking the kinds of questions you see in fanzines and stuff.

'What's the best thing about touring?'

'Playing a good show to a good crowd.'

'Worst?'

'Always eating in restaurants.'

'Sitting in a bus all day,' I added.

'Does your bus have beds, or just seats?'

'Beds and seats.'

'What's your favorite song, of your own?'

'Not this one.'

'Seriously, though.'

'"Wild Mizzourye."'

'"John Henry."'

'Not "Yankee Doodle?"'

'Yeah, okay, that, too.'

'What would you like to say to your father?'

Owen lifted his middle finger.

'What about you?'

What about me? I stared into the black circle, imagining my father was inside there somewhere. I could feel the blood pushing through the veins in my neck. I didn't know what I wanted to say to my father or my mother, or even if there was anything I could say. I almost never thought about them. I thought about them now, though, and I wondered what they were doing, what they were having for breakfast and what they thought of me, whether they knew what I was doing, and where I was. 'I don't know.' I shoveled too much scrambled egg into my mouth, little pieces of curdled yellow protein falling from the corners and back onto my plate.

'If you could change one thing, what would it be?'

Owen looked out into the street. It was cold and gray and raining, the drops slicing down at an angle and pelting the glass, making a tapping sound like when you touch a microphone to see if it's on. 'The one thing I'd change,' he said, still looking through the water-beaded glass, 'Would be to have her back. To not have fucked that up. I don't care about the other things as much, because I can't do them without her. She always used to tell me when I was being stupid, and she'd listen to me whine without telling me to shut up, and I think I could actually do better things if she were still here. She listened to me.' Ed brought his head out from behind the camera and looked at me to see if he should keep recording, then slowly lowered the camera from his shoulder. 'And I listened to her. I hardly ever listen to anyone. I think we just knew each other, how each other thought. But I fucked it up, I was too stupid, I —' Owen slapped both of his palms on the table making the plates and silverware jump and pushed himself out of his chair. 'Holy shit.' He raced from the café and into the rainy street, looked both left and right, then ran down the block and out of sight.

We drove up to Boston after breakfast and played a show there, then left immediately for Buffalo. After Owen had come back to the café, he told us why he'd run out. He'd seen someone walking in a blue and green raincoat with the hood pulled over. He'd seen a glimpse of her face and had run down the block, blowing away the little drops of rain that fell on his lips, trying to find that blue and green raincoat. He'd run seven blocks, all the way to Houston. But he hadn't found her. Had she been to the show? Had she walked by there on purpose knowing that it was the only place we'd be the morning after a New York City gig? He'd come back into the café soaked, his gray T-shirt darkened with rain, his hair matted to his forehead and over his ears. Ed had picked the camera back up and filmed Owen as he walked across the narrow dining area to our table. Owen put his hand out towards the lens, but didn't touch it, just slowly waved at it. 'Put that thing away, Ed,' he said in a normal, tired voice. 'Just turn it off and put it away.'

The bus rolled west towards Buffalo through the

forested foothills of the Adirondacks, and I lay in my bed – it was dark, and there was little, if anything, to see – listening to the hum of the tires, feeling the little bumps as we crossed each section of concrete, trying to sleep. I was too tired to sleep and lay there in the dark with my eyes open, staring into nothing. I heard a rustling and scraping noise and then Owen was in front of me on his hands and knees, at eye level, and even in the dark I could see that his eyes were red, that he was about to cry.

'Are you awake?' he whispered.

'Yes.'

Without saying anything else he climbed into my bed and I moved over to make space for him without even thinking about it. We lay there about three inches apart, face to face, and I could see Owen's tears catching what little light there was as they rolled down his cheeks. We were silent for a long time, the only sound our breathing and the hum of the tires.

'I miss her,' Owen said softly, his voice cracking. 'I want her back.' He wiped his nose with the shoulder of his T-shirt. 'Everything I've had I've fucked up. When she came home that day, when she was mad, I thought, what's her problem, it's no big deal, it's nothing, and she's over-reacting.' He didn't say anything for a long time, and we just stared at each other. 'I really thought I saw her walking by on the street, and my whole body just convulsed, like somebody had poured boiling milk into my veins. Does that make sense? And I ran, knowing that if I could just find her, I could tell her – I don't know.' Owen wiped his eyes and nose on his shoulder again. 'I just want her back. I need her back. I'd quit playing music, if it meant I could spend every single day with Anna.' Owen's chest shook as he tried to stop himself from crying, wrapping his arms around himself. Then I put my arms around him, pulling him closer, whispering shhhh, like I was calming an infant, until we both fell asleep.

We awoke in a parking lot in Buffalo, the sunlight filling the bus and making it hot. We were both sweaty with body heat and sun. And hungry. I got out of the bed and walked along the aisle towards the front of the bus, looking out into the small parking lot of the place where we were playing that night. Ron wasn't on the bus and neither was Rory, our bus driver, and the door was locked. I wasn't sure what time it was. It was either late morning or early afternoon. I looked up at the sun and then at the brick wall of the building. Owen came down the aisle and stood next to me, both of us silent and waiting. For what, I don't know.

Rory came back about an hour later, and Owen and I were still standing there feeling like maybe we'd never move again. His keys jangled as he put the right one into the lock and opened the door. He climbed up into the bus, grinning. Rory was always grinning. He was about forty, I'd guess, small and skinny, with a spider web tattoo spread across his left arm and several others on his right. He'd been a cook or something in the Navy but was honorably discharged after an accident involving frying oil that had burned his left hand so badly the pinkie and ring fingers were fused together.

'You boys sleep well?' he asked, sweeping his hair across his bald spot with the fused finger.

'Yeah,' Owen said. 'I guess so.'

'Good, good. Long drive last night. Best thing to do was sleep.' He was still grinning. 'Almost fell asleep myself – no, just kidding.' He gave a phlegmy laugh, then took a pack of cigarettes from his shirt pocket and slid one out with the fused finger.

When we got to Cleveland four days later there was a message for us to call Stuart Means. Owen phoned but then held the phone to me.

'He wants to talk to you.'

'Can't you do it? Or Ron? Isn't that his job?'

'That's what I said. He said he's got to talk to you.'

I took the phone and asked Stuart what was so important.

'You haven't seen any newspapers, have you?'

'No.' I was immediately nervous. Newspapers, it seemed, were always telling us things we should have learned somewhere else. 'Why?'

'Look,' Stuart said, his voice becoming quieter and slower. 'I know you don't like me very much, and this is not something you're going to want to hear, especially not from me. But I have to tell you this –'

'Stuart, what?'

There was a long pause during which I could hear Stuart breathing slowly. Owen was staring at me with one eyebrow arched in a quizzical look.

'There's an AP report in the *Times* today. Your – parents' house burned down. Your parents, they – were in there. They died. I'm sorry to be the one to tell you.'

'Stuart,' I said, and then didn't know what else to say. I held the phone to my ear for a long time, looking at Owen and trying to remember what my house looked like and my parents' faces, the phone to my ear, trying to remember where I was, who I was and trying to make it seem real.

USA Today, October 1, 1998:

HOUSE FIRE CLAIMS LIVES OF ROCKSTAR'S PARENTS

(AP) Delphi, Indiana – An overnight blaze in this small Midwest town has claimed the lives of Robert and Jean Brannigan, the parents of rocker Marauder, one half of the top-selling duo Owen Noone and the Marauder. Faulty electrical wiring is being blamed for the fire, which started at approximately three a.m. local time Thursday, according to fire department investigators. Arson has been ruled out.

Owen Noone and the Marauder are currently on a national tour. Their label refused to comment until the band had been notified.

The incident pushes the duo to non-music related national attention once again. Last year they began making headlines for their opposition to California Senatorial candidate Jack Noone, estranged father of singer/guitarist Owen Noone.

No funeral plans have yet been made.

'I have to stop the tour,' I said to Owen. We were sitting with Ron at the bar of the place we were supposed to play that night, drinking Coke and staring at the newspaper Owen had run out and bought. 'I can't play.'

'I leave this decision to you,' Owen said. 'This – I don't know what the right thing to say is. Whatever you do, whatever you want to do – I'll do what you want. I'll do whatever you tell me to.'

The gig was supposed to start in about four hours. Ron said I should do what I thought was best. I called Stuart Means back to apologize for hanging up on him and to tell him that we'd be taking a few days out from our tour, after tonight. We'd play in Cleveland, I decided. There was no reason not to play. But then we'd skip Detroit and Chicago and Milwaukee and probably Madison, too, depending on what happened. I had no idea what all the legal things I was supposed to do were. Suddenly this was all I could think about. So we'd play in Cleveland but that was it until I figured out what was going on, until after the funeral. I wondered when the funeral was going to be, and then realized that that was probably something I had to decide. What was even left, I wondered. What would be shown at a funeral? I didn't even really know who I was supposed to invite. Or whether people were invited to funerals, or just showed up. I knew a few of my parents' friends, people I remembered vaguely from growing up, but I didn't know who their new friends might be. I didn't even, if I was honest, know who my parents were anymore, what changes had happened in the past couple years. And they didn't know who I was. And they wouldn't.

So we played that night in Cleveland, and it was horrible. I just stood in one place moving my arm across the strings and making the shapes of the chords like a robot. Everybody in the audience knew what happened. At least, that's the way I felt. I looked out and saw all these strangers' faces looking at me, and I imagined they were all pitying me. Maybe I wanted them to pity me. When Owen announced that the next song was "Wanderin'," somebody shouted, We love you, Marauder. I almost said, No, you don't, into the microphone, but caught myself. They didn't love me. They didn't even know my real name. We love you, Marauder. No, you don't. And I sang:

> *My daddy was an engineer,*
> *My brother drove a hack,*
> *My sister takes in washin'*

And the baby balls the jack.
And it looks like
I ain't never gonna cease my wanderin'.

It didn't even make sense, I started thinking. None of this made any sense. None at all.

The house I grew up in, where my parents lived for however long, was nothing. It was just a blackened frame, parts of walls, some cement and charred linoleum. These are not the kinds of things you're supposed to see.

I stood on the sidewalk in front of the house. A couple of fire investigators were climbing over the debris on the ground floor and there was that yellow plastic tape all around the property and a police car in the driveway. A policeman stood next to me but neither of us was talking. I could feel the neighbors peering through their curtains, clucking their tongues, shaking their heads, saying to themselves how sad it was and what a horrible son I was that it took something like this to get me to come back home. The day was cold but bright, and I stood looking at the burned house, shading my eyes with my hand.

I don't think I'd eaten since Stuart had phoned, and my stomach felt like someone was pressing a fist into it and holding it there. I met with all kinds of people: the undertaker, the police, neighbors, the minister at the church, a lawyer, and after two days there was a funeral, with whatever was left of my parents' remains. They were buried in the same graveyard as their parents, all of whom had lived in Delphi, too. Lots of people told me they were sorry and I nodded, my mind blank, my body feeling like it belonged to someone else. There might have been a couple of reporters there from the local newspaper, or maybe from the Associated Press. I don't know. It was as though I did everything by reflex. Owen had gone on to Chicago. I'd told him not to come.

I left Delphi after two days. I felt wrong, like I should stay. But I went. There was nothing else I could do. I went to Chicago.

Owen and I met in a restaurant called Ed Debevic's. It had a theme. It was supposed to be an authentic representation of a place like Randall's, the roadside diner near Mammoth Cave, except it was very big and very loud and the wait staff were rude to you. This was part of the charm, apparently.

I had to push my way through all the people standing around to find the booth where Owen was sitting. There seemed to be too many not eating, not working, just talking. I slid onto the bench opposite him and felt happy to see my friend. I felt like I was back in a situation in which I knew what to do, how to act and what was expected of me.

'I don't know whether to show you this or not,' Owen said, his hand on a folded newspaper that lay on the table. Buddy Holly was singing "That'll Be the Day," and we had to shout to hear each other.

'It can't be anything worse than usual,' I said. 'What's Jack Noone done now?'

'Not Jack Noone,' Owen said. 'Rory.'

'The bus driver?'

'He's not our bus driver anymore.'

I tapped the table with my index finger. 'What did he do? Drunk driving or something?'

'No, no. It's nothing like that.'

I didn't understand why Owen didn't just show me the

newspaper. I suddenly imagined Rory being a serial killer or something. A waitress came over and sat down next to me.

'How're you boys doin' today?' She chewed a large piece of gum like it was cud.

'I've been better,' I said.

'Aww, too bad,' she said, patting my shoulder. I started to wish she'd go away. 'So, what do you boys do? Students?'

'We're rockstars,' Owen said.

She rolled her eyes. 'Right. Big time rockstars. What are you called?'

'Owen Noone and the Marauder.'

The waitress slapped the table. 'Bullshit.'

'That's not exactly professional,' I said.

'Bull-shit. You guys are not Owen Noone and the Marauder. Your tour was cancelled or whatever. I was supposed to go. You're full of shit.'

'We're them,' Owen said.

'Prove it.'

Owen picked up the newspaper and as he unfolded it I realized it was the *National Enquirer*. I was suddenly tense. The paper fell open and on the front page was a picture of two men laying arm in arm in a narrow bed. Owen and me.

National Enquirer, October 3, 1998:

OUT OF THE CLOSET!
SHOCKING TRUTH ABOUT OWEN NOONE AND THE MARAUDER

This exclusive photograph uncovers the truth behind the secret lives of rock 'n' rollers Owen Noone and the Marauder. Snapped by a source close to the duo, this photo obtained by the *Enquirer* proves that they are in fact more than just bandmates. The source, who prefers to remain anonymous but who has accompanied the rockers throughout their current tour, said, 'We knew something was up between those two, but I was surprised to find out the truth.'

Apparently the two lie arm-in-arm every night as they travel from city to city. Sources suggest that an earlier relationship between Owen Noone and actress Ellen Trelaine – a story first broken by the *Enquirer* – may have been no more than a stunt on the part of Owen to deflect any questions about his and his partner's sexuality.

The duo's record label, Pacific, did not wish to comment on the most sensational 'outing' since George Michael, stating simply that the band was currently taking a personal hiatus and would be resuming their tour soon.

'So is it true?'

Owen and I both stared at the waitress.

'What do you think?'

'Seems unlikely.'

Owen had told Ron to fire Rory immediately. Rory'd shaken Owen's hand when he left and grinned, saying, 'No hard feelings, eh?' Owen didn't say anything and just watched him walk away. Then he called Stuart Means.

'Stuart, have you seen this thing?'

'I saw it. They phoned me about it before it went out.'

'Why didn't you deny it?'

'I didn't know what they had – whether it was true.'

'Stuart, you dickhead. Do you ever do anything for us? Anything at all? Or do you just think, "Well, Pacific will get its name in the paper – any publicity is good publicity?" Do you actually give a shit about what happens to us?'

'Of course. I just didn't know. If I'd been able to get in touch with you guys, I would've countered.'

'Right. We're not going to start the tour again until Lawrence. Send us a new bus driver. Tell him if he so much as thinks about bringing his fucking camera with him, I'll throw him in the road and drive the goddamn bus over him. And tell Ron to do his fucking job. Isn't he supposed to keep these things from happening?'

'Okay, Owen. It's not that big of a deal, you know. Threaten them with a lawsuit. They'll settle and print an apology.'

'I don't want an apology. I don't want to be in any more newspapers. I don't want to be lied about anymore. I'm sick of it. We're sick of it. Send a new bus driver.'

'Okay. Good news, by the way. Your album is number one on *Billboard*.'

Owen hung up.

Our new bus driver was a man called Darryl who was old enough to be our grandfather and called everyone 'chief.' He met us in Chicago and gave us a package of forwarded mail from Stuart Means.

'I'm supposed to tell you I don't have no camera, chief,' he said. 'I don't have no camera.'

'Good,' Owen said. 'Then we'll get along fine.'

We were going to go to Lawrence, a town we'd never been to, and maybe practice a little but mostly we planned to sit around. As Darryl drove us through Chicago towards the interstate, we started sifting through the envelopes in the bag Stuart Means had sent.

'Uh-oh,' Owen said. 'This one is for you.'

I took the envelope from his hand and immediately understood why he'd said uh-oh. It was addressed to me. Not to the Marauder, but to me, using my real name. The return address was my parents'. My hands began to tremble as I looked at it, not sure whether I wanted to open it. I turned it over several times as though I could just keep doing this for ever. I pulled one of the corners of the flap loose and wriggled my little finger inside, then slid it along the seal. There was a single piece of paper in the envelope. I took it out and before I unfolded it, I looked across the aisle to Owen, who was watching me.

'We can't go straight to Lawrence,' I said.

'I was thinking that, too. Iowa City?'

'Yes.'

'Darryl,' he shouted to the front of the bus, 'Do you know how to get to Iowa City?'

'I can look at the map.'

'Good. We're going to Iowa City.'

'You're the boss, chief.'

Ron looked back at us from his seat near the front but didn't say anything.

I pinched the fold of the paper between my thumb and forefinger and re-creased it several times. I wanted to read the letter as much as I didn't want to read it, wanted to know what was in it as much as I never wanted to find out what it said. I could never respond and that thought kept me paralyzed. Owen reached across and took the piece of paper from me, unfolded it and put it back in my hands. I looked down at it and started to read the letter. Aside from royalty checks and contracts, it was the only thing I'd seen with my real name on it in almost two years.

Dear Brian,

This is a difficult letter for us to write, because it has been so long. At church somebody's son had a CD of the band Owen Noone and the Marauder, and they showed it to us and said, doesn't it look like your son, this picture? Well, we knew straight away it was you and that when you'd phoned us that day from Iowa, that last time, that you'd stuck to your dream.

You'd worked just as hard at it as you always did at every-
thing, and we'd been wrong to think otherwise.

We're proud of you, son, and we wanted to tell you that.
Also that we love you, and always have despite the last two
years, which have been difficult for all three of us. But we're
proud of your success and glad that things have worked out
the way you wanted.

We listened to the CD and tried to like it. There were some
parts that were nice, but it wasn't really our cup of tea. But
we're proud that you've made something that so many other
people like and listen to.

We hope that maybe this Christmas you could come home
for a few days, so we could have a family dinner. You could
bring your friend Owen, too. We'd like to meet him very much.

We're proud of you and love you. Please drop us a line soon
to say hello, even if it's just a postcard. We miss you.

Love,
MOM & DAD

I read the letter again and again, too many times, staring at
some of the words for several minutes, thinking about
whether what I was doing and what my parents saw were
the same thing. Whether things had actually worked out the
way I wanted or whether I'd actually worked hard for
anything. I showed the letter to Owen.

'You're lucky,' he said, 'To have parents like that.'

'Dead.'

'But they were proud of you. They loved you. They
believed you were great. They knew you were great.'

'They were wrong.'

'No. They were right. Imagine, they spent two years
thinking about you, wondering how you were, hoping for

you, and then they find out that their son has gone on to do exactly what he told them and made a success of himself. And they don't begrudge him. They don't say it won't last or anything. They say great, good, our son is happy and so we're happy. They always loved you, even when they doubted you. You can't change the fact that they died, but you can know that all those things you wanted to say to them, you don't even have to say because they knew and they felt them, too. You've got this letter. You're lucky. You could have nothing. Or you could have television footage. You have this.' Owen folded the letter and pressed it against my chest. 'Don't lose it.'

We returned for the second time to Iowa City and I felt the tension ease out of my mind and body. All I wanted to do, and all Owen wanted to do, probably, was go to Fuzzy's, drink a couple beers and play "Yankee Doodle" like we had only one chance in the world. We knew Mike would let us play. This dingy bar in this Midwestern college town was our only real home and Mike was like an uncle or older brother who kept an open door and let us be ourselves. The first time we'd walked into Fuzzy's we were petrified, unrehearsed, just wanting to play music. Now we went into big clubs, bored, over-rehearsed and just wanting to leave. Just thinking about playing at Fuzzy's made us remember that first time, Owen Noone and the Marauder, psuedopunkfolk, (Famous in Peoria), two kids who wanted to bang on their Telecasters and scream into microphones, to feel blood and adrenaline pumping through every vein, to make people sing along to a nearly dead national song, to make people believe in rock 'n' roll and leprechauns.

We directed Darryl through the streets of Iowa City

to Fuzzy's. As he drove, he began to hum quietly, almost mumbling.

'What a minute – what song is that?' Owen asked.

'That's "Careless Love," chief. My mother used to sing it all the time.'

'You've never listened to our music, have you?'

'No. Don't care much about rock music, chief.'

'Do you like singing?'

'Sure do.'

'Do you want to sing "Careless Love" with me tonight?'

'Oh, I don't know about that. I ain't much of a singer.'

'We can't sing, either. Come on, it'd mean a lot if you'd sing it with us.'

Darryl turned the last corner and pulled around behind Fuzzy's, the brakes squeaking as the bus came to a stop. 'Yeah, all right. Not much else I can do this evening, is there?'

Owen slapped him on the back. 'It'll be great,' he said.

We walked into the darkness, waiting at the door for our pupils to adjust. Mike was behind the bar, his back to us.

'You got a band here tonight?' Owen shouted from the door, and we started towards the bar.

'Yeah,' Mike said without turning around. 'That's what the sign outside says.'

'How much would it cost to make them not play?'

'What's your problem?' He still hadn't turned around.

'I don't want to fucking hear them, that's what.'

'Listen, pal –' Mike turned around. 'Holy shit. Owen.' He smiled and laughed and clapped his hands on our shoulders. 'You guys want a drink? You want to play here tonight? I can arrange something with the other band – they can

268

play tomorrow or something.' He turned to me. 'I'm sorry about your parents. Really.'

I thanked him.

We paid the band that was scheduled twice what they would have made from the door. They moaned about how much they'd been practicing until we offered the money. Then they stopped. We went on at eight, Owen belting out the opening words of "John Henry" and the jangle and clash of our guitars speeding out of our amplifiers, a bar-full of students clapping and singing along. It felt like August 29, 1997 again. Like we were just starting out, except we weren't nervous or scared, we were just doing what we were supposed to be doing, playing these songs to a roomful of strangers, making them clap and shout and making ourselves happy with the adrenaline pouring through our chests and arms, down to our fingers and into the guitars, burned into electricity and screaming out of amplifiers and into the air.

Darryl sang along on "Careless Love," holding my microphone between his large hands as though it were a flower, and croaking the words in a beautiful dissonance with Owen. It was completely different from the way Anna's voice used to float above Owen's, but somehow it worked. He grinned the whole time, his eyelids slightly closed, eyebrows arched up on his forehead, the words coming without effort, spilling out into the bar:

> Lord, I wish that train would come,
> Lord, I wish that train would come,
> How I wish that train would come
> And take me back where I come from.

'This probably isn't the place to say it,' Owen said before we played the last song, 'But the past few months – the past few weeks – have been very hard for us. It's made me think a lot of things, and I'm not even sure about all of them. The thing I am sure of, though, is that you should always believe in your friends. That's all you've got. I don't know if that makes sense, but I hope it does. Everything people tell you – if they're not your friends, it doesn't matter. But you have to hold onto your friends, you have to trust your friends. It's the only thing that's made sense since – well, for a long time.'

Somebody shouted, Yeah, and a few people clapped, but then the bar was silent. Owen stared out into the space above their heads, and I stared at Owen. Then I looked into the audience and thought about the first time I'd looked into an audience at Fuzzy's, and how much it had scared me. If I hadn't followed Owen out to Iowa City that day, after my graduation, I wouldn't ever have known what I knew at this moment: that so much of what I'd spent my life learning and worrying about was nothing but dust on the top of a table. It could be easily wiped away, and under-neath was what really mattered, the wood, the shining varnish, the pattern of the grain. All that you needed was an Owen Noone, somebody to lean on, somebody to lean on you, and you could figure this out for yourself. We didn't need the Jack Noones, the Ellen Trelaines, the Stuart Meanses or anybody else to tell us who we were and what we were doing. We were Owen Noone and the Marauder and we were alive.

'This song,' I said, 'Is our first and our last. Sing along as loud as you can.' I played the introduction and the audi-ence joined in, beginning with the verse everybody knows,

'Yankee Doodle went to town.' When we got to the end, we played the chorus three times, louder each time, and then, instead of ending, I started singing the last verse again:

> *Yankee Doodle is the tune,*
> *Americans delight in,*
> *'Twill do to whistle, sing or play*
> *And just the thing for fightin'.*

We left the next morning for Lawrence, where we would still have a few days of nothing before we had to play. The last part of the tour, where we headed to the Northwest and came down the coast back to L.A., had more off days built into it, because the cities were further apart, and they were smaller, and so we had to play on certain nights in order to get the largest possible crowd. When we got to L.A., we'd have a whole week off before New Year's Eve and the end of the tour, the end of the traveling, the end of living on a bus, and, we hoped, the beginning of something else.

On Election Night we were driving between Boise and Seattle, a long drive across the mountains of the northeast corner of Oregon and all the way across Washington. We'd forgotten that it was even going on and weren't thinking about it. Neither of us had read a newspaper since that *National Enquirer* in Chicago. I was tired of finding out about myself in the newspaper and of other people knowing facts and lies about me long before I did. When we started the fight against Jack Noone the newspaper seemed like a great ally, especially after the interview with Paul Danielson; and the interviews with music critics always seemed fun, like we were giving exactly the information and image of ourselves we wanted to, but lately they just seemed to bring trouble. It wasn't until the next morning, when we were sitting in a diner in Richland, Washington, about two-thirds of the way to Seattle, that we found out. Darryl spotted the paper sitting on the table next to ours.

'Ain't it your father that was running for Senate?'

'Yeah. I've given up on that. I don't care anymore and I can't make any difference. Neither will he.'

'Paper there says the election was yesterday.'

Owen stopped spooning his oatmeal and looked over at the newspaper. All it said on the front was REPUBLICANS HOLD CONGRESS. FULL ELECTION RESULTS INSIDE. I reached over and unfolded it in front of Owen. All of us – Ron and the roadies were there, too – scanned it to see if there was an article about California. On the last page before all the listings, we found it.

USA Today, November 4, 1998:

California: NOONE SQUEAKS IN

Los Angeles – In the most public and bizarre Senatorial race in the country, Republican Jack Noone edged out his Democrat opponent, Benjamin Steffens, by just a 3 percent margin.

At his victory rally, Senator-elect Noone congratulated his opponent on running a clean, issue-based campaign before going on to say, 'Tonight represents a victory not just for me, not just for the Republicans, not just for the State of California, but for the moral causes that I have so strongly defended and promoted.'

Mr. Noone's campaign was fraught with controversy, most notably the constant accusations made by his estranged son, the rock musician Owen Noone. Asked about his son, Mr. Noone stated, 'Owen and I still have some things to reconcile, but I hope and pray and am confident that in the coming months we will come to a better understanding of each other.'

'Well, I guess that's it,' Owen said, folding the newspaper over so that the short article was on top and running his finger along the folds to crease them. 'I don't feel like I thought I would. I thought I'd throw a fit or something, at least be angry. But I'm not. I just feel empty, like after losing an unimportant baseball game. I guess that's good. It doesn't affect me much. It's not important.' He pushed his finger along the crease again. 'It's strange to admit that.'

When we got to Seattle, a package from Stuart Means was waiting for us. Ed had worked quickly and our video was ready. It didn't really matter in terms of promotion, since our album was still number one and the single, "Will You Wear Red?," was in the Top Ten. But here it was, another document of ourselves. The bus had a video player that we'd never used. We put in the tape and watched.

It began with footage from the breakfast after the show, with Owen and me sitting next to each other, just after Ed asked what the best thing about touring was. You didn't hear his question, just Owen's response: 'Playing a good show to a good crowd.' The song started immediately, Owen's first syllable followed by my banging guitar:

> O will you wear red, O my dear, O my dear?
> Will you wear red, Jennie Jenkins?
> I won't wear red, it's the color of my head.
> I'll buy me a twirley-whirley, sookey-lookey,
> Sally-Katty, double-lolly,
> Roll-the-find-me, roll, Jennie Jenkins, roll.

The picture froze on Owen and me in the café until the chorus, when it switched to the live footage and alternated frantically between Owen and me and from both of us to the crowd, always showing us both during the chorus, which we both sang. Not all of the footage was from when we were playing the song, it was from other songs, which made it odd in a good way, because the actions didn't always correspond to the music and our mouths. At one point, when Owen was singing the fifth verse, the image was of me singing "Wanderin'," which made it seem like I had Owen's voice. After the last 'Roll-the-find-me, roll, Jennie Jenkins, roll' the images switched back to the café, zooming in on Owen as he stared out the window preparing to answer Ed's unheard question about what one thing he'd change. 'The one thing I'd change,' Owen said on the screen, watching the rain hit the window, 'Would be to have her back.' The video ended and the screen turned to snow.

Ron shut off the VCR and turned to us. 'I like it, guys. Really cool. What do you think?'

'I like it,' Owen said after a long silence. 'Do you like it?'

'Yeah.' I was thinking about those last words and Owen staring out the window. I was thinking about Anna.

'You married, Darryl?' Owen asked.

'Yessir, chief. She died, though. Five years ago next week.' Darryl watched the interference on the television. 'I remember that last time I saw her. Never forget it. Visited her in that hospital room and she was asleep, or unconscious. She was almost dead, you see, and I just sat there holding that tiny, light hand, just talking to her about my day. After an hour I had to leave. Visiting hours were over so I got up and walked to the door, but when I got to the hallway I remembered something, what I hadn't told her, after talking about all those dumb things I'd done during the last day. So I went back to the room, peeked my head in and said, I love you, baby. But I couldn't see her. The nurse was blocking my view, and sometime that night she was gone, disappeared, dead.' Darryl wiped his forehead with his palm. 'I always thought it was dumb, that the last thing I said to her was that I'd mowed the lawn.'

MTV played the video nonstop, and the fans we talked to before and after shows would tell us how much they liked it. After being on television we were recognized more, and it was harder to eat in restaurants without people asking us for autographs or to take a picture. The last week of the tour was the busiest of the whole four months, because even though there was nothing else – no interviews, no houses burning, no newspaper articles surprising us, no elections – we were never alone. Our anonymity was gone. People pointed from across the street, interrupted our meals and crowded around our bus in little groups before and after our concerts. We wanted to be alone more than anything. We were tired of attention. We looked forward to Los Angeles when we could just sit in our house all day with nobody else around, no television, the radio off, just silence.

So we played Seattle and San Francisco, and then finally we were driving into Los Angeles. We were home. Darryl parked the bus in front of our house and he and Ron helped us carry our gear into the living room. Owen and I took Darryl and Ron and the roadies to a restaurant and bought them dinner, and afterwards we said goodbye. Darryl was staying in a hotel in Los Angeles that night and flying back home to Georgia the next morning. And now that we were back in Los Angeles, Ron's job was done.

Owen and I walked home, happy for the peace, happy not to be riding on the bus, happy to be able to sleep in our own beds for the first time since August, to sleep on something that wasn't going to move, to fall asleep in the same place we'd wake up. I wished we could see stars, but the sky was violet from the city lights. Looking at it reminded me of the color schemes of romance novel covers. I kept my eyes on the sidewalk in front of me and concentrated on not stepping on the cracks.

'What should we do after next week?' Owen asked.

I'd been thinking about it too. 'I don't know. Go away somewhere. Get out of L.A. for good I think.'

'Where?'

'I don't know. I feel like I should go back to Indiana, but I don't know why. I own an empty lot there now. I guess I should just sell it and never go back, but I don't know.'

'We could go back to Charlotte. Or Iowa City. Someplace quiet.'

'Someplace quiet. Where we don't have to do anything.'

'We can learn some new songs. Or start writing our own. We ought to be able to write our own by now.'

'I'd like it back in Iowa I think. We could play at Fuzzy's,' I said.

'Do you think Stuart is going to make us get another album out real fast?'

'Can't we just tell him to fuck off? We've made enough of a success out of him. He can claim all kinds of responsibility for us that he doesn't deserve, and his bosses will lap it up. I think he owes it to us to leave us alone.'

'I'd like to go find Anna. I'd like to try and tell her I'm sorry. I'd like to tell her I love her and all those other things, like Darryl said. I just mowed the lawn today or I went to the beach and the sunset was nice. I don't think those things are dumb. If I thought it would work I'd go to New York to her parents' farm and I'd just ask her to forgive me. I don't think I have the courage though.' Owen stopped walking. 'Would you help me write a letter?'

I stopped a few paces ahead of him. I'd helped him write a letter to his father. I wasn't going to help him write one to Anna. I didn't know what he wanted to say, and I didn't want to write what he told me.

'This is you. Owen Noone.' I poked my finger into his chest. 'No, I won't do it.'

Owen scratched the side of his face. 'I could sing a song for her, I could sing "Careless Love."'

'No! You can't!' I was shouting. 'That's bullshit — somebody else. Maybe it means something, maybe it means a little, but it doesn't mean you. If you weren't such a coward you'd just go, thinking about all the things you wanted to say, practicing a thousand different scenarios in your head, and then, when you got there, you'd see Anna and not even know what to say anymore, so you'd just say the fucking truth. You'd tell her that you love her, that you fucked up and then you'd run out of things to say because mostly what you want to say are things that don't have the right words to attach to them. That's what you should do. What you won't do.' I started walking again and the gap between us grew wider. 'Even I know that,' I muttered, not sure if Owen could hear me anymore, and I left him to walk home by himself.

I woke up late the next morning in my own bed, so glad to be in my own bed, and lay there for another hour watching the slice between the curtains, the dust falling through the shaft of sunlight that cut across the room. When I finally made it downstairs I saw Owen's breakfast littering the kitchen. Empty milk carton, dirty bowl, glass and soggy wheat flakes were plastered around the drain. I poured myself a mug of coffee and leaned against the counter, drinking slowly, enjoying the fact that there was nowhere to go and nothing to do.

Owen returned while I was drinking my second cup, waving some pieces of paper in the air like a stockbroker. 'I did it,' he said as he walked across the kitchen and stopped in front of me. 'I did it. I booked a flight to Syracuse. And rented a car, and I'll drive to Anna's parents' farm just like you said. That's what I'm going to do, leaving on New Year's Day.' He was still waving the paper around. 'I'm going to pull everything together. I'm going to make everything okay.' He stopped and took a step back. 'Let's play some songs.'

We set up our equipment in the living room and spent most of the day messing around, playing the songs we liked best and trying out a few new ones. We decided to pick something brand new, something we'd never played, for the New Year's Eve gig, to make it special. We decided on "Hallelujah, I'm a Bum." It was just a little song about being a tramp, like "The Big Rock Candy Mountains." We played it several times, and got it down. It was only two chords, so we fooled around with the pacing and style to make it fun. Learning a new song and thinking about playing it in front of people made me look forward to New Year's Eve. I hadn't really been looking forward to it otherwise, it just seemed like another thing we had to do, the final obstacle before we could just relax and try to be ourselves again.

When New Year's Eve arrived Owen and I were excited, energetic, ready to play, ready to make it our best performance, ready to have fun and then to disappear for a while. Two other bands played before us, so Owen and I spent most of the time backstage. We had a couple beers, but not enough to get drunk. We wanted to be in control of ourselves, to be sharp and to be able to channel the energy exactly as we wanted. Stuart Means was backstage as well, and we were in such good humor that we were nice to him. We'd seen him at Pacific headquarters earlier in the week and had told him we were taking at least six months off, if not the year, before we made another album. He agreed.

What we wanted tonight was to be memorable, to play our songs and make people happy, make them move, make them adore us. When we were introduced by Stuart the noise was so loud I thought, for a second, they'd never hear us over their own screaming. It got louder when we walked out and picked up our guitars, and I looked over at Owen. I could feel my pulse beating in my neck and wrists, the adrenaline spreading through my body. There wasn't anything else I would rather have been doing that night than playing guitar to a thousand people with my friend, Owen Noone.

We stood facing the crowd, listening to their cheers and applause. Without looking at me or giving any signal, Owen started to sing "John Henry," that long first syllable stretching out into the air, and I slammed my hand across the strings and listened as the chord came flying out of the amplifiers behind me, hurtling across the room where our fans pushed forward, greedily soaking in our noise, their bodies pressed against the stage. We didn't stop when the song ended, but launched into "Green Corn," playing even faster, more urgently than on "John Henry," as though if we didn't play it just right, just this way, the whole world would stop spinning and collapse.

'This is a song,' Owen said before we played

"Hallelujah, I'm a Bum," 'that you've never heard because we've never played it before.' Some people cheered, then grew silent in expectation. 'We learned it last week.'

I started strumming the D-chord and the crowd began clapping, keeping a beat to this song they didn't know. Owen stepped on his distortion pedal and played a few bars before he started singing:

> *When springtime has come,*
> *O won't we have fun,*
> *We'll git out of jail,*
> *And we'll go on the bum.*

On the last line of the verse they cheered, as though going on the bum was a great sentiment, some great life lesson to be handed out through song. Owen stepped on his distortion pedal again at the chorus, which we played more quietly, but just as fast:

> *Hallelujah, I'm a bum,*
> *Hallelujah, bum again,*
> *Hallelujah, give us a handout,*
> *To revive us again.*

The clapping of our fans continued to drive the song forward, but we had a surprise for them, a disturbance in the verse-chorus-verse-chorus pattern: we ended the song after the seventh verse, omitting the last chorus, cutting the song short of its natural rhythm. The sound of Owen's guitar crackled and clashed against mine, and I stopped playing at the last two lines leaving just Owen, the white noise buzz of his guitar and his sandpaper voice:

Someday a freight train
Will run over my head,
And the sawbones will say,
"Old One Finger's dead."

On the last line Owen stopped playing, holding the neck of his guitar in his left hand and raising his right middle finger in a meaningless rock 'n' roll gesture to the crowd, who roared and applauded their approval.

The last song we played before midnight was "Careless Love." 'This is the last time I'll ever need to sing this song,' Owen said before we started, 'And the last time we'll ever play it.' He started stamping his foot and the crowd grew silent, the only sound that of Owen's voice and Owen's foot hitting the floorboards all the way through until the second verse, when we both started playing. Owen kept stamping. We continued until the last verse when we just stopped, and Owen was left singing a cappella:

Now my apron strings won't pin,
Now my apron strings won't pin,
Now my apron strings won't pin,
You pass my door and don't look in.
It's love, oh love, oh careless love,
It's love, oh love, oh careless love,
It's love, oh love, oh careless love,
You see what careless love will do.

It was almost 1999. Owen and I had decided during the week that, as soon as the New Year had started, right when everybody was shouting 'Happy New Year!' and hugging and kissing each other and spilling their cheap champagne, we'd start playing "Yankee Doodle." The soundtrack to the New Year would be our first and our last song. We'd begin the year and end the show with a thousand people singing the unofficial first national anthem, and then we'd leave the stage.

We stood mute above the crowd with nothing to do. A voice – I'm not sure whose it was – announced that the New Year was just two minutes away. I started to worry that we'd made a mistake, that we'd lost all the momentum we'd built up during the show, everything that propelled us towards "Yankee Doodle." Owen and I just stood watching the people who were watching the large clock that had been mounted above us. The noise of the audience started to grow more excited as the numbers got closer to midnight.

'Owen, we should've just played it. We'll never get their attention again.'

'Relax. As soon as we play, we'll have them back.'

'But they'll all be shouting, they won't hear –'

'Relax. It'll be fine.'

'But they won't care anymore, they'll be too –'

'Relax. We're not just a couple of guys playing songs, you know.' The countdown started, and Owen had to shout into my ear to be heard. 'We're not just Brian and a washed-up baseball player playing their silly songs on their guitars,' he said. 'We're Owen Noone and the Marauder. And those people –' he pointed out to the people below, all of whom had their champagne glasses raised and who were now down to five – 'will pay attention to everything we do.'

HAPPY NEW YEAR!

There was no "Auld Lang Syne." As soon as the cheer went up and the glasses were sloshed and drunk, our hands came down on our strings and the opening strains of

"Yankee Doodle" blasted from our amps. A new cheer raised from the crowd and as Owen stepped to his microphone, everyone began to sing:

> Yankee Doodle went to town,
> A-ridin' on a pony,
> He stuck a feather in his cap
> And called it Macaroni

The voices got louder when we arrived at the chorus:

> Yankee Doodle, keep it up,
> Yankee Doodle Dandy,
> Mind the music and the step
> And with the girls be handy.

And then, when we started into the second verse, people dancing and singing below us, it happened.

Los Angeles Times, January 2, 1999:

ROCKER NOONE COLLAPSES ONSTAGE

Controversial rocker Owen Noone collapsed onstage at the Hollywood Palladium just after midnight of the New Year. Noone was performing a New Year's Eve show with his band, Owen Noone and the Marauder, currently one of the most popular groups in the country.

Events surrounding the incident are uncertain, but Noone was said to be in critical but stable condition on arrival at St. Sebastian's Hospital. Information from witnesses suggests that faulty equipment electrocuted Noone as the band performed one of its final songs of the evening. Frank Dineri of Anaheim, who attended the show, said: "There was a shower of sparks and a loud buzzing or crackling sound and then Owen just fell down. Nobody knew what was happening – we'd just rung in the New Year – and then some people rushed onstage and carried him off."

Detailed comment was not available from Noone's bandmate, the Marauder, from the venue or from his record label. Stuart Means of Pacific Records said, "Everyone in the Pacific family is obviously shocked and upset, and we prefer to wait until the facts become clear before making any further statements."

Early on Saturday afternoon, fans of the band began to gather both outside the Palladium and near the hospital. Policemen at the hospital were keeping the fans from blocking emergency vehicle entrances. By evening, around one thousand mostly black-clad teenagers had assembled and stood huddled in groups, consoling each other and holding candles. Already hundreds of get well messages have flooded into the hospital. Many fans fought back tears as they sang some of the band's better-known songs, such as "Careless Love" and their most popular tune, "Yankee Doodle." Many were reluctant to speak to journalists trying to get information, but one teenager, who asked to remain anonymous, said, "Owen Noone is more than just a singer or a guitar player. He understands us, he says things that we want to say, and he says it in these really beautiful songs."

Los Angeles Times, January 4, 1999:

ROCKER NOONE AWOL

Rockstar Owen Noone, who collapsed onstage at the Palladium shortly after midnight of the New Year, disappeared from St. Sebastian's Hospital yesterday afternoon just hours after being moved from the intensive care unit and having his condition downgraded to stable. His whereabouts are unknown.

"Mr. Noone regained consciousness on Sunday morning, was alert and conversing with staff, and was moved to a new ward," said a hospital spokesperson. "A nurse making rounds two hours later reported his bed empty. We contacted Mr. Noone's home, but he had not been heard from."

The news is the latest turn

in a story that has taken Mr. Noone from unknown musician to political activist to national media star.

USA Today, January 5, 1999:

NOONE PRAISES MISSING SON

LOS ANGELES – Senator-elect Jack Noone yesterday called a press conference to remark on the disappearance of his son, the controversial rocker Owen Noone. In a fifteen-minute statement, Senator-elect Noone said that despite their fraught family history, he had come to respect and love his son in the past several months, and was "personally devastated" by his collapse and subsequent disappearance from the hospital. "Owen's disappearance is upsetting for me, and also for those many fans of his music, who admire Owen and his energy and commitment," he said. "I hope and pray that he is okay, wherever he is, and that he contacts somebody soon."

The Senator-elect bore no ill-will yesterday. "Owen is a passionate boy. Sometimes his passion, his commitment to his beliefs, leads him in the wrong direction. But I believe he has learned from his mistakes, and he is a boy of integrity. I was always proud of him and continue to be, and hope that he will return soon."

After the fifteenth phone call on New Year's Day I pulled the phone out of the jack and threw it across the room, hitting the wall and making a web of cracked paint. I drew the curtains and became convinced that journalists were going to use X-ray cameras or something to see inside, to see the mourning Marauder, to get the pictures they wanted for magazines and television. I couldn't leave the house and wouldn't let anybody in. Eventually the journalists went away, but the handful of fans who figured out where we lived were there all day Friday and Saturday, just standing around in groups on the lawn, hugging each other and holding candles; occasionally they'd put something through the letter slot. Photographs taken at shows, letters and poems piled up in front of the door. At first I read a few or looked at the pictures, but I couldn't stand it so I just left them there. I sat on the sofa watching the wall, afraid to turn on the radio, just sitting and waiting. I wanted to go to the hospital, but I didn't want to see Owen lying on his back with machines around him. So I plugged the phone back in, hoping he'd call, that somebody I knew would call to tell me he was okay – but Owen was really the only person I knew.

Then the hospital called. Somehow I knew he wasn't coming back. If he was, he would've come straight home. He would've told me to plug in the guitars, the four-track, to get out the songbook, and we would've spent a few hours playing new songs. His plane ticket for Syracuse was sitting on the coffee table. I realized that my only friend was gone for good, the only person I trusted and loved. All I could do was sit on the sofa and stare at nothing and hope I'd fall asleep.

The telephone woke me Wednesday morning, and I panicked. I didn't know whether I wanted to answer it. I didn't think it was Owen, but I wanted it to be.

'The television told me. The television.' It was Anna. Her voice sounded worn out, as though she'd been talking nonstop for days. 'How could I learn about Owen on television? Or newspapers. Or any of that shit. I wanted to come back. I was going to come back. But after all those months –'

I wished she were standing next to me, so I could put my arms around her and not feel alone. 'He ran all over the Lower East Side in the rain because he thought he saw you when we were there,' I said, wondering if I was saying the right thing, if there was a right thing to say, if I should be saying anything at all.

Los Angeles Times, February 2, 1999:

VIGIL FOR MISSING ROCKER NOONE

One month after he went missing, friends of Owen Noone gathered yesterday at Dockweiler State Beach to hold a public vigil for the controversial rocker. Noone was electrocuted by faulty equipment during a performance at a Hollywood nightclub on New Year's Eve, then disappeared from St. Sebastian's hospital two days later.

The ceremony was attended by a number of Noone's celebrity friends, but not, notably, by his musical partner, the Marauder. His estranged wife, Anna Penatio, did not attend either, but his one-time girlfriend, actress Ellen Trelaine did, along with a number of representatives from Pacific Records and some unknown friends and relatives. Significantly, Noone's father, Senator-elect Jack Noone, did not attend, due to unavoidable conflicts in his schedule, his spokeswoman said. The group held candles in relative silence for an hour, after which a wreath of carnations was placed in the ocean.

The Los Angeles Police Department roped off an area of the beach for the ceremony, and thirty officers created a barrier between the vigil-keepers and the hundreds of fans and media who arrived to witness the ceremony. The event passed peacefully.

Ms. Trelaine, whose relationship with Mr. Noone made tabloid headlines, said, "Owen is very special to a lot of us, a really talented guy who we love, and who is missed by everyone who's heard his music, and everyone, like me, who has been fortunate enough to share part of his life. We really want him back and hope he is safe."

Stuart Means, representing Pacific Records, read from a prepared statement. "Owen Noone is an energetic, exciting person to be around, someone with a vision, and a sense of purpose, all of which came through in his music. More than anything, it is this that all of us in the Pacific Records family and, indeed, the wider world as well, miss. We were lucky to have Owen for a time, however brief, and his spirit will live on every time someone plays one of his songs. Hopefully he will return soon, to continue to enliven our lives."

The Marauder has not made a public statement since his partner's disappearance.

The vigil was Stuart Means's idea. I told him there was no way I would go along with it. I didn't want to be involved in the circus anymore. Rumors of Owen Noone sightings had already started, and I wanted to believe and disbelieve every one of them, and also wanted them to stop. Owen was in Charlotte, walking around in Washington with a sandwich board, crossing the border into Canada, eating in a diner outside Norman, Oklahoma. And Pacific had that ceremony with a long list of invited guests, and I spent the whole thing at home. Dave Ferris phoned and told me he would have come if he could. Ed couldn't be there, either. It was nice of them to call, and of course I didn't blame them. I didn't blame Anna, either. Vic Reems went. The rest seemed to be the same crowd that showed up to our record-release parties and told us how great everything was. Now they were all talking like he was dead. Like he was Elvis. Reporters kept calling the house and asking for comments, so I had to unplug the phone again. What could I tell them? Owen's gone. You don't know him. These people don't know him. They like to pretend they do, because it makes them look good. I spent every day with Owen for two years. Sometimes it felt like we were married and sometimes it felt like we were brothers. Nobody came to watch me bury my parents, but everybody wanted to watch me bury Owen Noone, even though he wasn't dead.

I suppose to them, though, he was dead, because he wasn't playing music and that was the only thing that made him exist for them. And then they wanted me to tell them how I felt. I didn't want to be watched anymore. I wanted to disappear.

I left Los Angeles two days after Owen's vigil, packed up the truck and drove East, trying to put as many miles between myself and the Pacific Ocean as I could. I left early in the morning and drove through the night, ending up eighteen hours later somewhere near Albuquerque. A few days later I was walking into Fuzzy's, in Iowa City, the only place I could think to go. Mike let me stay in a room above the bar until I could find a place to live.

I started working behind the bar at Fuzzy's. Not many people recognized me, and those who did didn't say much, but they'd smile knowingly, as if we were in on some secret together. Every so often I'd get a royalty check from Pacific. They were huge. In the week after Owen disappeared, another one million of our records sold. Everybody wanted to be in on it now, the mystique. They wanted to say they were fans, they knew the genius, if only they'd seen him play live once. Stuart Means phoned and asked me to write liner notes for the live album, which Pacific wanted to get out right away. This is what I wrote:

Owen Noone and the Marauder started in a small room in Peoria, Illinois in 1995 and ended on a stage in Los Angeles, California on January 1, 1999. Every show we played started with "John Henry." Every show ended with "Yankee Doodle," except the last one.

There was nothing else to say.

The live album was released in April. It had the whole New Year's Eve show except for "Yankee Doodle," since we'd only played the beginning. Pacific added a version of it from another gig, to which I agreed, since it seemed weird not to have it at all. The album spent two weeks in the Top Ten then dropped. I don't know if any of it was played on the radio because I'd stopped listening.

Three or four nights a week there'd be a band at Fuzzy's, and most of them weren't very good. Mike asked me a few times if I'd play, but I didn't feel much like standing on a stage by myself. I couldn't play those songs on my own, they didn't belong to me, I was only half of it, so I told him no every time and he stopped asking. I hadn't played my guitar since that night. I didn't want to.

A couple of weeks ago, in June, I went to a flea market and someone was selling those Russian dolls where there are about five or six dolls inside of each other, each one smaller than the next. He had ones that were presidents, the British royal family, baseball players and movie stars. One caught my eye. The outside doll was Owen Noone. It looked just like him, carefully painted features, his shaggy sand-colored hair, even the orange T-shirt that he always seemed to be wearing. I picked it up.

The guy smiled. 'That's a good one. One of my favorites. I paint 'em all myself, you know.'

I pulled Owen's head and he came apart at the waist. Inside of him was Kurt Cobain. Inside Kurt Cobain was John Lennon and inside John Lennon was Elvis Presley and inside him was Buddy Holly, the smallest doll. I put them all back together, Kurt Cobain disappearing under Owen's head.

'Who's the one on the outside?' I asked.

The guy gave me a confused look. 'Oh, come on. You must know him. Everybody your age knows him.'

I shrugged.

'That's Owen Noone,' he said. 'Owen Noone. The boy who collapsed playing his guitar onstage and then disappeared. The boy who played "Yankee Doodle." Owen Noone. You've got to know him.'

'Yeah, I guess I do. I've heard of him, anyway. But he's not dead. All the others are.'

The guy shrugged. 'Might as well be.'

That evening I was working at the bar. All the students were gone, except for the few who stuck around for the summer. There were maybe fifteen people sitting in small groups at tables. I'd found our first album earlier, the one we'd made for Pulley. I put it in and pressed play. Owen's voice jumped out of the speakers and filled the bar with the long opening syllable of "John Henry," and then the guitars came in, jangling and fast until the line, 'Gonna be a steel-drivin' man, Lawd, Lawd,' when Owen stepped on the distortion pedal and the speakers pulsed with the beautiful noise of our fake folk rock 'n' roll. It made my heart beat faster to listen to it. It was the first time I'd heard these songs since we'd last played them. I leaned my elbows on the bar, looked at the stage where we'd played our first paid gig, where we'd always felt at home, and I smiled.

A kid who I'd seen around a few times came over and ordered a beer. As he took it, he pointed to one of the speakers and said, 'Come on, man, nobody wants to listen to that anymore. Turn that old shit off.'

I would if it would bring back my friend. I would, I would, I would, I would, I would.